The House with Too Many Rooms

by

Mel Stein

Cara Samuel Books

For Sam and Cara

Table of Contents

The House with Too Many Rooms .... *i*

Prologue *1*

Chapter 1 .... *3*

Chapter 2 .... *6*

Chapter 3 .... *10*

Chapter 4 .... *15*

Chapter 5 .... *18*

Chapter 6 .... *22*

Chapter 7 .... *26*

Chapter 8 .... *31*

Chapter 9 .... *34*

Chapter 10 .... *36*

Chapter 11 .... *41*

Chapter 12 .... *48*

Chapter 13 .... *51*

Chapter 14 .... *56*

Chapter 15 .... *59*

Chapter 16 .... *63*

Chapter 17 .... *67*

Chapter 18 .... *72*

Chapter 19 .... *77*

Chapter 20 .... *83*

Chapter 21 .... *90*

Chapter 22 .... *95*

Chapter 23 .... *100*

Chapter 24 .... *106*

Chapter 25 .... *109*

Chapter 26 .... *114*

Chapter 27 .... *120*

Chapter 28 .... *124*

Chapter 29 .... *127*

Chapter 30 .... *131*

Chapter 31 .... *135*

Chapter 32 .... *139*

Chapter 33 .... *144*

Chapter 34 .... *148*

Chapter 35 .... *152*

Chapter 36 .... *155*

Chapter 37 .... *160*

Chapter 38 .... *166*

Chapter 39 .... *171*
Chapter 40 .... *177*
Chapter 41 .... *183*
Chapter 42 .... *188*
Chapter 43 .... *192*
Chapter 44 .... *197*
Chapter 45 .... *202*
Chapter 46 .... *206*
Chapter 47 .... *210*
Chapter 48 .... *212*
Chapter 49 .... *217*
Chapter 50 .... *221*
Chapter 51 .... *224*
Chapter 52 .... *228*
Chapter 53 .... *232*
Chapter 54 .... *237*
Chapter 55 .... *243*
Chapter 56 .... *250*
Chapter 57 .... *255*
Chapter 58 .... *260*
Chapter 59 .... *265*

Chapter 60 .... *270*

Chapter 61 .... *275*

Chapter 62 .... *280*

Chapter 63 .... *283*

Chapter 64 .... *288*

Epilogue *293*

  Copyright 295

Prologue

It was as if I wasn't there. At the funeral, I mean. We were burying Helen, my wife of some forty years, and all I could think of was the domino with the mark of the dog's teeth that had belonged to my grandmother. Both the domino and the dog that is. Although, by the time I played with them in her dark and somewhat damp basement flat, they were memories of better times long past. The domino in question was a double six. I've always been good with numbers.

I have no idea why that particular image sprang to mind. Perhaps, the tombstones reminded me of a row of dominoes, just waiting for somebody to push one over before they all fell down. I had turned away from the grave by then. I'd shoveled in the traditional first three clods of clay, buried the shovel so deep into the wet ground that my son, Adam, had difficulty in extracting it and doing what he needed to do. I'd tried not to break down, had focused on the clear May sky looking for a cloud that stupidly I thought, might have assumed Helen's human form.

Adam embraced me then, leaning down the necessary four or five inches from his six feet height. I could not recall the last time he had done that. He's thirty-five years old and lives in New York and neither of us were ever ones to be touchy-feely with each other. He'd not let me kiss him since he put on long trousers, but now he held me so tight that I could feel his heart beating through his shirt and jacket, his dark curly hair, so much like mine when I was his age, scratching my cheek. Helen had always been the emotional one, the one who knew just when to reach out if a cuddle or a kiss were needed. And Helen was in a pine box, which by then had disappeared between the earth which had pounded on the lid as the other men filled in the grave.

My two daughters, Chloe and Lauren, joined the group hug, one fair like Helen, one almost swarthy like me. It was as if we were preparing for a contest. I'd seen footballers and cricketers make the same physical contact before a match, hyping themselves up for what was to come, promising to be there for each other. I had thought it absurd, but now I understood. This is what humans do to get through the unthinkable. This is what they do when words are not enough, when there are no words. This physical bonding together was one, long, primal scream. Only, at that moment, I doubted that anybody was listening. Helen was gone and despite the proximity of my three children I knew that I would have to face the future on my own and I was one of the least equipped men on earth to be able to do that.

Chapter 1

"He won't cope," said Lauren. "He's absolutely useless. He doesn't even know how to boil an egg or how the central heating works or even how to turn on the oven, let alone use it," as she sat next to her siblings on the low and exceedingly uncomfortable *shivah* chairs. For her part she would have dispensed with the week of mourning. It was all mumbo-jumbo this whole Jewish thing and despite having gone to two Jewish schools she'd met her non-Jewish husband at Exeter University and despite the histrionics of her mother and the anger of her father, she'd gone ahead and married him. She and Luke now lived down in Devon with their two small children, Callum, seven and Peta, five. Although her parents had been talking to her again by the time her mother died, the wounds she had caused had never really healed.

"I suppose it's all going to fall on my shoulders," Chloe said, as if she were starting a totally new conversation. "I'm the only one in London."

"Will you ask him to come and live with you?" Adam asked. He was the oldest of the three and had lived in the States for the past ten years. He had an American accent which his sisters thought was for show, but which, in fact, he had gradually developed after his own marriage. That marriage was over, leaving two young boys, Ben and Casey in its wake and selfish though it was, all Adam could think of was that whilst he was here, he was missing his weekend with them. There was no way his ex-wife Carly was going to make that good. She'd never liked his parents and she never hesitated to tell him so. Perhaps his mother had been right when she'd told him that all Americans had in common with the English was the language and sometimes not even that. He'd never been prepared to admit that to her whilst she was alive and now it was too late.

"I don't think that's going to work," Chloe replied. She glanced at the door and satisfied herself that her father was still upstairs in the bathroom. He seemed to spend a lot of time in the bathroom and none of the children could decide whether or not it was just a place to cry and then wash or if he had some physical problem that dragged him back time and time again.

"Why not?" asked Adam sharply. Chloe as the baby of the family, only just thirty, had always been spoiled and now it seemed she was being true to character.

"Well, I would, like a shot, but you know what Damien is like."

"What *is* he like? "asked Lauren, aggressively. "I mean, we've never really got to know him although you've been married, what is it, ten years now?"

Chloe neatly side stepped the confrontation. She took after her mother, not just in looks (pale skin, fair hair, vividly blue eyes) but in nature as well. Helen had always avoided a fight. She just wanted everybody to get on with everybody else and the friction between her children had been the biggest regret she had taken with her to her grave.

"He's like, Dad. Only Jewish son. Set in his ways. Hates change. He would agree to please me, but it would be a formula for disaster. We've enough problems with Tommy."

Her brother and sister exchanged glances. Tommy's "problem" was that he was he was autistic. Neither of them had seen a lot of him, but he seemed a bright kid, if a little over enthusiastic.

"Surely, Tommy at what age is he now? …" Lauren began,

"Eight" replied Chloe, knowing what was coming next and wondering how best to counter it.

"Well, at eight wouldn't it be good to spend more time with his Grandfather? And it would be good for Dad as well to take his mind off things and you get a free child-minder" Lauren finished off.

"Nice of you to arrange our lives for us so neatly, sister dear." Chloe said, still in control, but as near to losing her temper as she ever was and at that moment, Daniel reappeared, his brown eyes red, his greying hair, still thick, wet with water and slicked back, but with a slight stoop that none of them had noticed before.

"It's good to see the three of you getting on so well," he said, "Mum would have liked that." And as a few well-wishers began to fill the room they each turned to their individual visitors to exchange the usual platitudes that those who grieve share with those who don't.

Chapter 2

Of course I knew they were talking about me when I came back into the room. I guessed they were wondering what I was going to do, but as I didn't have a clue myself, I couldn't enlighten them. The thing about Jewish deaths is that they don't give you time to think. Helen had died on Monday night. It was like a bolt from the blue. We'd sat and watched a bit of television as we often did when we were at home. She'd had a hot chocolate before she went to bed and I'd had nothing as I find that a drink at that time of night guarantees a visit to the loo in the small hours of the morning. I was going to say the wee small hours, but that's the sort of joke that had made my family groan for years. But then it's been a long time since we really were a family.

Those holidays when the kids were small belong to the time of black and white movies. The traditions, like buying the buckets and spades on the first day at the seaside, the toy soldiers for the boys to bury in the sand (we'd start with a hundred and end with a dozen or so and never take the other stuff home, just abandon it to other families at the hotel) and start all over again the following year. I tried to take myself back to those Mediterranean nights, the children in bed (in those days we felt we could leave them safely on their own) whilst Helen and I took a deep breath and settled down to a well-earned dinner and a bottle of wine. Just the two of us. And now just the one. I tried to conjure her up, but her portrait was already fading, receding even as I desperately reached out my hands to keep a hold on her image. My Helen, petite, dark brown hair, streaked with grey when she needed a trip to the hairdressers, gentle hazel eyes without a hint of malice, an almost oval face with a chin that could tilt in defiance when she felt she obliged to make a point, her nose that I adored, but which she hated because of its slight kink from a tricycle fall when she was five, breasts that we had joked about when they did not travel South like those of so many of her friends, her bottom that she always thought was too big (which woman doesn't?) and her lovely legs topping off those delicate ankles. And all of them now lying beneath the ground which we had piled upon her. I had tried to shovel on the earth delicately but shoveling delicately is somewhat of an oxymoron. There is no nice way to bury somebody you love. Have loved, I should say.

After she died, we raced around getting death certificates, making arrangements with the Burial Society and by Tuesday afternoon we were at the cemetery laying her to rest. I've often wondered in the past how so many people manage to get to a funeral at such short notice and Helen's was no exception. There must have been over two hundred people there, so many that they had to leave the doors to the prayer hall open at the back as people kept arriving.

It was like watching an episode of 'This is Your Life', or more like 'This is Your Death'.

People I hadn't seen for years. Ex-neighbors, work colleagues, relatives who I only ever saw at weddings, bar mitzvahs and funerals, her childhood friends, and some who I simply did not know. No siblings, as we were both only children, but men and women who'd volunteered alongside her in the various good causes she supported, friends of my children, some still recognisable from the grubby urchins who'd passed through Helen's kitchen filling themselves up on their way, with her home-baked cakes and biscuits.

The house was never empty then and as one by one our own offspring fled the nest I simply did not notice it emptying out. They left, but their clothes, their books, their childhood toys never did. They'd come back from time to time after one crisis or another. A failed romance, a matrimonial tiff, a lost job. And then suddenly it was just

Helen and I and the kids stopped coming back. Except for Chloe who would pop in once or twice a week and bring both the grandchildren with her, assuming Helen would be able to look after them. Always Helen, never me.

"Just for an hour or so Mum," which turned into hours or even a day while the children ate us out of house and home until Chloe returned with effusive apologies and a bunch of flowers and bundled them half asleep into her car without any real explanation as to why she had been so long. She never shared her day with us. On reflection she never shared her life with us. Maybe she did tell Helen things that she never shared with me and maybe Helen wanted to spare me from the more painful of the revelations. Maybe it was the same with the other two as well, as they staggered through the traumas of their personal lives. Even as we were trapped together for this week I could not see them sharing any of that with me. They wouldn't talk to me. They would just talk about me and if I was the catalyst for bringing them together then, perhaps, Helen's death hadn't been totally in vain.

Who was I kidding? Of course, it had been in vain. A sudden heart attack. Yes, she'd taken tablets, yes, she'd only visited the doctor a few days before, which was what enabled us to get the funeral arranged so quickly. The doctor had been a family friend for years and came to the funeral and confided to me that he'd been concerned for her. But she had said nothing. She would not have wanted to worry me.

Then after the funeral the pace continued. The week of *shivah*. The services at home. The *kaddish,* the mourning prayer, with Adam stumbling over the words despite his Jewish education. And all those people who had come to bury her and those who'd only heard after the event all pressing into the room where we were sitting. All day long, all night long, until we staggered exhausted up to bed (or home in Chloe's case) and started the process all over again the following day.

No, there was no time to think, although rubbing the beard that had already started to thicken after just a few days of not shaving as demanded of a Jewish mourner, I appeared to be deep in thought most of the time. But soon the *shivah* would be over. Lauren would return to Devon, Adam to New York, Chloe to her family just a few miles away in Hatch End and I would be left here. Picking up the pieces and trying to answer the question that none of the three of them had raised the courage to ask. What do I do now?

Chapter 3

"Tough day?" Damien asked as Chloe came through the door.

"You could say that," she replied. "I got there, at what? Ten. Left twelve hours later and in between had to make small talk with people I either didn't know or hadn't seen since I was twelve. I've had my hand squeezed by some individuals who haven't had a bath for a week and been kissed on my cheek alongside deliveries of stubble and halitosis. And you?"

"Yeah," her husband replied, scratching his head, as if thinking how best to answer. "Sorry, I couldn't get there for the evening prayers…"

"That was the third most asked question. Where's Damien?"

"And the first two?"

"How did she die? I've answered that so often that I might as well play a recording and lip-sync."

"And the other?" Damien asked.

"Well the winner continues to be, what's Dad going to do now he's on his own?"

"Was there an answer to that?"

"From most people apart from Dad, yes. But he says nothing about it. In fact, he says very little at all. He's shown no interest in anything since Mum died. He won't even talk about her except in the present tense. It's as if she's just popped out for a loaf of bread and a pint of milk. He picks at his food, he answers with a yes or a no or a maybe. Even David couldn't get any response from him and he's been his best friend and business partner for about a hundred years.

"So he's not even asking about the business?" Damien queried in some astonishment.

His father-in-law had lived and breathed the successful property business he and his childhood friend, David Segal had built up over the past forty years. They made a perfect match. Daniel had an unerring eye for property, knowing the right price to pay, what it would cost to tart it up and how much they would make on the deal. David was the manager of the projects, able to create and read a spreadsheet, negotiate with contractors and estate agents alike, as brilliant with figures as he was with technology. Daniel struggled to use a mobile phone and Damien couldn't remember receiving a single email from him in the twelve years he'd known him (two before the marriage to his daughter and ten since). His mother-in-law had done all that. The social arrangements, the messages on Facebook and WhatsApp, the electronic greetings and New Year cards. He doubted that Daniel even knew at all that social media even existed. Well, maybe he'd have to find out now.

Chloe collapsed into an armchair and kicked off her shoes.

"Be an angel and pour me a drink. All they do in the kitchen is make endless cups of tea and lousy coffee. There must be some unwritten law that says you can't open a bottle of wine when you're in mourning. So, a dry white for me please. And no, he's not asking about the business."

She heard the satisfactory sound of the cork coming clean from the bottle followed very closely by Damien returning with an almost full glass. She noticed that even though he was at home, just waiting for her, that he looked ready to go out to a smart party. An expensive blue cashmere jumper topping the inevitable Brooks Brothers button-down shirt, fitted Calvin Klein jeans and loafers he'd bought at Saks Fifth Avenue on their last trip to New York. His dark hair neatly trimmed, his skin smooth, after what must have been a very recent shave and not an ounce of fat on his athletic frame. Just standing there he made her feel fat and dirty although she was certainly not over-weight and until this chaotic week had managed to fit in a visit to the gym and a personal trainer most days.

"Nothing for you?" Chloe asked.

"I've got a headache. Our son tends to have that effect."

"I'm sorry you had Tommy all day long. Believe me I didn't ask for this."

"I know" her husband replied leaning over to kiss the top of her head.

"I assume Scarlett was no problem," she said referring to their six-year old daughter.

"A little angel. Even offered to help feed Tommy when he was throwing his food around."

She sighed deeply and drank even more so.

"Adam and Lauren think Dad should move in here," she said quickly and without making eye contact.

"Do they?" Damien replied in a tone that could have meant anything.

"They do."

"And what gives them the right to suggest that? Do they think it's better for your dad or more convenient for them? Lauren tucked away down in the West Country, Adam on the West Coast…"

"He's in New York," Chloe interrupted.

"I know, but the West Coast sounded better," Damien continued. "Look, love, if you really want him here, then I'll do my best to make it work…"

"But it won't work, will it? They made it sound like a perfect fix, Dad has some family around, he gets the food he likes while I copy Mum's recipes, he bonds with the kids and we get some life back when he looks after them..."

"But they don't know what it's like living with Tommy, do they?" Damien said sadly, sitting down beside her and putting his arm around her shoulder.

"No, they don't. And, you know what, I couldn't tell them either. It's not the sort of thing you can explain. You have to live it and we do every day. And I'm not sure it's fair to ask anybody to share that with us, even if it is his grandfather. I have a feeling that Mum shielded him from the worst, from the reality. But then, she shielded him from everything. And now his shield is gone, and it must be unbearable..."

It was impossible to explain how much she missed her mother and how guilty she felt that she'd not told her the extent of her love when she could. And now it was all too late. She began to cry and as the sobs racked her body she was unable to finish the sentence.

Damien gently took the wine glass from her hand and stroked her hair, "Hey, it's going to be alright, I promise you," he said but she pulled away both from his touch and his voice.

"No, Damien, it's not going to be alright and you shouldn't make promises you can't keep. Nothing's ever going to be alright ever again," and with that she picked up the glass of wine and emptied it in one gulp.

"I'm going to bed. I'm tired beyond tired." She kissed him absent-mindedly on the top of his head, then threw over her shoulder, "Are you coming?"

"In a bit, I'm just going to watch some footie highlights," he said, not even realising that what he'd just said was insensitive and wandered into the kitchen to make himself a coffee. Caffeine and football weren't the best combination to have before he went to bed, but he needed to think rather than to sleep.

Mel Stein

Chapter 4

I looked at my watch. I'd found myself doing that a lot as if my looking at it made time move. But it didn't. Time stood still for me, frozen in that moment she died and although the week of *shivah* was almost over I still had no idea what to do next.

Adam was flying home the next day, Lauren was being collected later by her husband (who'd been noticeably absent all week – and I didn't know if he'd been tactful or uncaring) and Chloe had asked me if I wanted to stay with them for a while. An indefinite while. It was kind, but I sensed it was not really what either she or Damien really wanted although when she asked there was a chorus of approval from her brother and sister.

Actually, it wasn't what I wanted either. There was too much of Helen there for me to abandon this house, to abandon her. I'd had this absurd idea that when they'd all gone, family, friends, neighbors, well-wishers, when it would be just me and my, our, familiar things that I'd be able to conjure her up. You can't live somewhere for over thirty years and not become part of its fabric.

I remembered watching a ghost play on television years ago when the long-deceased inhabitants of a house became a part of it, their voices recorded in the stone of the steps. Maybe, that's not just the imagination of a science-fiction writer, maybe that's what actually happens. If I wander from room to room, looking for her, calling her name then there must surely be one place where the memory of her will answer me. However futile an exercise it may be, I knew I had to try it. For her sake as well as mine. I couldn't believe she wasn't trying to reach out to me, to tell me not to worry, to make the best of it. That's what Helen always did. She made the best of everything. Even me. And I am not a good person.

So, I thanked them for the offer and declined and watched as they struggled to hide the relief from their faces, just as Lauren and Adam tried to persuade me otherwise. To keep them quiet and get them off my back I lied to them and told them I'd consider it. That I just needed a bit of time on my own. Some space. I'd told Helen that, what, twenty years ago?

"I just need some space," as I packed a small bag and left her crying and distraught at the kitchen table. Of course, I came back. Space isn't what it's cut out to be. Now I had enough space to last me a lifetime and it occurred to me that I had some limited control over how long that lifetime might be. It was an option and I need to consider all my options.

On the face of it I needed never to be alone. I could get in the car and drive over to Chloe whenever I wanted. I could go into the office and catch up with all the backlog that had to be waiting for me there. I had the best neighbors in the world and there would always be somebody around with whom I could share a coffee. Helen was the center of the microcosm of a community that was our small street. Her best friend Marsha had tried to arrange a meal rota. I neither said nor did anything to encourage this; but then I'd not declined the invitations either, though I could see myself putting on weight from the sudden glut of what would, doubtless be, huge meals as each wife tried to emulate the excellent cooking of Helen. As I thought about it she was always cooking. Meals to put in the freezer, all carefully labelled, cakes so that she would always have something to offer the unexpected visitor, biscuits for the grandchildren, some put into packets and mailed down to Lauren and her brood. The fact that they often arrived in pieces never once put her off.

"You have to break them to eat them," was one of her mantras.

I could hear her voice saying that now and I didn't want to leave the conversation that was going on in my head, but Adam was talking to me and it seems expecting an answer.

"So will you be ok, Dad?" he asked.

I saw the shadow cross Chloe's face in the knowledge that if I wasn't ok, then she would be the one who had to deal with it, not her brother or her sister.

"I'll be fine Adam, just fine. I'm not as useless as everybody seems to think," but later that evening, when the house echoed to Helen's absence, when I'd tried to heat up some soup (I'd turned down Marsha's invite to come in whenever I was ready) when I'd finally got the hob to work and then burned both the soup and the toast I was making to go with it, when I realised I had no idea how to adjust the timer on the central heating, that was when it dawned on me that I was even more useless than everybody thought and I was a million light years away from "ok".

Chapter 5

As Adam's plane landed at JFK he reached for his phone and switched it on as he always did at the earliest opportunity. He'd never been able to understand why you could get Wi-Fi on Transatlantic flights, but still not be allowed to use your phone in case it interfered with the plane's electronic equipment. He'd flown in a two-seater across Florida and his friend Matt, who was piloting was quite happy to let him make calls.

"It's nothing to do with their systems mate. They just don't want a few hundred passengers all yammering away together in a confined space. Haven't you notice how they always manage to put the seatbelt sign on just before they serve a meal. It's the same principle. They don't want the aisles clogged up for the trollies. Flying is all about the crew, not the passengers, never forget that." And with that he'd put the tiny plane into a massive side roll for his own amusement making Adam dig his nails so deeply into his flesh that he drew blood.

Even at thirty-five years of age Adam had always texted or emailed his mother to let her know he'd landed safely, and he was half-way through the message when he remembered that it was no longer necessary. He deleted the message and instead sent his father a one-liner,

"At JFK. Speak later." He paused and then added a kiss. It felt odd, but without it the message seemed so stark as if he was just telling a business colleague that he would be on time for a meeting.

He knew he would have to call or FaceTime his father later (he'd tried to teach him the basic rudiments of his late mother's laptop and phone) although he hadn't a clue what he would say. He'd spent nearly two weeks with his family, and he felt he'd run out of subjects of conversation after the first day. It wasn't completely his fault as all his sisters seemed to do was snipe at him as if he had run away to the States and abrogated all responsibility, not just for his parents, but for them too. It was as if they thought that, as the oldest, he was the one who should have been responsibility for holding everything together. Yet, at the moment he had enough problems in just holding his own life together.

It wasn't his fault that his firm had sent him to New York in the first place or that he'd been so efficient in turning the office around that they'd insisted he'd stayed. Of course, he could have refused, there were wealth management companies back home who'd have jumped at the chance to employ him. But the financial package was so attractive and by then he'd signed up for the Manhattan lifestyle and what he thought was going to be a lifetime relationship with Carly.

His mother had been so pleased that he'd met a Jewish girl after all the *shikses* he'd dated, that any reservations she'd had about her only son living thousands of miles away, had flown out of the window. However, when it turned out that Carly had been the prototype Jewish American Princess who could do no wrong in the eyes of her adoring parents, who'd assumed that Adam could keep her in the custom to which her millionaire father had accommodated her and who could scarcely be bothered to arrange for the grandsons Ben and Casey to skype their English grandparents, then some of the non-Jewish girls Adam had been out with seemed ever more attractive.

Adam had heard an audible sigh of relief from his mother when he'd told her he was getting divorced and both she and his father had supported him every step of the way during what proved to be a less than amicable parting of the ways. All of a sudden, the money that her father had poured into her lap had dried up. It seemed his business was no longer doing so well; even though it made a miraculous recovery before the ink was dry on the more than generous divorce settlement that left her in the four-bedroomed apartment overlooking the Hudson, down near the trendy Meat-Packing District and him looking to rent anywhere he could in Brooklyn.

He'd flown back for his mother's funeral half-contemplating job-hunting with a view to coming home, but that week of the *shivah* had made him realise that was easier thought than done. His children were in the States and however difficult Carly was making it for him to develop a working relationship with them, there was a relationship there and not a bad one at that. Whilst the relationship with his sisters was a little like walking a tightrope. One wrong step and he would fall to certain death.

And then there was his father. His relationship with him had never been fractious, but it had never been the normal Jewish father, Jewish son either. Daniel had never been on the touchline on a Sunday morning cheering Adam on as he scored goal after goal for a variety of youth clubs. There'd never been the opportunity of a shared season-ticket at Arsenal or Spurs which so many of his school friends enjoyed. Adam had drifted towards supporting Chelsea, but unable to go on his own, even that had now tailed off to watching the odd game on the American cable channels which showed Premier League football, or soccer as they insisted on calling it here. He'd bought both his sons replica shirts for their kick-abouts in Central Park on his days with them, but Carly was never going to be a Soccer-Mom so for him it was just another way to bond rather than a religious passion to be handed down from father to son.

It was hard to remember now, as he sat in the cab battling through the traffic to Brooklyn, exactly what he had shared with his father growing up. His mother had been the one to take them to the cinema or the theatre as they got older. She'd even got him tickets to see Springsteen when the singer had first grabbed his imagination. So why was that? Was it because his father was always too busy with his work? Or because he just couldn't be bothered? Or worst of all that he'd just not wanted him or liked him when he got him? Whatever it was, it had made Adam all the more determined not to make the same mistakes with his own boys.

    His sisters were right in their way. It was sort of ok for him. He wouldn't have the responsibility of looking after his father and yet he felt a little guilty about leaving him on his own. He felt even more guilty about the following thought, that he'd lost the wrong parent. Tears began to well up in his eyes for the first time since they'd covered in his mother's grave. She would not have wanted him to abandon his father, of that he was sure. She would have wanted him to try to make things better and he owed her that. He owed her far more than that. He owed her everything and he accepted, as the cab stopped outside the brownstone that contained his apartment, that was a debt that he had yet still to pay.

Chapter 6

I knew I had to get back into the office some time, but I did not envisage that it would be such an effort. I'd convinced myself that my work was going to keep me sane and I'd throw myself into it. Yet, now I realised that over the years, I'd allowed my work to take control of my life. And looking back at all those years of missed opportunities to do something better with my time I understood just what I'd not only missed, but had lost forever.

How many times had the kids, Adam in particular, asked me to do something with them in an evening or a weekend and how many times had I said that I'd had work to do? A property to look at, a deal to chase, finance to pin down, another business lunch or dinner. I've never been that religious, but I couldn't help but think of the long song written by King David which somebody précised into "Turn, Turn Turn." Everything is vanity. The final conclusion is dust. Helen was turning into dust every day. I'd read somewhere it took about three months for a body to become a skeleton. I could only survive by not believing that we buried Helen to that end. We buried a shell. Her spirit was indestructible. Only I hadn't truly appreciated that when she was alive. Despite everything, I thought I might be searching for something beyond human understanding, a greater Being, a divinity. If only to be able to reason with him, to ask him why, to berate him whatever might be the reply. In the unlikely event of any reply at all.

We didn't have a huge office, David and I, for our company which we had imaginatively named, Kengal Properties (Kent and Segal combined in case you didn't get it). Nor a huge staff either. There was Amanda Strauss, our secretary who liked to call herself our PA and I suppose she was because she did far more than typing. She's a large lady in her mid-forties with a smoker's cough and a laugh that fills the room. She's a fading blonde who must have been attractive when she was younger and I suppose probably might still be attractive to a particular kind of man who liked large breasts and bums, but I wasn't that kind of man. I wasn't when Helen was alive and certainly wasn't now she was dead, so if Amanda thought that by crushing me in a bear-hug of sympathy that she might have some kind of chance with a lonely widower she was very much mistaken. Indeed, the one thought I'd not had since Helen died was that there might, sometime in the future, in the very distant future, be any kind of replacement.

"I'm so sorry, Daniel," Amanda said, the smell of cigarettes that always lingered on her clothes making me want to cough. "I was at the funeral, you know but there were just too many people there for me to get to you."

I pulled myself free and gave her what I intended to be a grateful, understanding look and it seemed that I got the message across as she replaced her hold on my whole body with just a grip of both hands and looking me straight in the eyes said, "If there's anything I can, anything at all. You know you only need to ask."

"Thanks Amanda," I said, actually quite touched by her obvious sincerity. "Everybody's been very kind."

The two lads we used to source property, referred to by David and I as Bill and Ben as they were fairly inter-changeable, but who were actually called Jason Lehrman and Sam Birns, moved towards me and I assumed, quite correctly, that I was about to be in for a bit of man love. At least neither of them smoked although Jason at twenty-five the elder of the two, was a bit heavy-handed with his after-shave that engulfed me in an invisible cloud.

"What can I say?" Jason said, rather than asked. He was in his late-twenties and had been with us for nearly ten years and was on a generous salary topped off with commission that reflected his contribution to the success of our company.

"She was a lovely lady." Sam added and then immediately turned back to his computer screen as that was a fairly long speech for him.

David also threw his arms around me and as he did, sort of tugged me back towards what passed for our office.

He began to call out for a coffee for each of us, but Amanda was ahead of the game and brought in two cups. Black for me, white for David with his two sweeteners.

"I thought you might need a sugar rush," she said pointing to the half a dozen chocolate biscuits she'd put on a plate and then carefully closed the door behind her to give us some privacy.

"How are you doing, Dan?" David asked, even though we'd spoken on the phone just the night before when I'd told him I was coming in.

"Taking it day by day," I replied

"You know, if you want some time off, we can cope here," David said, devouring first one and then a second biscuit almost in one bite. "Do you want one before I scoff the lot?" he asked pushing the plate in my direction, but I shook my head. I needed to lose some weight after the sedentary days at home, days accompanied by the Jewish mantra that food was the remedy for everything

"Time off is the last thing I need," I found myself replying although that wasn't what I'd intended to say, "I need to fill my head with stuff that doesn't come back to Helen at the moment."

David nodded. We'd been best friends since our Primary School days and had an instinctive understanding of what the other wanted or needed. If we'd been gay we'd have made the perfect couple, but we'd both always had a healthy appetite for the opposite sex, often when we were younger going out with the same girl, in the case of one teenage crush both at the same time.

"Understood. We've been working on a couple of new projects whilst you've been off. Shall I fill you in?"

"Yes please, that would be good." I replied, but when we were joined by Sam and Jason and when Amanda refilled my cup and when I realised that I'd actually eaten two of the biscuits myself I also suddenly became aware that I'd not heard a word any of them had said.

Chapter 7

Lauren breathed a sigh of relief as she closed the car door having just dropped Callum and Peta off to school. Their teacher, Miss Fraser had made a big point of telling her how sorry she'd been to learn of the death of her mother.

"I made a special effort with the children whilst you've been away, Mrs Campbell" she'd said and Lauren also had to make an effort to realise just who Mrs Campbell was. Her, of course, but these days back in London with the family and all their Jewish friends had made her think of herself as Lauren Kent. Lauren Kent. The life and the soul of the party, the clever girl at JFS, the Jewish Free School, the wild girl at parties. The one who'd got away, first to Exeter University to read Politics of all things and then down here to Barnstaple after she'd met and married Luke. Yes, Luke Campbell. That was how she'd got this very non-Jewish name and this non-Jewish life where her kids picked bacon off their father's plate every morning.

Those days of mourning had left her discomfited. Not just because she was devastated by the death of her mother, but because she realised how much she missed her life in London. Or rather the life that could have been had she not been so bloody stubborn in taking the path signposted to danger. She remembered a day on the river when she'd been steering a boatload full of friends and had aimed straight for the sign that said "To the Weir" because it sounded interesting. Robby had grabbed the wheel and guided them back to safety. Robby always guided her to safety and that's why she'd chosen Luke rather than him. If she'd married Robby, as he'd wanted, she'd be living now somewhere like Bushey or Radlett or Boreham Wood or Hatch End alongside her sister, in a large detached house enjoying her

2.5 children and all the material trappings that came with being married to a successful lawyer.

But she hadn't chosen the safe option. She'd chosen Luke. Tall, gangly, red-haired, very much not Jewish, Luke who she'd met on her course at University. His left-wing views had mellowed a little, but not a lot. He still campaigned actively for the Labour Party, loved Jeremy Corbyn to bits and couldn't understand how Lauren could possibly have any feelings for an occupying State like Israel. It had come to the point where they simply didn't discuss the Middle East. Or politics at all for that matter. He regarded her family as right-wing Fascists, which, together with the sudden urge to be responsible for the children, was a good excuse for not even coming to the funeral let alone the *shivah*.

The only problem was that Right-Wing Fascists earned a damn sight more than Left-Wing Activists and had a far more attractive lifestyle. She couldn't help but compare her father's six-bedroomed house with their tiny single-storey, rented cottage where the kids had to share a bedroom and there was nowhere for her to have any me-time at all. Although Luke did not seem to understand or accept, she also wanted to have some kind of life. She may have studied Politics, but she just as easily could have done English or Creative Writing, although nowadays she did not feel she had a creative bone left in her body. That was what pro-creation did to you.

Yet, she'd had time to think, sitting on that hard, low stool for a week. Think and reflect and the reflection had led her to some decisions, none of which would meet Luke's approval. But then, not a lot of what she did or said nowadays met with his approval. She ought to leave, she knew that. Bring the whole sorry mess to an end and admit she had made a huge mistake. At the end of the day she was just a nice North-West London girl who'd tried to be a rebel. However, there were three things stopping her. The children for two. And then the thought of going back to London with her tail between her legs and admitting everybody else had been right when they'd said neither Luke, nor a penniless life in the country were for her.

Chloe had realised at once that things weren't right for her. Adam had his own problems and as for her Dad, how could she expect him to cope with another failed Kent marriage to add to the loss of his wife. Then there was the thought that the one person who would have welcomed her back the most was no longer there. That was the hardest fact of all to face. She'd hurt both of her parents when she'd chosen to marry out and not just to marry out, but to cut all her ties with everything Jewish.

Luke despised organised religion. He didn't quite say it was the opiate of the masses, but if it hadn't been such a cliché then he would have. She'd wanted to have the boys circumcised, just in case they'd ever wanted to return to the fold, but he was having none of it. He'd refused even a plain surgical procedure saying it was all barbaric mumbo-jumbo and that he wouldn't let his children be brain-washed by nonsense like that. It had been one of the hardest conversations Lauren had endured with her parents and indeed, the kids had grown up hardly knowing their maternal grandparents.

They'd had generous birthday presents from them, Seasonal gifts deliberately timed to arrive at Chanukah rather than Christmas, but until a recent session at school on comparative religions they'd not even known what Chanukah was, let alone seen a candle lit. Helen and Daniel would make an expedition down a couple of times a year and Luke had always found a reason not to meet up with them, but just before her mother had died she'd taken to arranging FaceTime and Skype sessions between her parents and the kids before Luke got home from work.

Work was a generous description of what Luke did. He was most certainly not stupid, but had made it clear that any job that paid good money had by its very nature to be part of a capitalist conspiracy against the common man. So, every day he went down to the harbor and used his hands for all sorts of odd jobs that barely allowed them to scrape a living. She'd survived on the cash that her father pressed into her hands when he came down and which she meted out sparingly so that Luke simply would not know that she was taking money from a business based on property and thus the exploitation of the poor.

Chloe had whispered in her father's ear and so she'd returned with nearly a thousand pounds in cash which she'd secreted in her underwear drawer. The lingerie itself reflected where she found herself now. Marks and Spencer knickers washed so often that their colours were faded and unidentifiable. Bras that needed urgent replacement as they no longer did their job. Nothing alluring, nothing sexy and she doubted Luke found her to be either anyway.

She got home and realised that the place needed cleaning. Luke was not one for house-keeping and when she'd first got back she'd found that his method of domesticity was to work his way through their entire collection of china, cutlery and glasses until there was nothing clean left in the cupboard. He'd timed it to perfection and her first task on returning home was to wash everything up, scraping off grease and bits of food that clung to the surfaces after several days. She'd thought wistfully of her parents' home with its state-of-the-art dishwasher and had knew that even if they could have afforded one Luke would still have plumped for the old-fashioned method, that left her hands red and chapped despite the use of plastic gloves.

She idly traced her finger over the dust that lay on the surfaces and then very slowly and very carefully wrote the words. "I must get away" in that self-same dust before blowing them away in a cloud that almost choked her. The words might have disappeared, but the thought would not and clearing a space on the kitchen table that served for the children's home-work space and her old computer, she began to formulate a plan for her escape.

Chapter 8

The month during which I'd been obliged to say *kaddish,* the mourner's prayer was nearly over. It was one of the vagaries of the Jewish religion that a husband goes to synagogue every day for 30 days to mourn his wife, but the male children have to keep it up for eleven months. The Rabbi explained that away easily,

"A man can get another wife, but a son has only one mother." He'd paused then and added, "when you're ready Daniel, my wife the *Rebbetzin,* is always good at matching people up."

At first, I thought it was a bad joke, but then our Rabbi Ezra Klein was not really a man for jokes, bad or otherwise and I realised he was perfectly serious. I bit back what I was about to say. He was a Rabbi and deserved some respect and that was the way the Orthodox lived their lives. But I was a long way from being strictly orthodox and at the moment the wounds left by Helen's death were still open and painful. Maybe he was right, maybe there would come a day. Helen had always said that.

"If I go first, you'll find somebody else."

I'd denied it with a joke, telling her she'd live forever, that only the good died young, but she was good, and she did. That certainly felt like a bad joke now. Yet, looking back at her prediction, was she looking forward or looking back? I wanted to be able to ask her that question, but it was too late for that.

The fact of the matter is that I hadn't minded the weeks of getting up early to go to synagogue. I had to be there at a little after seven every day and I found myself actually looking forward to the forty-five minutes of being part of the *minyan,* the ten men or more who made up the necessary congregation to say the *kaddish*. In fact, on the few days that we were exactly ten I felt a sense of pride, of achievement in the fact that I was actually contributing to the congregation and helping other who, like myself, had lost someone.

My fellow congregants were a mixed bag. The Rabbi, himself was always there although invariably late after dropping his kids off at school. There were several old boys who also sought company, found it hard to sleep and used their attendance as a way to start and partially fill the day. There were the few who were deeply religious and came not just in the morning but in the afternoon and evenings as well and then there were those like me, passing through, having lost a loved one. Not once did we fail to get the required numbers and I also found myself going back at night to help out in ensuring we had enough, my beard thickening to the point that I was beginning to look like some Old Testament prophet.

The night-times were harder physically, but easier mentally. I was tired at the end of the day. People had their lives. The elderly morning regulars did not like to venture out at night. The younger ones who had lost a parent rather than a spouse had a life to live and often felt they'd done more than enough in saying the prayer once a day. Nobody but me had lost a wife. Once again, I felt I was set apart, but the easier element was because it helped to make the evenings pass more swiftly.

At first, I got the usual murmurs of sympathy and then, that too, passed. I was just another member of a club whose only requirement for membership was to have suffered a loss. The synagogue visits became part of my daily ritual and I swopped pleasantries with the other attendees, got to know a bit about them and although I never actually became a part of the inner circle, I was certainly accepted enough to get a few invitations for Friday night dinner or Saturday lunches, all of which I politely declined.

The Rabbi might have been humourless, but he wasn't stupid and often overheard the conversations.

"You don't want to close too many doors, Daniel. People get tired of asking if they get rejected too often. You might not want to see new people now, but just tell them maybe another time and convince them that you mean it. And then take them up on it or get their numbers and say you'll call when you're ready."

He'd obviously been there before, and it was good advice. What surprised me was that I knew I would keep on going even after my obligatory time was up. I had never asked Adam if he was actually saying *kaddish* or how long he intended doing so. It was just another example of how little I know of him and his life in the States that I couldn't even hazard a guess. But, what I did know was, whether or not there was some kind of afterlife or not, I couldn't take the risk of having nobody speak for Helen. I just felt that every time I recited the prayer which ended, "May He who makes peace in His High places, make peace for us and all Israel, and say: Amen.", that it gave some comfort to the dear departed soul of my wife. And I knew, selfishly, that it gave some comfort to me.

Chapter 9

"I think he's losing the plot," Chloe said to Damien. "I asked him over Friday night, and he said that he was going to the Rabbi's house to eat. And he's going to *shool* first. *Shool,* for heaven's sake. He never even called it that. Synagogue it was when we were growing up. We had to go to synagogue three times a year. New Year and the Day of Atonement. And even then we'd take the car and we weren't even made to go into the Children's Services. What's going on Damien? Is he having some kind of religious break-down?"

Damien turned up the volume on the television a little louder. He was watching football and his team, Arsenal were losing to Liverpool and he obviously felt the need to concentrate to help them score an equalizing goal.

"Damien," Chloe said shrilly, "did you hear a word I said?"

"Yes. Your father is undergoing some kind of religious awakening. Is that a bad thing? If it's helping him get through this then why interfere?"

"Because maybe he's getting brain-washed. He's susceptible at the moment. If they get hold of him anything could happen."

"They?" Damien queried, cursing under his breath as the Gunners missed an open goal, "who are '*they*'? Last time I checked Judaism isn't some kind of a cult. You don't sign away your worldly possessions as a pre-condition of being allowed to go to *shool*. We go to *shool*. Our kids go to *shool*. I had a *barmitzvah*. You had a *batmitzvah*. The presents were good and as I recall I even got to snog Amy Levine at my party round the back of the hall. It's not a bad thing. It's just him taking a different direction."

Chloe sighed. She should never have raised the subject when Damien was watching football. He would give her about ten per cent of his attention and she needed one hundred and ten percent. She didn't dare tell him about the problems she'd had with Tommy during the day or the thoughts of her mother that kept running through her head. She wasn't coping, but he'd hate her for it if she ruined his game. He claimed it was the only recreation he had, but that simply wasn't true. He had loads of outlets that she was denied.

He had his work for one. He was successful at what he did. He had set up his web-design business at a time when there was far less competition than there was now and had managed to grow the company and retain his clients in the face of ever-growing and expanding rivals in the industry. The work created a social life of its own and she was now resigned to a supper for one after putting the kids to bed when he was out on his self-created expense account wining and dining some actual or prospective client. Then there was his season-ticket at the Emirates, the home of his beloved Arsenal. And in the summer there was cricket at Lords where his MCC Membership had finally come through after years on the waiting list. Oh, and the tennis at his sports club, and the actual playing of the cricket when they were "just one man short and I can't let them down."

She brooded on that for a moment. She knew her sister had made a bad marriage and was suffering the consequences. Her brother too and that had cost him a small fortune and threatened to cost him his children as well. Had all three of the Kent children failed to emulate the happy relationship of their parents? Her situation was different she told herself. She and Damien still had an active and rewarding sex-life. They had friends. They managed to squeeze a decent social life into their busy lifestyles. Or at least his busy lifestyle. She always had space in her diary for a visit to the theatre or the cinema or a dinner party. The only problem was that she knew that she would nod off within minutes of slumping down into a comfortable seat however good the play or the film or would find herself looking at her watch after the first glass of wine at a friend's house and wondering when they could decently make their escape and get to bed.

She used to read before falling asleep, but now every book took her an eternity to get through as very often she had to start it all over again having forgotten the plot. It was the same with television and even Radio 4, which had been her best friend during both pregnancies, now only acted as an instant cure for the insomnia she did not have. She couldn't remember the word for the opposite of insomnia, but whatever it was she had it to the point of embarrassment when she could nod off mid-sentence whether it was that of a companion or even her own. Narcolepsy, that was it and she felt a momentary sense of relief that she wasn't losing it all together.

She looked at her watch. It was twenty to ten. The match couldn't have much time left. At least it was up in Liverpool although he had been tempted to go until she'd given him what he called "the look". She didn't want to be known as that kind of wife, the kind who always stopped her husband enjoying himself just because she, herself, wasn't enjoying whatever he was doing. She'd tried to go with him to football, to get into it, but she didn't like the noise, the cold, the foul language of the unwitty chanting, the smell of beer and sweaty bodies, the tattoos on the players' arms, their silly haircuts and peacock strutting. And most of all, the fact they earned more in a week than she could have earned in a year even if she'd had the time to go back to teaching. So when Damien told her he had a spare ticket she just told him to take one of his friends who would actually enjoy it. Another father might have taken their son but there was no way Tommy could or would concentrate for ninety minutes. Or even nine minutes for that matter. And that was what she wanted to discuss with her husband, apart from the newly found religious fervor of her father, but as Arsenal conceded another goal and he kicked the footrest from one side of the room to the other she knew that this was most certainly not the moment, nor the moment to tell him that despite the support of her immediate family, without her mother she could not see or feel beyond the gaping deep, dark well of loneliness.

Chapter 10

The eating tour set up by our (correction, my, I am having to get myself used to thinking in the singular) neighbour, Marsha had been a challenge, but I had got through it.

All our friends knew I wasn't exactly a foodie and basically at dinner parties there were all too many of those, "It's just Daniel being difficult" moments. In truth, I don't think I am that difficult to feed. It's just that can only eat what I like and can't force myself to eat anything that I don't fancy. I'm not one of those people who live to eat. I simply eat to live.

There came a week I was invited both to my daughter Chloe and to the Rabbi on Friday night and much to my surprise, having chosen the Rabbi as being closer to my home, I found myself really enjoying it. On an one to one basis he was by no means as lacking in humour as I'd led myself to believe. I loved the emotional warmth of their home, the interaction with their four children ranging from ten down to five, as one by one they climbed up on to his lap and told him what they'd been up to all week. I suspected that his job kept him so busy that this was the first opportunity for him to get involved with them all and in return for their updates he threw questions at them with a treat for every correct answer. To my great shame I would have ended the evening treatless had they been addressed to me.

His American wife, Rachel or the Rebbetzin or Rochelli as he called her, was lovely in both senses of the word. She wore a snood to cover her hair rather than the more traditional wig or *sheitl* as it was called in Yiddish. She had a pretty face, with eyes that on another woman would have been considered sexy and alluring. She managed to move on past that by giving no indication whatsoever that any man other than her husband might find her attractive. Even with all those children she'd kept her figure and she told me she worked out every day in a women's only health club and did Pilates and yoga.

I found myself envying the Rabbi, not just for having an attractive wife and one that was still alive, but for so clearly being in love with the mother of his children. I began to have some unseemly thoughts for the Sabbath. This couple would share a bed that night and hold each other close. I'd once been told by an Orthodox friend that it was a *mitzvah,* a blessing to have sex on Friday night and so, perhaps, my thoughts were not so unspiritual after all.

It transpired that Rebbetzin Rachel was originally from New York, had been a bit of a wild child and had been sent to Israel by her ultra-orthodox parents. That had been a good move on their part because there she had met her future husband and now seemed perfectly at home in London. I suspect she was the sort of woman who would have fitted in perfectly anywhere in the world and she certainly succeeded in making me feel at home. For the first time since the Black Day as I thought of it, I actually forgot for a few brief moments that I was on my own in life.

For the meal, after the blessing over the wine and the bread, which she'd baked herself (I got a bit confused over the washing of the hands and having mumbled an approximation of that blessing I forgot you couldn't talk until the bread bit had been dealt with) she started us off with chopped liver and egg and onion, then chicken soup, with matzah balls as she said, betraying her American heritage. Helen called them *kneidlech* as did every kosher or kosher style Jewish restaurant, but I couldn't bring myself to correct her. She continued with roast chicken, kugel, red cabbage and a choice of desserts that would have filled a page in a restaurant menu.

At ten, the Rabbi yawned, and I realised it was a signal for me to leave given that he had an early start in the morning. I said my reluctant goodbyes and walked the few streets to where I had discretely left my car. My hosts had not asked me how I'd got there, and I'd not volunteered the information, but truth to tell I felt a little ashamed of myself. The Rabbi's home was within perfectly reasonable walking distance from where I lived, and I'd just been lazy and unthinking. I'd assumed that the way we'd lived was acceptable for me on my own and that was becoming an all too familiar feeling. Everything I did made me feel guilty. Just being alive when Helen was not made me feel guilty.

Chapter 11

How had it come to this, Adam wondered as he sat in the office of his ex-wife's lawyer? The paintings on the walls of the meeting room into which they'd been shown looked expensive, as did the furniture. The coffee that was served was freshly made and as his own lawyer, Kelly McGuire handed him a cup he noted that it was Wedgewood bone china. Even the biscuits were hand-made and individually wrapped, bought in (and doubtless hand delivered as well) from an exclusive bakery on the Upper East side that he could not afford to frequent.

And the fact of the matter was that, although he had done nothing wrong, he knew he would be paying for all this, or at least making a sizeable contribution through Carly's legal bill that would doubtless one day soon be making its way through his mailbox. Up close, Kelly looked awfully young. Most of his dealings with her had been through emails or on the phone and this would be the first time he had seen her in action. No pressure there, then. She had been recommended to him as a rising star in the divorce field, but he would much rather that she had been fully risen to her zenith.

His feeling of unease grew as Carly came in with her own adviser, Mark Rockman. Kelly had never said as much, but other divorced friends had told him that he was known as "The Rock" in the profession for his indestructability in negotiations. He was built like one as well, a big, solid man in every sense of the words. A huge head, seemingly carved from granite, perched on a bull-dog neck with shoulders filling every inch of his hand-made mohair suit that must have cost more than all of the clothes in Adam's wardrobe put together.

He nodded and the earth seemed to move in Adam's imagination. It was a vague acknowledgement of the presence of the others in the room. He ignored Adam and looked Kelly up and down as if sizing her up before devouring her in one huge bite. He took a chair at the end of the table, tossing the files from it on to the floor. He'd nabbed that seat, Adam realised just like the Germans with their towels by the side of the Spanish swimming pools and in a way that normalised him. He settled into his seat which had clearly been tailor-made to meet his specific requirements. Adam wondered what would have happened if he had chosen to sit there. It would not have been the perfect start to the meeting he decided. Rockman was a man used to getting his own way, underlined by the way a young female assistant hurried over and made him a coffee, mindful of getting it exactly right. She returned, placed it before him, careful not to spill a drop on the highly polished surface. He lifted the cup and sniffed, appraising it in much the same way as he'd dealt with Kelly and Adam and then finding the drink to his satisfaction took a sip.

Adam could not contain himself recalling an advert from his childhood for tinned fruit and said aloud,

"The man from Del Monte, he says yes."

Rockman gave no indication he had heard or understood the reference as who on earth ate tinned fruit nowadays. Adam's mother had given it to him for a treat with custard and for a moment all he could think of was her face as she served it to him as a dessert. Oblivious to Adam's feelings, Rockman simply said,

"Ok. I'm going to record this meeting if nobody minds,"

" I mind," Kelly said calmly, "we didn't agree to anything of the kind and I can't see the purpose. This meeting is without prejudice and simply exploratory. Recording it puts it into a whole different ballpark."

Rockman lifted an eyebrow in a gesture that he might well have rehearsed time and time again in front of his bathroom mirror.

"Can you not, young lady?" he said finally

"Can you please address me as either Ms. McGuire or Counsel. And that is on the record. I'm not your young lady. Or anybody else's for that matter."

"Did they teach you posturing at Law School, my dear?..."

"Did they teach you manners anywhere? And 'my dear' doesn't grab me either," Kelly said, in that same calm tone she'd adopted from the start.

Adam just hoped that she knew what she was doing. It appeared to him to be a little like poking a tiger before one had tested the bars of its cage. If this was a ploy deliberately to wind up her opponent, he feared it would fail. The thought that she was just showing she was no easy touch was more reassuring.

Rockman shifted in his chair, took another contemplative sip of his coffee and then pushed a brand-new writing pad in front of his harassed assistant. He set another before himself and removed an old-fashioned gold fountain pen from his pocket and with a deep sigh wrote the date and time on the first sheet. As the meeting developed Adam could not but help notice that Rockman's pad remained dismissively blank whilst his assistant (whose name proved to be Rebekah) covered sheet after sheet with her own brand of shorthand.

"Given that you want to create work for everybody, Ms. McGuire," Rockman had said, "let us at least agree we will both have our notes typed up, exchange copies and try and agree a definitive version. I thought you young people were all in favour of progress and technology..."

He saw the expression on Kelly's face and sensing she was about to warn him about possible sexual harassment he paused in mid-sentence.

"I'll come to the point. It took us a lot of time and effort and costs to finalise the financial arrangements of the divorce and the arrangements for the children. And now, my client has had enough of pussyfooting about. Your client takes off whenever he wants without notice then expects his access rights to be tailored to his needs rather than the mutual good of the children."

"My mother died, for fuck's sake," Adam shouted, "I had to go home."

"Can you please ask your client to restrain himself and moderate his language when there are ladies present." He turned to his assistant, "I apologise that you had to hear that…"

"I suspect she's heard that and worse before," Kelly interrupted, but Rockman ignored her.

"It is interesting that your client talks of his parents' house in England as 'home'. This is exactly the point I am making. He is unstable and unreliable, always putting his own interests first, which is why my client has come to the decision that it is simply not in the interest of the children for him to have any access at all until they are older. She has suggested a supervised Skype or FaceTime conversation once a week, the subjects of which would be pre-agreed. And given that your client thinks that England is his home he might well find that an attractive offer."

Adam opened his mouth to speak, but Kelly put a restraining hand on his arm.

"That, counsellor, is totally unacceptable as you well knew even before you suggested it. I'd like to know what your agenda is here before we proceed further."

"Agenda?" Rockman said, his tone innocent and affronted, "there is no agenda other than the well-being of the children, American children, I may add, who have already been so traumatized by the break-up of their parents' marriage that they are in regular therapy."

"The therapy is her idea," Adam said pointing at his ex-wife, "and it's unnecessary. They're fine. She's just getting me to pay for something else and undermine my relationship with them."

Kelly stopped him there and continued herself.

"I note that you've not sought to introduce any reports from the therapist. I wonder why that might be? Could it be because they say the children adore their father? That they are actually well-balanced kids?"

"The reports are irrelevant," Rockman said gruffly and Kelly knew he was right, "the therapy is at an early stage and we need to wait until the course is concluded before there can be anything relevant here."

Kelly snorted derisively, "And where will your client be residing when my client speaks to his children by scripted video-links? In the same Upper East Side apartment which he's struggling to maintain for her and these allegedly traumatized children?"

Rockman leaned back in the chair, which tilted slightly with his weight before re-adjusting itself. He dropped the pen casually and then crossed his hands across his ample stomach.

"Ah, I was coming to that. My client will be making an application to the court to remove the children from the jurisdiction. She believes that to broaden their horizons it might be better for them to live in Europe for a while. Her father has substantial business interests there and would make available one of his apartments in Monaco where I am given to understand excellent schooling is available as well as providing a safe haven from the daily threats we suffer here in the

States. Not to mention being considerably nearer to Mr Kent's 'home' as and when he earns the right to resume access."

Kelly and Adam exchanged glances. Neither had anticipated this turn of events and neither was prepared. It was Kelly who gathered herself together first.

"I cannot believe that you allowed us to come here today, incurring substantial expense, without giving us some warning of what you had in mind. This is simply not acceptable. Your professional conduct is also unacceptable." She swept her papers together with a dramatic flourish and rose to her feet, her small, slight frame quivering with rage.

"We're leaving…"

"So I see," Rockman said smiling, looking at Carly rather than Adam and Kelly as if expecting some applause from his client for his performance.

"I take it that your sudden departure means that you will be considering our proposal." He then did take in both Adam and Kelly with a stony expression on his face. "You really should, you know. This is a fight that you can't and won't win. My client's father has a very deep pocket."

"Are you threatening us, counsellor?" Kelly asked although she already knew the answer.

"Threaten you? Heaven forbid?" Rockman raised his eyes and his arms to the sky in a quasi-religious gesture. "Now that *would* be unprofessional conduct. But don't let me keep you. You were on your way out and I think we were about done anyway. So just let me know when you come around to our way of thinking."

'When' not 'if' Adam noted and feeling sick followed Kelly into the subtly lit corridor thinking it looked more like a five star hotel than a legal practice.

"That went well." Adam said despondently as they faced up to the huge bank of elevators.

Kelly put a finger to her lips. She knew better than to discuss a case on opposition turf. You never knew who might be listening. It was only when they came out to the bright lights and noise and bustle of Fifth Avenue that she answered him.

"You may not realise this, Adam, but it went well enough. You have to trust me. I'll get you through this."

Even as she spoke, Adam could hear his mother's voice saying exactly the same words to his tearful, younger self. Only her, he'd believed. He just wasn't so sure about his lawyer.

Chapter 12

Lauren looked at her watch for the umpteenth time. She'd begun her vigil straight after lunch, although lunch was a very generous way of describing a glass of milk and an apple. What was she? Five years old again? She wished. She kept searching for a way to tell her kids what a wonderful grandmother they had lost, one they'd never got to know very well because of her own stubbornness and stupidity and the jealousy of their father. Just because he'd had a miserable childhood, he thought it only right and proper that his own offspring should replicate that. Not having loving and caring grandparents was part of that regime.

Peta came out of school at three-thirty. Callum ten minutes later. It was going to be tight to collect them, have a cab waiting and hustle them on to the London train. What happened after that she had no idea. She was possibly committing all sorts of offences that Luke would want to use against her in any divorce proceedings. Divorce? She'd not really thought about that either. She just wanted to get away and if divorce was to be the consequence of her escape then so be it.

This was just another example of her rushing into things in her life. She'd picked a course and a university just to leave home with no real thought as to whether she would like the city or the subject or, indeed, whether she'd be able to get a job afterwards. She'd then rushed into her relationship with Luke and look where that had got her. She'd flung herself headlong into motherhood as well, without even considering what responsibilities that might entail. Well, she'd found that out quickly enough.

And now this. She'd met her friend Natalie Dennis for lunch and for the first time had lowered her guard and fully opened up as to the state of her marriage. She'd first met Nat at the antenatal clinic and then the mother and baby group and she was as close as she got to having a best friend. The two women had a lot in common. Nat also came from a Jewish background (Manchester) had also married out and had two kids. But there the similarities stopped. Her husband was a successful heart surgeon and the whole of Lauren's cottage could have fitted into the lounge of Natalie's house with room to spare. However, she was a good listener and Lauren gave her no opportunity to do anything but listen. When she was done, Nat had reached across the table and covered Lauren's hand with her own.

"Oh, you poor thing. I had no idea. I am so sorry that I haven't bothered to ask once in the seven years that we've known each other how things were for you. I'm always just so pleased to see you that it's never occurred to me just how unhappy you've been. You should get a job on the stage, Lauren, because I have to tell you that you are one hell of a convincing actress."

Lauren had felt her eyes fill with tears. She'd barely cried when her mother had died, yet here she was blubbering over her own fate with somebody she'd known for just a few years. She should have lifted the phone and confided in her mother when she'd had the chance. Or, better still just got on a train and spent a day with her in London. But that would have needed explaining to Luke. Everything needed to be explained to Luke, every expense justified.

He didn't get the whole family thing. His own father had walked out when he was not yet seven. His mother had blamed her children for the failure of her marriage and although she was still alive and thriving, he never bothered to contact her, nor she him. Luke just bottled everything up, believing that, when it came to family, every kind of emotion was a sign of weakness. And lately, that had extended to him showing any sign of love and kindness towards her. It was as if he was angry that she was sad because her mother had died.

"You have to leave, Lauren, you have to leave soon. And take the children with you. I truly believe that if you hesitate then you're lost."

Lauren had tried to find every excuse under the sun to say it was impossible. Any excuse, just one. But none of them had worked so here she was, bags packed, train booked waiting for the minicab. It was as easy as that, although she was not so delusional as to think this was anything other than the first stage of her journey. She peered out of the window waiting for the cab to appear from around the corner. Any minute now. The money her father had given her meant that she had enough to pay the fare and enough to buy some food on the train for the kids and get her home. She still could not think of the house that her father now occupied alone as 'home'. Indeed, her mother had always complained that she needed finally to get her stuff out of her room after the years at uni and then of marriage. However, it didn't seem to matter how long she'd been away. Deep down it was still her room. All those belongings still there, books, cd's, posters on the wall, the ancient television and the even older music system that still took cassettes, even her favourite, battered doll, Sally, tucked into the bed. As long as they were all there then it was still her sanctuary and one in which she was about to seek refuge.

She heard a noise from outside. It had to be the driver. Her cases were already in the hall. She took a deep breath and went to open the door, only distantly realising she had no need as a key was already turning in the lock. There was her husband, home early, his mouth a perfect circle as he took everything in.

"What the fuck?" he said and as he pushed her back into the house she realised that she would not be leaving today. Or anytime soon.

Chapter 13

It's odd how I now needed to fill the days on weekends. When Helen was alive the time seemed to fly by. We always found something to do whether it was a film (she hated anybody English calling them movies) or the theatre (she was out of the traps like a greyhound when priority booking opened always wondering how she could possibly be seven hundred and twenty third in the queue). Then there were galleries. I don't like art particularly, but Helen always made them fun and read up before she went so she could act as my guide, arguing with herself as she looked at a painting a critic had admired and arguing gently with anybody else she met in the coffee shops.

When intellectual pursuits failed there was always the television with her huge store of recordings that she would eventually delete to make room for more. Yet, once she got hooked on a series, she was obsessive and she knew that I would gradually get sucked in as well despite my protestations. I had hardly watched anything since she had died, but somehow could not bring myself to delete anything she might have wanted to watch. There would come a time when I would sit down and work my way through them all, imagining what she might have said, but that time was not yet.

Even six weeks after her death I was finding it hard to concentrate. I'd done virtually nothing with the garden, but as I sat out in the mildly warm June sunshine, I could see that some of her efforts from previous years were starting to flourish once again. We normally had a contract gardener come in every couple of weeks, but having cancelled him for the week of mourning when he was due to come, I'd not bothered to re-book him. Most of the neighbours used him as well and he clearly knew of her passing because he had put a very sweet condolence card through the letterbox. Yet, he was obviously sensitive enough not to push for a date for his next visit, but I made a note on the pad by the phone to call him in the morning to get him in before things got totally out of hand.

I added that call to my list. I've always been a list person, but now I'd become obsessive. I wrote everything down. Take out rubbish on Monday night for collection on Tuesday. Sort the newspapers for recycling. Helen was a great recycler and I know I drove her mad by my total indifference to saving the planet, but now this was another thing my guilty conscience was forcing me to do on a daily basis during the week and almost every hour on weekends. Finish a toilet-roll. Recycle it. Empty the milk. Wash the container and in it goes. Envelopes ripped open and the contents removed which I had previously tossed into the rubbish bin (I did at least do that) now found their way into the recycling along with every sheet of the newspapers and colour magazines.

Helen loved the weekend papers. She would cut out recipes, circle the tv programmes she wanted to record, make note of the books she intended to read. Not for her, Amazon. She would go to Waterstones or Daunt Books or any small independent book shop she could find and leave with her bag full of reading material. She constantly told me off for buying a plastic carrier bag for five pence or whatever it cost. She always had an old shopping bag or some ancient reusable bag she'd acquired years before and kept either in the boot of her car or folded up in her handbag. So now, I found myself doing exactly the same and adding to any shopping list the magic words, "Take bag".

You don't need to tell me that I was living somebody else's life. I knew I was. It was a calculated decision because now that she was gone I could see that her life was far, far better than my own even though it would appear that I had contributed so little to it other than fathering three children and putting a comfortable roof over her head.

For her sake I was trying to keep in touch with the children. I had got myself a WhatsApp account and building on Adam's basic lesson had learned how to use FaceTime and Skype so that should have been easy. In fact, it was a challenge.

Tracking them down was hard. Adam was in a different time zone so there was some excuse there. I didn't like to try too early his time because I didn't want to wake him and often I'd fall asleep on the sofa at night and then realise that if I called him he'd be at work.

Chloe seemed to be in perpetual motion. Whenever I called, she was in the middle of something. Taking the kids to school, collecting them, at the gym or her trainer (she had to be the fittest person in Hatch End), at the child psychologist with Tommy, taking my granddaughter to ballet or piano lessons (though she did not seem to be particularly talented at either) and I was told it was a peer pressure thing. Just tracking her movements made me feel exhausted and I wondered how she had always found time to meet Helen for a coffee after which I got the family news second hand. And in which, I have to confess, I never appeared to be very interested.

The one that worried me was Lauren. Before her marriage, 'The Disaster' as Helen capitalised and called it, she had always been the most outgoing of the three. Although we'd not seen as much of her as Helen would have liked, she had always been bright and breezy on the phone, insisting that we speak to the children who reluctantly muttered some terms of prompted endearment when pressed to do so. Yet, now I was Facetiming her and the kids and I noticed that she never picked up unless Luke, her husband was around. I would catch a glimpse of him, a looming background figure, who would shout a "how are you" to me and then say nothing more.

It was as if my conversations with Lauren were now scripted at her end. If I tried to move on to a subject that I wanted to discuss I was guided back to where she wanted to take me. I use the word 'wanted' but I am not sure it's the right one. She did not seem to want anything. There were times when she was on automatic pilot, as if she had been brain-washed and was just going through the motions. Every time I suggested she come up to London or I come down for a few days I could almost see her looking to Luke for guidance as to how she should answer.

The problem was that I had no idea what to do. Helen would have known, so I tried to put myself into her mind. Helen would have realised that she was going to get nowhere other than by a face to face conversation without Luke's presence. Helen would have been decisive and just got into the car or onto the train and gone down there. So, without giving Lauren any notice whatsoever that was exactly what I decided I would do. The decision had been made for me by Helen, just as she had made so many of my decisions when she was alive.

I looked at my diary, filled with business meetings for the week ahead, many of them important, but only important in a business sense. I lifted the phone and called David and told him I needed to take a few days off the following week. Just as ever he asked no questions but told me he would cover whatever was needed to cover. I had never made a train booking online before, but this seemed as good a place as any to start. After thirty minutes and many false starts I finally found a way through the maze of options, times and prices wondering at the end of it why anybody would ever pay full price for any rail fare. It was only when I was on the train to Barnstaple the following Tuesday and chatting to some fellow passengers that I realised that not only nobody did, but also that nobody in my carriage had paid the same fare for the same journey. It was yet another everyday truth that everybody seemed to know, except me.

However interesting and useful that was, there was only one truth I wanted to find out. What, apart from the death of her mother, was troubling my daughter, Lauren? And then, how I could make it better?

Chapter 14

Chloe had been here before. There was a loop to the life of her son Tommy. For a while all seemed well. He was getting on with his classmates at school, he was behaving as well as could be expected of an eight-year-old at home, he was actually acknowledging the existence of his younger sister, and then suddenly they were back to square one.

A call from the teacher to collect him because he was out of control and disruptive. The reduction of Scarlett to tears and a trail of smashed toys that she wanted replaced immediately. It had begun when it was apparent to him that Grandma Helen was no longer picking him up from school on a Tuesday and a Thursday, that she was no longer bringing him treats in the shape of his favourite biscuits and there was no more home-made chicken soup being brought for his supper.

Chloe had given it a few weeks and the weeks had turned into two months and it was just unbearable. So, here she was in the waiting room of the child psychologist, just as she had been so many times before in his short and troubled life. It wasn't that Tommy had learning difficulties. He was bright, very bright, probably the brightest in his class when he was on song and concentrating. But the death of his favourite Grandma (Damien's lived in Marbella and drifted in and out of his life with absent-minded affection) had clearly had an effect and one that could not be cured by kindness and understanding.

It was bad enough trying to explain the death of an elderly relative or pet to a child, but in modern day terms Helen had not been elderly and there had been no warning, no long drawn out illness to give the family time to prepare. This was not one of those deaths where you could say it was a kindness, that "Grandma had been in pain". No, this was a sharp and sudden knife wound to the heart and Tommy, of all the family, was the most vulnerable when it came to matters of the heart. Perhaps he'd also sensed how Chloe was feeling because she was struggling on every front. So, it was hardly surprising that poor Tommy, with all his personal issues, was finding it so hard to come to terms with the latest cruel hand he'd been dealt by fate.

Natasha Gower, the psychologist had treated Tommy ever since it was first noticed that he was not exactly like other children. He never stayed still for long. Getting him to sit through a film or a pantomime was well-nigh impossible. He was up and about, pacing, wandering, standing rather than sitting, ever vocal, ever questioning. When it came to the time for him to go to nursery school, they had been the ones to diagnose him as a child with special needs. Nobody ever used the 'A' word and indeed, although he was on the spectrum, he was not classically autistic. But then, as Natasha had explained, every demonstration of autistic tendencies was different.

He had terrible mood swings, the babyish tantrums turned into real childish rage when at times he seemed as if he might be a danger not only to himself, but others. So far, that had not come about and Chloe had to negotiate very hard to keep him in school with his more "normal" peers. Her argument that he had real friends there (true) and that they accepted him for what he was (also true - children can be cruel, but they can also be very understanding and sensitive) finally won through. There were times when he needed a teacher specially assigned to him and there were times when he was indistinguishable from his classmates (apart from the fact that he was always one step ahead of them). Yet, since Helen's death, Chloe was beginning to feel she was fighting a losing battle.

Damien was no real help at all. She didn't know whether he was just in denial, but he always accused her of making too great a fuss.

"Just leave the boy alone. He'll grow out of it. It's hard being both clever and sensitive."

"You mean like you were," Chloe had replied sarcastically, but she just did not have the stomach to open another battle-front at this stage.

Normally Natasha saw her and Tommy together, but today she'd asked to see him on his own first and they'd been together a good twenty minutes when the door to her room opened and she signaled Chloe in.

"Well?" Chloe asked almost belligerently, feeling slightly jealous that this woman, this stranger could communicate better with her son than she herself.

"I'll let Tommy tell you himself what the problem is," Natasha said, leaning back in her chair and cupping her hands around her chin.

"Go on Tommy, you've been really good today and I think we know now what's been troubling you."

Both women looked expectantly at the child. Not for the first time Chloe marveled about how beautiful he was. His thick dark hair glistened, his perfect eyebrows topped those long lashes that his Grandmother had always said were wasted on a boy, his eyes were an unusual sea-green, his complexion was Mediterranean olive and his smile was destined to break a thousand hearts. Yet, right now he avoided her gaze and studied some invisible mark on the ceiling, and she could see he was blinking back tears and trying desperately not to cry.

"Tommy?" Chloe prompted him, "come on you can tell me. I won't be cross, I promise. We can't make it better if you don't tell me."

"I miss Grandma Helen", he finally stammered out and then the tears came and when she realised it was that simple and that she could not make it better, Chloe also broke into floods of tears.

Chapter 15

I am not a man of violence. In fact, I've never hit anybody in my life. Not a child or a grandchild, not a man in a bar or on a plane who may have provoked me, not even a yobbo in the street who has called out some anti-Semitic jibe. And certainly not my wife, although there was one occasion when she'd had too much to drink at a party and did slap my face when we got home for no good reason whatsoever. She had no recollection of it in the morning and I was certainly not going to bring up the subject.

Yet, within an hour of arriving at the home of Lauren and Luke and seeing the state of my daughter, I was prepared to make an exception in the case of my son-in-law. Even calling him that stuck in my throat. How on earth she ever chose him, let alone married him, I simply did not know.

"What are you doing here?" was Luke's greeting to me when he opened the door. I have to admit that I had hoped to have judged my arrival for a time when he was at work. Most family providers are out earning the corn at noon, which was when I got there, but he did not look like he'd been to work or was going any time soon. He was unshaven, his hair a mess and his clothes looked as if he might well have slept in them. I didn't really want to get up close to him, but when he pushed his face belligerently towards mine, I could smell drink and stale cigarettes and a general unwashed odour of decay. He was a man in freefall and when I saw my daughter hovering nervously in the background, I knew that he had her firmly by the ankles as he tumbled towards the ground and beyond.

"Dad," she said, nervously, "you need to go. This isn't a good time."

I was going to ask when was a good time, but I thought I knew the answer to that already. Never, as long as he was around or as long as she was around him. My grandchildren hovered in the background almost clinging to their mother's dress which I could see was stained and torn and looked like it had come from a charity shop. Or maybe the rejects from a charity shop.

This was Lauren, my daughter, with her love of clothes and makeup and all the creature comforts she'd enjoyed at home before she'd become radicalized and seemingly brainwashed, as she eased her way to a First in Politics at Exeter. This was my oh-so-clever Lauren, with bruises showing on her wrists and doubtless also concealed by the long sleeves of the dress, with the fading bruise on her left cheek and the remnants of a black eye.

"You heard Lori," Luke said. 'Lori'. She had always hated any abbreviation of her name, any babyish diminutive. From the very first when she had gone to nursery school at our local synagogue, she had always insisted on being called, 'Lauren'. There was nothing affectionate in Luke's tone. 'Lori' was just another example of her subjugation, that I got at once.

I dug my nails deep into the palms of my hand to prevent myself from bunching them into fists. I ignored them both and called out to my grandchildren, "Callum. Peta. Are you ok?"

Even as I said the names, I knew for sure that they had not been chosen by my daughter. She would have gone for something traditional, probably biblical even though her life had taken a path away from organised religion. But she would have wanted to please her mother and it was that thought of Helen that got me under control.

"Come and give your old grandpa a hug," I said to them, "and see what he's brought you from London Town."

They looked at their father and I could see that they were terrified of what might befall if they disobeyed him. There was violence loitering not too far under his skin and I could not help but think that he had inflicted it on them as well as my darling daughter.

"Stay where you are," Luke growled at the children, "if you know what's good for you,"

He turned his rage on me then,

"Who do you think you are coming here without any warning and bringing your charity for my family. We don't need anything from you. Was it your idea to get my wife thinking it was a good idea to abandon her family? You know what, I bet it was. You Jews and your families. She'd left all that nonsense behind her until you started filling her head with nonsense and mumbo jumbo after her mother died. She probably took something to end it all just to get away from your crazy creed."

"There's only one crazy person here, Luke and that's you. You need to get some psychiatric help. Now we can do this nicely or nastily. Nicely is that Lauren packs up some stuff for herself and for the kids and comes back to London with me. Nastily is I close the door behind me and call the police and Social Services and then my solicitor to get an injunction against you. Which is it to be?"

"Fuck off before I put you in hospital," he said and I realised that he was either drunk or on drugs and that we could all be in danger if I didn't handle this right. What would Helen have done, I asked myself and the frank answer was that I really hadn't got a clue. There was only so far that her kind, calm and loving nature would have taken her, but for her sake and the sake of my daughter and grandchildren I had to try to get inside her head.

"Lauren, just do as I say and everything will be fine. Trust me. I'm your father and I've never let you down."

Even though that was far from true, at that moment I even managed to convince myself and something must have clicked because my daughter began to back away with the children in tow, I assumed in the general direction of the bedrooms.

"Luke, I'm not here to threaten you or bribe you, but you have to understand they need to come with me. Now. Do you understand that. We can talk about the future when you've calmed down. And we will, I promise you. Nobody is taking your children away for good. Nobody is interfering in your marriage or your life…"

The words were in my voice, but they were Helen's for all that. For a moment I thought he was going to launch himself at me and had he done so I have no idea what I would have done. Helen had always teased me by saying,

"You're a lover, not a fighter…"

Instead Luke just collapsed into a worn armchair which creaked as it took his not inconsiderate weight. Now I could see his beer belly and could hear him panting for breath I realised he was hopelessly out of condition and that even if he had come for me that I would have stood a chance.

"Take her," he mumbled, "take the whole bunch of them. You deserve the miserable fucking cow and the moaning brats. And good luck to you with them." He lowered his voice until he was muttering to himself, "Fucking Yids. They always stick together," and as Lauren reappeared with a hastily assembled bag for the three of them, I realised that was the only thing that he had said which made any sense at all.

Chapter 16

The judge was a woman. Adam thought that was a bad sign, but Kelly thought otherwise and as his lawyer he desperately wanted to believe her. She was Afro-American, probably in her early fifties, but with smooth ebony coloured skin and an eccentric hairstyle that suggested she might be fun to meet in another context. Only, whichever way you looked at it, today was going to be anything but fun.

It had been a couple of weeks since the meeting in Rockman's office and despite every effort that Kelly McGuire had made to negotiate, Rockman and his client had refused to budge. Carly wanted to move to Monaco, she wanted the children to be educated there and it wouldn't cost Adam a dime. The price he would have to pay was having his children thousands of miles away if he wanted to continue working and living in the States. He wished he could have spoken to his mother. She would have come up with some good advice and probably a solution. But that was no longer possible and as for his father, he did not feel it fair to put any more pressure on him.

His dad was fragile, he realised that. Adam had taken to speaking to him far more often than when his mother was alive and although he was putting on a brave front Adam sensed, it could take just one more catastrophe to split him into a thousand pieces. He was like the windscreen of a car, chipped by a stone and liable to shatter at any time. So, this was one crisis he had to face alone, well, alone that was, save for his lawyer.

Judge Marjorie Callum had a reputation for being hard but fair. She also had a reputation for being short-tempered and not suffering fools gladly. As soon as Mark Rockman stood up to make his application Adam knew they were in trouble. Judge Callum and he seemed to be on exceedingly good terms whilst Kelly had admitted she had never appeared before her before and knew her only from hearsay.

Rockman's speech was short and to the point and even Adam had to admit to himself that the man was good. But then he had never really doubted that Carly would get herself the best. She had been used to the best since she was a small child. She wanted the most expensive doll's house at the late lamented FAO Schwartz and she got it. She wanted a pony and she got it. She wanted skating lessons, tennis lessons, ski lessons; her father got her the best animal he could find and the best instructors. Nothing was too much trouble to indulge the whims of his only daughter. And marrying Adam, with his cute English accent and his seeming ability to handle her had been a whim. It had all too soon become apparent that she did not want to be handled and an accent is an accent and if you become bored with somebody then it really did not matter in which language you said that. And ultimately, he had proved to be very far from the best as far as she and her father were concerned.

Judge Callum leaned back in her chair listening intently as Rockman painted a picture of a man who had always been too busy to spend quality time with his children and who had flown off to England for nearly a fortnight without notice after the death of his mother. Somehow, he managed to remove all the emotional points that Kelly had been prepared to make in a few sentences.

"Obviously, my client was saddened by the loss of her mother-in-law with whom she had an excellent relationship. Yet, although her ex-husband had never shown any great interest in the Jewish tradition whilst they had been together, suddenly he is born again and has to sit in mourning for a whole week. When my client's own mother so sadly passed away very young early in their marriage, she and her father merely observed the shivah period for one night and Mr Kent raised no object to that. However, if that were the only reason for my application, I would be embarrassed to raise it. But, it forms part of a much bigger picture where everything and anything that occurs in Mr Kent's life is seen as an opportunity by him to abandon his family. I have supplied the Court with copies of the relevant judgements in the divorce hearing and Your Honour (he looked straight at the Judge to underline his sincerity) will see that Mr Kent was not totally honest when it came to disclosure of his worldwide assets..." (Adam leaned across to Kelly and said, "that's not true" and got a stern gaze from the Judge for his troubles which sent the message that she did not like interruptions in her court room from anybody)

Rockman's pause and condemnatory silence was effective and elicited a nod from the Judge that he could continue.

"As you will note, Your Honour, my client's lifestyle and that of her children, Mr Kent's children as well, has had to be substantially subsidised by her father as she simply could not come close to sustaining it upon what Mr Kent claimed he could afford to give her."

He underlined the word "claimed" as if Adam had been part of some dark conspiracy to hold back a hidden fortune from Carly and his own children.

"Despite all this, my client," Rockman continued, "is not seeking to deny Mr Kent access. All she wants, all she has ever wanted is the best for her children and after great thought and research her father, who, as you are aware, is a well-known philanthropist..."

Ah, thought Adam, so that's it. Carly's old man gives to causes dear to this judge's heart and she knows it and Rockman knows it and they are going to make some mileage of it. He only half listened to the rest of Rockman's speech. Carly was there, of course, sitting alongside him and her father too, Benjamin Gilbert (formerly Goldberg until he had Americanised it) looking like butter would not melt in his mouth, an expression of concern on his face for the well-being of his daughter and his grandchildren.

Adam had hardly ever seen that look before. Gilbert had begun life as a wholesaler of electrical goods and then built that business into a nationwide retail brand. He was ruthless in business and any generosity he showed had a selfish purpose. Just before the marriage he had waved a prenuptial agreement in Adam's face almost as they were entering the wedding venue. What could Adam have done? He did not know then what he knew now about Carly. Then it was love's sweet dream, the Great American Romance and as Rockman finished and the Judge almost beamed at him as Kelly rose to oppose the application, he realised that the dream was about to become an even greater nightmare than it already was.

Chapter 17

It was odd having one of the children back home. Well, hardly a child. A grown woman really, although she had brought children with her, of course, in the shape of Callum and Peta. My grandchildren. That part, at least, of Lauren's arrival, I was enjoying. Lauren, herself, was a challenge. It seemed Luke did not permit her to grieve once she was back with him and all that grief has grown like tumour within her and I had to find a way to cut it out. And I was not a surgeon.

When the children first came into my house they were like little ghosts. They tiptoed around almost soundlessly, flinching every time I tried to touch them, only speaking when asked a direct question and then answering in monosyllables. At the table they sat bolt upright, eating with a concentrated mechanical movement, leaving nothing, although there were times when I could see they were forcing themselves to clear their plates.

I could only guess at the level of treatment they'd experienced at the hands of their father. They did not mention him and Lauren also refused to open up. It was a slow process of healing for them all. The bruises on Lauren's arms with which she had arrived gradually faded. The children got a bit of colour back in their faces and even sat with me, watching some cartoons on television with characters of which they seemed totally unaware.

I arranged for them to get into a local school, which, as it happened, was the Jewish Primary. I knew the Head Mistress, explained the situation and she didn't seem at all fazed that their father wasn't of the faith.

"We've lots of kids like that here," Hazel Brown told me breezily.

"Some of the dads have converted in one form or another and even those that haven't still take an interest in their children's religious education. Our only requirement is that the mum is one of us. Although, we've also had to take in some kids who aren't Jewish at all as the Local Authority puts us under pressure as we have spare places. Nobody seems to question these little Asian kids celebrating Pesach and wearing *kippot* and *tzitzes*."

I raised a smile at the thought, but understood what she was saying. In the Jewish religion the children take the succession from their mother on the basis that one always knew who the mother was even if the paternity was in doubt.

"The kids know nothing, Hazel," I continued, "absolutely nothing. Until they came to live with me I'm not even sure they realised they were Jewish. When my darling daughter married out she went the whole hog. If you'll excuse the pun."

Hazel had smiled politely, but without any great appreciation of my sense of humour.

"And is she returning to the fold?" the Headmistress asked.

"You know, I'm not sure. I know this sounds crazy, but we've yet to have a real conversation since she's been back."

"And that's been what? A month?" Hazel asked.

"About that. I just can't bring myself to ask her anything…" I hesitated, but Hazel didn't offer to fill the void so I had to continue.

"I guess it's because I really don't want to know too much. I mean I really want to kill this guy."

"Your son-in-law you mean," Hazel prompted, "and I wouldn't share that thought with too many people. From the little you've told me about him it doesn't sound as if he's Mr Popularity in the area and you don't want somebody else bumping him off and you ending up high on the list of suspects."

"You're right, of course, Hazel. But as to whether I'm getting my Lauren back or will ever get her back, I'm just not sure. There are a few positive signs. I mean since Helen passed away I seem to have been invited out almost every Friday night, but before I leave the house I always light the *shabbas* candles because that's what my Helen used to do and if I didn't it would feel as if I were letting her down. Last week Lauren took matters out of my hand and did it herself and although she clearly didn't want me to see I could just about hear that she was murmuring the blessing on the candles under her breath. When the kids were little they always argued about who was going to blow out the match. But then, as soon as the girls were old enough, Helen bought them their own little sets of candlesticks and that brought the fighting to an end. Although even then, I remember they had a competition as to whose candles would burn the longest."

"And Adam?" Hazel asked. She'd known my family since the children were small and had actually taught them Hebrew.

"Adam?" I echoed her, searching for the right words. "Adam has always marched to his own parade. You never knew what he was thinking and it was only a year or so after his bar mitzvah when he turned fourteen that he told us that he thought the whole religion thing was mumbo jumbo and he didn't want to be a part of any Medieval superstition. Helen breathed a sigh of relief when he married somebody Jewish. Little did she know how that was going to turn out."

"And how did it turn out?" Hazel probed.

I was tempted to clam up. As I spoke about my children, I was beginning to realise what a disaster they were. Was it my fault? I knew that it certainly wasn't Helen's. Should I have been there more for them? When did it all go so terribly wrong? Had I put in enough effort to keep the family together since our loss? Because it was our loss and not just mine although sometimes it just felt frighteningly personal. And as if reading my mind Hazel leaned across and touched my hand.

"There's no point in beating yourself up about it, Daniel. Helen did everything she could with them and for them and if she couldn't deliver then nobody could. Trust me, we all admired her mothering skills and you weren't the absent father any more than anybody else in our community. And at least Adam married in…"

Yes, I thought. He married in and look how that worked out, but I said nothing and just let her continue.

"Children grow up. They do what they want. You show them the path, but if they want to step off it and go their own way then there's nothing any parent can do about it."

Although I still said nothing, I knew she was speaking from her own bitter experience. Her only son had died from a drug overdose in his teens and she and her husband had thrown all their energies into a charity they'd set up in his name to help others avoid suffering the same gut-wrenching grief.

"And Chloe?" she asked brightly moving the conversation briskly away from dangerous ground.

I had felt more comfortable talking about Chloe who was the least problematic of my three.

"You know Chloe. She's Chloe. Living her life at a hundred miles an hour. Popping in and then rushing out again. She'd brought Tommy and Scarlett over to get to know their cousins and I have to say in that respect, it's Tommy with all his issues, who has been the surprise package. He's got on wonderfully well with Callum in particular and even shown a bit of tolerance and patience with Peta. I watched the four of them playing really nicely and all I could think of was how much that would have meant to Helen."

"That's the trouble, Daniel. We realise what truly matters all too late. Don't worry. I'm sure Callum and Peta will be fine here."

"It will be nice if you can teach them a bit of *Yiddishkeit* " I said, realising that I was sounding like my own grandparents by slipping into the language of their childhood.

"If we can just teach them how to be children, Daniel, then I think that might well be enough for the moment," she'd replied and as she rose from her chair to take Assembly I realised that it was time for me to go. There were very few people I absolutely trusted to do the right thing and with Helen gone, Hazel Brown was probably my best option.

Chapter 18

It was quite absurd, but Chloe was feeling jealous of her sister, Lauren. On the face of it, Chloe had everything. A nice husband, home, children, money and security, whilst Lauren had nothing. But, Lauren was now back living in the family home, a home she'd abandoned without a second thought for anybody, but herself. It was bloody typical of her. Go off and make a total mess of your life, then wait to be rescued and become the favourite all over again.

One part of Chloe had taken a smug satisfaction in seeing Lauren's life turn into a train crash almost immediately after she'd chosen and married that odd-bod Luke. It wasn't just because he wasn't Jewish, but nobody in the family had liked or trusted him from the off. Go tell Lauren that. Go tell Lauren anything. Yet, the other and nicer part of Chloe felt a permanent guilt that up to now she'd been reveling in the misery of her sister on a "told you so" basis.

It hadn't always been like that between them. Although as sisters they fought and squabbled as sisters do, there had always also been the 'us' against the world element in their relationship. 'Us' against Mum when she imposed an unreasonable curfew, or stopped 'Us' wearing inch-thick make up and eye mascara or six inch stiletto heels or dresses so short they left very little to the imagination. 'Us' against Dad when he showed, to the point of downright rudeness, that he didn't approve of a particular boyfriend… well, most boyfriends if she was being really honest. He'd never thought that the boy had been born who was good enough for his daughters. 'Us' against Adam when… well that hadn't really been the case. He was their big brother and he'd always looked out for them until that American bitch from hell came along and broke the bond.

"I told you so" would have been even more apposite as far as Carly was concerned. They'd both sensed she was predatory. Not in a financial sense, because money was the one thing of which she wasn't short. Yet, predatory for all that. In the way she'd sought out Adam as a trophy husband. Jewish which ticked her father's box, good-looking which ticked her own and intelligent which ticked every box for a while until she discovered just how much more intelligent he was than she herself. When that penny (or dime) dropped it was time to move on and seek a brand-new target, whose head she could mount and hang on her bedroom wall.

The worst thing was that almost as soon as they'd met her, she knew, that they knew, what and who she truly was. Only they couldn't tell Adam, at least not without driving a huge wedge between them. And Carly knew that as well. Adam was head over heels in love with her, or rather the person she had made him believe that she was, which, in fact, was a million light years away from the reality.

Chloe and Lauren had talked it through between themselves, balanced risk against reward and had eventually decided to share their feelings with their mother, Dad wouldn't have understood. Carly was attractive, witty and gave the appearance of being bright. Dad had also got on well with her father when they'd met and had been duly impressed when he'd said he was going to meet all the costs of the wedding. The downside was that the ceremony was going to be in the States. But all too many of the parents of Adam's friends had ended up paying for their sons' weddings (or at least making a substantial contribution).

The previous generation of Jewish parents knew they were doomed to pay for their daughters' weddings, with the boys' parents picking up the tab for the flowers and the cars and maybe the bride's veil. However, as kosher weddings got more and more expensive the insurance policies that the girls' fathers had taken out at birth just didn't cover the extravagant dreams of their daughters and the groom's family (or rather his father) ended up contributing the shortfall which was often as much as half. And even half could be around fifty grand (the dreams really were extravagant in some cases). No man wanted to appear mean to the family with which they would one day be sharing grandchildren, but the offer which came from Benjamin Gilbert, Carly's father, seemed to be with no strings attached and why look a gift horse in the mouth?

It wasn't that Daniel was mean. Far from it. In the early days he'd made many personal sacrifices for his children before he began to make real money. It was just that when Benjamin turned up from Monaco in his personal jet, and drove to their door in his Porsche convertible and told Daniel he wouldn't have to worry about a thing, that he truly believed he'd died and gone to heaven.

Although the Gilberts came from New York, Carly had wanted the dramatic back drop of the Pacific for the wedding setting and what Carly wanted, as far as her father was concerned, Carly got. They didn't know then that she also thought she had the right to get whatever she wanted from anybody who crossed her path. Including her husband.

So, everybody had gathered near Carmel for the sumptuous beach wedding, which Benjamin had even agreed, without any argument, would be strictly kosher as a mark of respect to the Kent family. The Kents were told they could invite as many guests as they wanted, but as Benjamin's generosity did not extend to chartering a plane for his English guests or paying for their fares, inviting was one thing, being able to afford to come was quite another.

They'd been outnumbered like visiting fans from an obscure lower division football team visiting Old Trafford in the Cup. Even Daniel and Helen might have seen the warning signs when, deliberately or not, they'd been made to feel like the poor relations. Despite the casualness of the setting (beach, bathing and barbeque) the Americans wore designer dresses that must have cost thousands (and those that did actually strip off for an ocean dip wore custom made bikinis into which they poured sveldt figures that must have cost even more to achieve). The women had brought personal hairdressers and manicurists along and wore jewelry that fully justified the armed security guards installed by the father of the bride.

The men were also dripping in gems. Nothing cheaper than a Cartier between them and the gold necklaces that hung on chests from which the hair had been carefully (and no doubt expensively and painlessly) removed were twenty-four carat. In their tight Armani-type suits they all looked like a casting director's dream for a new Mafia movie.

Somehow or other, they'd all got through it. The Kents and the few friends and family who'd made the trip sat patiently while the wedding rehearsal dragged to its end, listened with seeming attention to the Toast and Roast speeches which meant nothing to them and swallowed back their objections when a lady Rabbi stepped forward to conduct the actual marriage ceremony (kosher food might be one concession but Benjamin Gilbert wanted the main officiant to be from his Reform Temple).

"I give it five years," Lauren had said to Chloe, but that comment and thought they'd not shared even with their mother, Helen, who'd endured the whole thing with seeming good grace for the sake of the son she'd adored. Although, there'd been a slight aura of sadness about Helen that day and not just because it wasn't really the wedding she had wanted for Adam. Was that because she'd felt deep down that her only son was marrying the wrong girl, or had she experienced some kind of premonition that she would not live long enough to see it all go so terribly wrong?

So, there it was. Adam was battling through the divorce. Lauren was about to embark on hers. Helen was dead and Daniel was a bereft widower, seemingly adrift on a sea on hopelessness. Which left her, Chloe, the last Kent standing. Only she wasn't a Kent anymore. She was a Gold. But, in name only she thought. Once a Kent family member, always a Kent family member. Right now, that felt a little like being a member of the Kennedy clan. Beset by tragedy, by assassins, struck asunder by a relentless divinity.

"I won't allow myself to be like them," she said to herself. "I really won't. My marriage is good and my husband, flawed though he might be, he loves me. And only me. And I love him. And I love my children."

But, even though she repeated the incantation, almost word for word, it still did not have a sufficient ring of truth about it to give her the merest crumb of comfort.

Chapter 19

Lauren had stopped looking at her phone. The only person she wanted to speak to was Natalie and she'd taken to calling her every day from the landline. At first, she had looked at all her messages, but then she found that as soon as she saw one from Luke in its terse, threatening tones (yes he had the ability to give even a phone text a certain vocal tone) that her stomach would fall away and her chest would tighten. Her childhood asthma had returned and she was now the possessor of a nice blue Ventolin inhaler and a Seretide disc (a matching shade of blue) courtesy of her father's private doctor.

She tried to imagine what he was planning. Luke was always planning (though not in any way that ever made them any money) and he was not the sort to give up easily. Or at all. Now that she was away from him she could see him in a much clearer light. And as that light illuminated him for what he was she had no idea why she had ever married him. Or even dated him. She tried to recall the early days of the relationship to see if there had ever been anything there, something that had changed. But now she could see he hadn't changed at all. Only she, herself, had.

It had started as something with which to annoy her parents, not to mention her perfect sister, who'd always toed the party line. Now she had kids herself and read them Horrid Henry stories she could see that she had been a female Henry, Horrid Henrietta, with Chloe cast as Perfect Peter. Yes, something to annoy her parents along with all the other things she calculatedly did to achieve the same result.

Yet, she'd never dated non-Jewish boys before even when she was at uni. It was a line she'd never wanted to cross. And everybody knew that it didn't count if you went off the straight and narrow between the ages of eighteen and twenty-one, particularly when you weren't living at home. And as for Chloe (Miss Goody Goody Two-Shoes... or dozens to be precise because her sister could never just pass by a shoe shop and had a collection to rival Imelda Marcos), she had never been tempted by forbidden fruit, or if she had then she'd kept very quiet about it. Not for her the experimental *goyishe* (as her late grandmother would have put it) shag. Not that her grandmother would even have known what a shag was.

Lucky Chloe, she was still living in her 'nice' large home, with Damien, her 'nice' quite good-looking Jewish husband and even if Tommy was supposed to be a bit of a problem Chloe was quite happily continuing to tick all the boxes in the questionnaire prepared by her parents. Or, parent now, she mused forlornly.

That was one of the reasons that Lauren now felt so awful. Her mother had not deserved to be on the receiving end of what she'd put her through and now there was no way of making any of it right. Her father had been more vocal in his objections to the wedding, but some of that, she realised now, had been to protect her mother. Maybe, 'protect' was the wrong word. Perhaps it was just plain anger at what she'd done to them after all they'd invested in her education, her welfare and her sense of being Jewish.

Like almost all of her contemporaries she'd spent a summer in Israel. "Being brain-washed" as Luke later put it contemptuously, but then he'd regarded everything she'd done pre-him with contempt. She'd gone with FZY, the Federation of Zionist Youth, a fairly moderate, middle-of-road sort of organisation, neither ultra-rightwing, nor ultra-orthodox, with most of the group being from similar middle class, respectable, boring backgrounds like her own. The trip was kosher and hardly rock 'n' roll although there'd been a fair bit of illicit drinking and smoking and a few soft drugs that got some of the kids sent home early.

They'd seen all of the sights that the organisers wanted them to see, Jerusalem, with its beautiful stone buildings, the famous Western Wall, the last surviving part of the Temple, where she'd felt obliged to offer up a written prayer and stuff the crumpled piece of paper between the bricks. Who on earth prayed to a wall, for goodness sake? Well, the Jews obviously and again she'd toed the party line. All the other kids shared what they'd written.

"Please make my Grandpa better."

"Please make me a better person."

"Please let me find a good husband" (that from the most orthodox of the group, at 17 for heaven's sake)

Lauren kept what she had written to herself. It hadn't been for the welfare of any member of her family. She had just asked to be a famous writer. It was what she wanted to do, what she had tried to do before she had met Luke, a whole bunch of juvenilia crap and then just one long block without a word.

Years later she had confessed all to Natalie who, in her down to earth way, had simply said,

"Forget all the Jewish guilt about thunderbolts coming from the heavens. Basically, it all comes down to the byline that you can't be a writer if you don't write. So just get on with it. Start with a hundred words a day. Build it up. Don't worry if it's any good or not. Just get it down on paper and you can edit it later. You aren't gonna win any Nobel Prizes for Literature so the best you can hope for is that one day somebody wants to publish it and somebody else (preferably plural) wants to buy it and read it."

Lauren had left her laptop down in the West Country and doubtless Luke was scouring its history to see if he could find anything that he could turn to his advantage against her. Well, good luck with that. She'd submerged herself in dreary domesticity when it came to doing anything online. Hunting around for the cheap option, even for things like nappies when the children were small, then toilet cleaners, tissues, bin liners and even clothes when she was too embarrassed to visit the charity shops. Living with a meagre budget had been a necessity when Luke found it so hard to keep down any job. How could he when he felt the world owed *him* a living? She had become simply too scared to indulge herself in anything that might be considered a luxury or, more to the point, that Luke might have considered a luxury. He had been stripping her down to her bare essentials, removing all the trappings of her past life just because she had allowed him to do so.

But, no more, she was back home now and enjoying the kind of lifestyle that her husband had despised largely because there was no way he could ever have been able to provide it. Not when he could hardly move for the gigantic chip on his shoulder. She knew that if she asked her father for anything, he would provide it, whether it be for her or the children. So, maybe, just like the one luxury item on 'Desert Island Discs', a programme her mother had so loved on a Sunday morning after 'The Archers' omnibus, she would ask for a new laptop. She would try to rekindle her ambition to write. The only thing stopping her (assuming the laptop fairy delivered) was the terrible fatigue she felt whenever she tried to do anything. She'd seen the GP at her old family practice. All her old favourites there had moved on and the girl who had examined her looked about twelve years old, but she did get right to the core of the matter.

"It's PTSD. You've had a trauma. You've done a brave thing and from what you've told me, also the right thing. But now you're geographically in your safe place your body and your mind needs to catch up. Just give it some time, Lauren. I'll write you out a prescription for some anti-depressants…

Lauren had made to protest, to say she was mentally fine, but the doctor waved her down, firmly, but kindly.

"And you might want some counselling as well…"

"I get that from my sister," Lauren said with a wan smile.

"I'm sure you do, only she's not professionally qualified…"

"My sister is convinced she's qualified at everything," Lauren said, realising she was only adding support to the doctor's advice.

"Give it a month and come and see me again," the doctor said, "take the pills and get yourself writing again. Enjoy the chance to pause and smell the roses. These breaks in life never last, so appreciate the opportunity while you can. And try to get to know your father again. He seems like a good guy."

The tablets did help. And she had an appointment with a counsellor the following week and not for marriage guidance either. That train had well and truly left the station. A grief counsellor might have been nearer the mark. She was determined not to take the tablets for too long, nor to get hooked on them. That would have played straight into Luke's hands. Not that he could afford a top-flight matrimonial lawyer to help play that card, but surely even the least competent local solicitor could make something of the fact she'd taken the children and run (not quite in the middle of the night, but almost) and was now popping pills and unable even to find a steady job, let alone keep one down. And all the while, Luke was the abandoned, righteous father who could offer a stable home by the sea in the beautiful West Country. And as for getting to know her father, well, first of all she needed to find a way to breach or climb the wall he'd built around himself. Whether he'd done that to keep people out or keep himself in, as yet she had not been able to figure out.

Even as those dark thoughts passed through her mind, it suddenly occurred to her that she didn't need to think up a plot for her first novel. She already had one in her own life story and she was writing a new chapter every single day.

Chapter 20

Until Lauren arrived with the children, I hadn't realised just how solitary I had become. I choose the word carefully. Solitary, not lonely. I was isolated despite all the well-meaning people who continue to strive to rescue me from my self-imposed confinement. Wandering from room to empty room had been my way of filling each evening when I got home after work. The invitations for dinner kept coming, but I kept turning them down until eventually to a man (or a woman) our friends- or rather my friends though, I couldn't help still thinking of them in the plural, said, words to the effect,

"Listen, Daniel. It's an open invitation as far as we are concerned. Just tell us when you want to come and you'll be welcome. In fact, don't even tell us, just turn up."

But, so far, I'd taken nobody up on the option, except the Rabbi and his wife where I enjoyed the occasional Friday night. I wore my solitude like an invisible cloak, concealing my pain and grief. And my guilt, if truth be told.

"Time's a great healer."

If I had a fiver for every time I'd heard that I could probably retire. In fact, if I were so minded then I could, but more time on my hands was the last thing I wanted. I'd not even mentioned it to the children, but without even telling me Helen had taken out substantial life insurance years ago whilst swearing our broker-friend, Matthew, to secrecy. She'd paid the premiums religiously from her own bank account and never saw fit to mention a word to anybody.

It was only by sheer chance that I found the policy when I was going through her drawers to begin the process of removing some of her things from the house. I contacted Matt who, although a little embarrassed at the deception, told me that there was a million pounds to be paid out on receipt of the death certificate.

"And when were you going to tell me that, Matt?" I asked him, "after you'd spent it all?" But he knew I was joking and all he said was, "Daniel, I was trying to find a way to tell you, but it was hard."

I understood. You don't call somebody you've known for years and say, "Hey, I'm sorry your wife is dead, but the good news is that you're a million quid better off." But I was and as it transpired in monetary terms Helen was worth far more to me dead than alive.

Not only did the money from the policy swell my bank account, but Lauren and the children seemed to swell out the house to bursting point as well. Disruptive though it was, I realised that it was good for me, because I'd begun to slip into a routine and not a good one. Helen had always called me a creature of habit.

"Why do you always have the same for breakfast, Daniel?" she'd ask, not unkindly, but with a little frustration. She was right though. However huge the buffet on offer, whichever the country we were in, I always sought out the grapefruit, the same cereal with a sliced banana, an orange juice and a cup of English breakfast tea. Occasionally, I'd push the boat out and have a croissant or a slice of toast, but that was pretty much that.

It was the same with the food at home or when we ate out. Helen once calculated that there were about half a dozen main courses that I rotated.

"Don't you want to try something different, Daniel." she'd ask in desperation, having cut a menu out of a magazine, but I'd just smile and shake my head leaving her muttering to herself that it wasn't worth cooking it for one.

I told her that at my age I'd eaten just about everything I liked and that any experiment would be a waste of time and money to which her reply of 'you'll never know if you don't try it' fell on stony ground. But she never pushed it because it just wasn't in her nature to do so.

It was the same with my clothes. Once I'd found a shop I liked I tended to buy there exclusively, only straying into Marksies for my socks and underwear. Truth to tell, I had a really low boredom threshold when it came to shopping and Helen could never understood how I invariably bought the first item I picked up.

"You take all the fun out of it." she'd said when she'd once bought the tenth hat she'd tried on (which coincidentally had also been the first). I had shaken my head in bewilderment.

"You've just spent an hour of your life, not to mention mine, choosing a hat, that you could have bought first off."

"But that's the fun of it." she'd replied.

I think I'd said something about an hour of our lives that we'd never get back. And now I regret the loss of that extra hour to her and rage about the too many hours that I have to fill.

My conservatism, extended to my reading tastes as well. I had my favourite writers, bought everything they wrote and when one died I was bereft. Well, I say bereft. I didn't really know what bereft was until I lost Helen.

I was the same with music. I was stuck in the years of my youth. Bowie, The Stones, Springsteen and although the kids would often call me in to their rooms to listen to some new artist or other, none of them really caught my fancy.

Fortunately, Helen and I shared the same taste in films, theatre, television and newspapers. We only ever bought 'The Times' and sweated our way through all Mind Games. Crosswords, easy, hard and impossible, Sudoku, quizzes and the polygon word game. Since I'd been left alone, I found I could solve just a couple of clues and then get stuck. With the pair of us working at them it had been a team effort. One on his own just did not equal a team.

I continued to attend the morning service at the synagogue and I felt myself sucked into the microcosm of life that existed on a parallel universe for less than an hour, six days a week. But, as far as the banter was concerned, those mourning a son or daughter, never joined in. Theirs was a different type of grief, making me feel almost and bizarrely grateful that I had merely lost a wife, something, unlike a child, that could be replaced. That doesn't sound right, but although I was still suffering the pain of an open wound and though still cynical of the suggestion that time was a great healer, I could convince myself that it was probably true. Yet, if I'd lost Lauren or Adam or Chloe, I knew, however much I complained about them or argued with them, that I would never recover. Losing a wife at Helen's age was outside the normal order of events. Losing a child must be beyond imagining. That's the story of the Jews really. We cope because things can always be worse.

Oddly, none of us who met on a virtual daily basis, socialised beyond that morning service. As Passover was in sight, one or two asked in a vague, general way if I was "all right for the *seder* nights", but never pursued that to a firm date. It didn't bother me. That wasn't why I went. It filled that first part of my day, eased me off to work. Just being there was enough, watching the days, the weeks, the months, the Festivals, begin to tick by was sort of satisfying.

I had fixed a date for the stone-setting, the tombstone consecration, some eleven months after she had died. That was a good long way away, but everybody told me I needed to book it. It seemed that the cemetery's diary filled up quickly. I had friends in Israel who did it thirty days after the funeral. I'd never really got that, but then they didn't use coffins there either and I certainly didn't get that. I knew that sooner or later I would have to go to choose a gravestone and give instructions to the stonemason for the inscription, but even some three months after Helen's death, I wasn't ready to do that, to carve her passing in stone.

But, back to my routine. After the morning prayers I went back home for my usual 'boring' breakfast (still no diversion from my set dietary perimeters) then off to work, going through the motions for the day, letting others lead whilst I just followed and assented. Grateful that I seemed to be making more money than ever, but not sure what to do with it. Helen's insurance money sat untouched in a low interest deposit account, because I could not be bothered to look around for anything better, or even to ask my Financial Advisor to look for me. I'd booked no holidays, nor even considered one. Helen and I had holidayed well and often, ticking off the countries enthusiastically, working our way through our respective bucket lists until her bucket sprung an irreparable leak.

I actively looked forward to getting home and engaging with my grandchildren. They were slowly adjusting and actually seemed to like, rather than just tolerate, me as was the case with Chloe's brood. Callum and Peta enjoyed me teaching them card games, looking up things on my iPad, downloading games, playing with them in the bath and reading them a goodnight story. Lauren never actually thanked me, but she looked grateful and I wondered what kind of nightmare these kids had been through when living with Luke.

It was only after they'd gone to bed, after I'd rushed through some make-do microwave-friendly food (Lauren had never been one for cooking) that the silence once again set in on the house. It was then it became hard to cope. Lauren either met up with some old friends or took to her room complaining that she was tired (though I was never quite sure what she did to knock herself out) and we'd still not had the conversation that needed to be had.

I still moved from room to room, adjusting an ornament here, a picture there, tracing a finger through dust between some photo frames as Helen might have done, making a mental note to speak to the cleaner as and when I actually saw her. Somehow, our paths rarely crossed and when they did, her limited English and the fact that she made me feel as if I was working for her had not created the best of relationships.

Basically, my life was still pretty much on hold with very little happening and after the big thing that had happened, after the drama of the rescue of Lauren and my grandchildren, that wasn't such a bad thing. The neighbours still sometimes popped in for a quick chat but, finding me unreceptive, never outstayed their welcome. When Helen had been here they'd just used their keys to gain entry as Helen had done with their houses. Now they rang the doorbell and if it wasn't them calling on me then it was either a charity collector, a door to door salesman or somebody asking me to sign a local petition in respect of a cause I neither knew, nor cared, about.

But, this evening, when the bell rang, those annoying chimes that had made Helen and I laugh when it was first fitted, it was none of them. Nine at night. I was expecting nobody. There'd been a few break-ins locally and the door was locked from the inside and Lauren would use her key to let herself in. I was always awake when she did so, unable to sleep until she was safely home. Helen had been like that and I'd followed in her footsteps. The kids were fast asleep. I felt a sense of irrational panic and peered out through the window to see who it might be. The last thing I wanted was to find myself held at knife point in my own home.

I went downstairs and unlocked the door but kept the safety chain on. I heard a voice that I'd not heard for years and had thought never to hear again, but which immediately brought back all sorts of memories, some painful, some exquisite.

"Hello, Daniel," the woman at the door said, "I didn't think you would take my call if I rang so I thought I'd just take a chance and pop round. Aren't you going to ask me in?"

What I should have done was to relock the door, turn away and climb back up the stairs. But, I didn't and that was a huge mistake I knew I would never be able to correct.

Chapter 21

Adam had always been aware that money brought power. Before the breakdown of his marriage he had felt pretty powerful himself. He'd gone to the States with a decent sum of money in his bank account, made considerably more once he was there and had then married into even greater wealth. Yet, the painful lesson he had learned was that there was always somebody with more money and consequently more power. And the even more poignant lesson was that however much money you had it still couldn't buy you everything. All the money in the world could not bring his mother back to life.

He could command his office staff, the concierge at his apartment building, the maître d' at top class restaurants. Even his sisters (well, until Lauren married that shit Luke) still seemed to be at his beck and call whenever he reached out to them. Yet, maybe that had nothing to do with how much money he had and was just because he was their brother.

But, he could not command Carly or her father, Benjamin Gilbert. He, for sure, was one of the Masters of the Universe, made so familiar by contemporary American literature. He could not say that money meant nothing to his father-in-law. In fact, it meant everything, everything that is except for his only child, his little girl, for whom he would do anything, destroy anybody. He simply did not care how her whims and fancies might cause collateral damage.

She'd once told him that the doorman hadn't held the door open for her for quite long enough and the next day he'd been gone. Neither she nor her father had even considered for a nanosecond that the poor man had a wife and three kids and without a reference would struggle to find another job. He was not a part of their world and consequently did not matter.

That was what was happening to Adam now. He was in the path of the Gilbert Family juggernaut and it wasn't bothering to stop when it reached him. He had been expelled from their world, but that was not enough to satisfy them. At least with the doorman it ended with his dismissal, but as far as Adam was concerned it could not just be left there. As long as he posed any kind of irritation, let alone a threat, he could not be allowed to survive. He supposed he should be grateful for the small mercy that he'd not been the subject of a murder contract, a very small mercy indeed, because right now it did feel that he might well be better off dead. Just about alive, Adam was making his way out of Eden to the accompaniment of a barrage of spears and stones.

His lawyer, Kelly, had said that Judge Marjorie Callum, was hard but fair. It had not seemed that way to Adam when she'd delivered her judgment. It felt as if Benjamin Gilbert had bought her body and soul, not to mention mind thrown into the bargain. It was not as if he could prove, nor as Kelly said in hushed tones in the coffee shop afterwards, even give voice to the thought in public. At least not unless he wanted to be charged with contempt of court to add to all his other problems. But in his heart he knew. Benjamin Gilbert had once again demonstrated exactly what money and power could do.

Carly's lawyer, Rockman had got everything he had requested, although the judge had tossed Adam a crumb by refusing the application for costs to be awarded against him. He guessed that was her way of demonstrating that she was being even-handed. The fact that the costs were nickels and dimes to a man such as Gilbert was irrelevant. The children would live with their mother in Monaco (or wherever else she though suitable). He assumed that ruled out Damascus and the Gaza Strip, but he wasn't entirely sure. He would have visiting rights twice a month, but would not be permitted to travel with them to the UK.

"In case he does not return them, they are after all American children (clearly one of his favourite phrases)," Rockman had argued persuasively in much the same tone he might have used to oppose bail for an alleged felon who could be deemed to be a flight risk.

"Can we not appeal?" he'd asked Kelly, who to be fair to her, appeared to be every bit as upset as he was.

"We can. But it will take a load of money and your ex and her father are banking on the fact that you won't want to spend it and possibly don't even have it to spend. I think you know exactly how deep his pockets are."

"I don't really," Adam muttered although the fact that he couldn't begin to guess at the Gilbert wealth told its own story. "But would we win?"

"Hey, come on Adam. You know every lawyer thinks they have a chance of winning. But I'm not going to dish up any crap. We should have won today. But we didn't..." she made to say more, but looked around the room, thought better of it and put a finger to her lips.

"I know what you're thinking. I said hard, but fair. But this isn't the place to discuss it. Too many court people around. It's obviously a favoured pre and post court venue for a coffee otherwise we wouldn't be here. It's not good enough for the Gilberts, but the courts are a village and this is a great spot to gather gossip. I think you probably have to accept it for the moment and bide your time. I don't really know your ex-wife, but I know her type. And her father's type as well. It's all about winning. They've done that although I've no idea how or why..." Her voice had dropped to a whisper and Adam guessed she had said more than she wanted to in those surroundings, "but they'll get bored. She, in particular. Do you really think she'll want to get lumbered on a daily basis with a couple of kids who'll cramp her lifestyle? As at today they are her trophies. Tomorrow they'll be her baggage. She'll have them nannied, meet somebody else from her sort of background, he might well have kids of his own that he doesn't know what to do with and that'll be the time to go back to court."

Adam drained his coffee cup, crumpled it and aimed for the trash can. He missed. It was that sort of day.

"Listen, Kelly, you did your best. And I appreciate it. But you can't play against the house, when the house is rigged. Just let me have your account and I'll settle it by return."

"It's ok, Adam. I've got money on account. It'll cover it."

"A lawyer with a generous streak. And a heart," Adam said with a rueful smile, "have I discovered an endangered species?"

Kelly smiled back at him and just for a second Adam wondered if there was something more in that smile than just sympathy. Did she not want the relationship to end here? For his part he didn't think it would be a great idea to embark on anything non-professional with his lawyer, however attractive she might be. He had an image of his late mother shaking her head in disapproval as he leapt from the frying pan of a Jewish wife (albeit a total bitch) into the fiery cauldron of somebody who was by any standards a total *shikse*. New York City might be the melting pot of religions and cultures but Kelly was almost certainly a woman who did not have a drop of Jewish blood running through her veins. Maybe the only one in the whole of the Big Apple.

But his mother wasn't here and he was feeling lonely and exposed so he chanced his arm.

"Listen, you've gone beyond the limits of what you needed to do. I know you're writing off a fair chunk of costs so maybe I can at least offer to buy you a dinner…"

"You really don't need to Adam…." and he immediately felt annoyed with himself that he'd given her the chance to knock him back, but then to his amazement and he had to admit, his elation, she was saying,

"But why not? I'm totally free tonight if you are."

'I'm free every night,' he thought, but all he said was,

"That's great. What do you like, Italian, Chinese, Sushi?"

"Unbelievably, considering I'm a lawyer and New York born and bred I've never been to a proper kosher joint, so why don't you find one that gives the whole experience from chicken soup to strudel and let me know when and where I need to meet you."

"And how many calories and how much cholesterol you'll be consuming?" he added, enjoying the exchange.

"Yeah, that too. And throw in some kosher wine. I once tried some Manishewitz at a friend's on a Friday night and so I've set the bar pretty low. Shall we aim for 7.30pm?"

" Fine," Adam replied and despite everything that had happened in the court-room, despite the fact that he had no idea when he would next see his kids, despite the fact that if his mother wasn't already dead she would be sticking her head in a gas-oven, he felt for the first time in years that he actually had something to which he could look forward.

Chapter 22

"You look older," Lizzie said, as I stood in the kitchen making her coffee.

"Did you just drop by to insult me?" I asked, but in that familiar tone that told her I wasn't really hurt at all. After all, I did look older. That's what the death of your wife does to you. And when you threw into the mix the problems with Lauren and Adam and Tommy's ongoing issues it was a minor miracle that I had the energy to get out of bed in the morning.

"Still black and strong?" I asked.

"Yes, like my men," she replied following a bygone routine. Then she gave me that lopsided smile that had started the whole thing off. The smile she'd given me at that property conference in Manchester and had then made me fall from grace. The smile that might well have destroyed not only my marriage, but my life. That was, if I had not looked down into the precipice to which the smile had drawn me like the Siren's song. Looked down and then stepped back.

I tried to remember what it was that had finally brought me to my senses. Had I grown to hate this woman who was now inhabiting the kitchen where Helen and I and the kids had shared so many breakfasts, had so many arguments, made so many decisions?

I looked at Lizzie closely for the first time since I had asked her in, all the while also asking her just why I had done that. Curiosity? Desire? Seeking a closure we had never really had? Or was it simply that I didn't want the neighbours, my personal security guard, to see her and start asking questions that I would not have been able to answer truthfully? The fact was that I had never been able to give a truthful answer about Lizzie. Not to her, not to our friends, not to Helen nor the kids and certainly not to myself.

She also looked older, but why was that a surprise? Whenever I had thought of her she had been frozen in time and yet it had been more than fifteen years. She had aged in a more subtle, more graceful way than had I. A few lines at the side of her eyes, yet they only succeeded in highlighting the vivid blue of the eyes themselves. If you looked carefully you could also see a few strands of grey in her hair, but not many. Lizzie had always gone to the best of hairdressers and clearly continued to do so. She wasn't vain, but she was a woman who liked always to look her best. Not in a 'hey I'm here to be picked up' kind of way, but just because she had self-esteem.

The hair, itself, was cut much shorter than I remembered, giving her an elfin look with a hint of Audrey Hepburn. She was still slim, her skin creamy smooth, her clothes looking casual but I knew they would have been expensive. She always spent more than she could afford on her clothes, the very antithesis of Helen. In that and in so many other ways. She was, in fact, the Lizzie of old. Taking her time in getting dressed, but making it appear that she'd flung on the first things that had come to hand and then taking a bow for the cohesive picture they formed.

Tonight, it was a dark-blue, crew-neck t-shirt, with snug, pale blue jeans, moulded to the bum that she always claimed was too big, but was in fact just right. She was bra-less as ever, her breasts a miracle of self-support and now, not in the least, affected by the passing of the years. Nothing was left to the imagination and it didn't need to be, because I had seen it all.

The hooped gold earrings set the outfit off perfectly. I recognised them immediately and I guess that had been Lizzie's intention. She seemed to be an off-the-cuff kind of girl, but generally everything was thought through. Cause and effect that had been her speciality. We'd bought the earrings together in Brighton and the young designer who'd owned the small shop had said,

"It's as if they were made for you," and had given her that look that said 'if I'd met you before I made them then that certainly would have been the case'. But, in fact, everything Lizzie wore, dresses, shoes, coats, jewellery, even her under-wear looked as if it had been designed with her in mind.

The thought of Brighton brought me back to earth with a resounding crash. Ever since Helen died I knew that I really needed to visit the apartment overlooking the sea that Helen and I had bought together. But, I had just not been able to bring myself to do it. Our neighbours and the cleaning lady had keys and as they'd not phoned in a panic, I assumed we'd not had a fire, a flood or a robbery.

Helen and I both loved our weekends there, as did the children when they were young. It was somewhere different and there was the beach to make it feel like a holiday. Then they grew up and declared it boring. And then I made the huge mistake of taking Lizzie there and everything was ruined. I've no idea what excuse I made to go away for the weekend and I soon realised the crazy risk I had taken when, by then, so many people in the block knew us. I got away with it, but the price I paid was horrendous.

After that, whenever Helen and I visited I felt like a criminal, worrying if he had covered his tracks. Were there any clues to suggest to Helen that I'd been there with another women? A stray hair on a pillow, a bottle of perfume or a shower gel that wasn't hers, a programme recorded that I would never have been seen dead watching (Lizzie had a penchant for Soaps like Coronation Street and Emmerdale and EastEnders which I'd always ridiculed) except when I sat, mindless of the programme and watched her face, relaxed and smiling, taking it all in as if the cast were her own beloved family.

I had obviously done too good a job when Helen commented that our regular cleaning lady had raised her standards, but that was as close as it came. Or, at least, I thought so.

"I'm sorry about your wife," Lizzie said

"How did you hear?" I asked, as we didn't exactly mix in the same social circles.

"Rob told me," she replied.

"I didn't realise you'd kept in touch. He never said anything."

"Well done, Rob, I did ask him to keep it to himself."

Rob Klein was a friend of mine from my university days and the only person I confided in about Lizzie.

"He asked me out, you know," Lizzie added.

"What? While we were together?" I said in a tone that could not conceal that this was unwelcome news to me. I felt betrayed though, of course, as the principal betrayer I had no right to the luxury of such a feeling.

"No. Afterwards. You broke my heart and there were so few people who I could confide in. Rob was very kind. Sat me down, made me tea, gave me one of those terrible cakes he used to try and bake and told me what a shit you had always been."

Great, I thought, and he's my friend. What are my enemies saying about me? Rob and his bloody cakes and his failed marriage and his succession of unsuitable girlfriends. He seemed to collect a never ending stream of them while muddling through his life as a freelance travel writer.

"And that's when he asked you out?"

"Well, not then, but later. That was after the bottle of wine we shared."

"Later? Wine? What else did you share?" It came out more sharply than I'd intended.

"Yes, wine. Yes later. Why are you repeating everything I say? And why are you homing in on the fact that your old friend Rob asked me out after you dumped me and went back to your cosy domestic existence as if you and I had never happened. Or if we had, then it had occurred in some parallel universe. Do you remember how we used to laugh at The Beautiful South when they sang, 'Don't Marry Her, Fuck Me.' They're playing our song, you said as we sang along. I still know all the words today though I turn it off when it pops up on the radio."

Yes, I remembered. I remembered everything about our parallel universe although I didn't repeat her words, nor did I start humming the song. "Think of you with pipe and slippers, think of her in bed, laying there just watching telly, think of me instead, I'll never grow so old and flabby, that could never be, don't marry her, fuck me"

I'd never smoked a pipe but I realised I was wearing carpet slippers. Helen had never had the chance to grow really old, but she had put on weight, unlike the Lizzie standing before me. I felt that old familiar feeling of guilt mixed with desire and returned to the question of why Lizzie had chosen to visit me at my home in my widower state. And whether or not I really wanted to know the answer.

Chapter 23

Chloe lay on her bed trying to focus on painting her toenails even though she was due to have them done professionally in a couple of days at her hairdresser. One was chipped and one was peeling, and she was planning to wear her strappy sandals that evening. She liked all her nails, toes and fingers, to be perfect. Over the years she'd spent so much on them that when she even mentioned to Damien that she had an appointment with either Paul, her hairdresser, or Tracey her manicurist and pedicurist, he merely shrugged. He'd given up making jokes about season tickets and second mortgages or getting the whole beauty team at the salon just to move into one of their spare bedrooms.

She had her phone balanced between ear and shoulder and was dipping in and out of a conversation with Lauren. Despite her slightly ambivalent feelings about Lauren's current situation, they were generally getting on much better than they'd done for years, united in the loss of their mother and their concern for their father.

"He's acting very strangely," Chloe said.

"He's been weird since mum died." Lauren replied.

Chloe wanted to ask how her sister would know since until their father had ridden his white horse to her rescue she had hardly been around him. Yet, she knew that if she went down that road it would end in a row and she wasn't looking for another argument today.

She'd started full on with Tommy being difficult and her being so irrational that even Scarlett had said in that annoying grown-up tone,

"Oh, Mummy, do leave it. It's not appropriate at this time of the morning."

Despite everything she'd had to raise a small smile at her daughter's turn of phrase. Where on earth had she picked that one up? But then where did Scarlett get anything from. She knew her daughter watched YouTube videos (heavily censored and controlled), children's TV shows (generally badly written and even more badly acted American rubbish) and also read avidly. Her tastes for a six-year-old, both in viewing and literature, were ridiculously mature. She was sort of a handful now, challenging, but not in the Tommy category.

The argument had begun, like most arguments with her son, over something totally trivial. Trivial to her, but of vital importance to him. Like his grandfather, he liked things to be just so. It was part of his condition, but given how her father was a slave to habit, it was also built into his genes.

"This porridge is too hot, too runny and too sweet," he'd complained even though she reckoned it looked exactly the same texture as every other morning. Well, maybe she had been careless with the sugar and over-generous with the milk, but not so that anybody, but her son would notice.

"Who are you, Goldilocks?" Chloe had snapped.

Big mistake. Tommy didn't get sarcasm and didn't take too kindly to being snapped at either. He liked those even less than he liked any variation in the substance and quality of his breakfast porridge. So, he simply upped the plate and tossed it all on the floor, before storming up to his room leaving his sister shaking her head as if to say, 'I told you so. That was never going to be a good idea.'

Chloe had been about to start in on her for no good reason other than the fact she was still there and an easy target, when Damien had come down for his breakfast, all showered and shaved and booted and suited for work, looking like a million dollars as he always did. Without offering to help or risk getting himself dirty he merely said,

"That obviously went well. Maybe you could get commissioned to write a book about how to cope with children on the spectrum."

Chloe was on her hands and knees by then, clearing up the mess, looking at her reflection in her husband's highly polished footwear and not liking what she saw. As if to erase it from her sight she could not resist taking the porridge-soaked cloth and wiping it over the shiny leather. That, fairly predictably, did not go down well either.

"Childish." Damien said, ignored his breakfast, ignored his son's screams coming from upstairs, ignored his daughter wearing her world-weary, 'I've seen all this before look' and ignored his wife as well. He simply turned on his heels, walked out of the room, tramping marks of porridge on the hall floor and then left the house, slamming the door behind him.

"Don't say a word," Chloe had shrieked at her innocent daughter who had by then, unusually, also burst into tears. And that was all before seven-thirty a.m.

Chloe hadn't bothered to relay all or any of this to her sister. It would all blow over. It always did. Tommy and Scarlett had gone off to school laughing and skipping without a care in the world. Damien had sent her a sad face emoji and she had sent him a kiss back. None of it was his fault, but she knew that he would bring her flowers that evening. He was well trained in feeling guilty for events that were not of his making. Life was just easier that way. However, it was the fact that all of this had happened before and would happen again and the lack of predictably and the aftermath that was so depressing and dispiriting.

"So, how strangely was he behaving on a scale of 1-10?"

She realised her sister was talking and that she might well have missed something whilst she had tuned out, but as the theme still seemed to be the same, Lauren couldn't have noticed. Indeed, it was odd for Lauren to notice anything that didn't relate to her, but she assumed that living in the same house meant that their father's 'strange' behavior could be classified as relating sufficiently to her for it to be a subject of her conversation.

"I came home the other day and there were two dirty cups in the kitchen. And one was stained with lip-stick…"

"So, one of the neighbours had come in," Chloe said without great interest, "you know how they keep an eagle eye on dad. We might as well just give them the key, or better still leave the door unlocked."

"The side-door into the garden is unlocked and they do have the front door key," Lauren continued. "To be perfectly honest Mum never seemed to mind, but I find it a bit unsettling when I am here on my own and suddenly someone like Marsha appears. I actually have to get myself up and dressed early just in case one of her old coven makes a surprise appearance."

"I'm not getting your point, Lauren," Chloe said, applying the finishing touch to her damaged nail, "Mum and Dad have known all of them forever. They've known us since we were babies. Why would Dad having a coffee with one or other of them be deemed strange behavior?"

"That's the thing. It wouldn't. But I don't think any of them was his mystery guest."

"Lauren, you're being obtuse. This isn't some cheap thriller or bodice ripper. There are loads of women Dad knows and I suspect they all wear lipstick and would have had a perfectly good reason for visiting for a cuppa. There's Hazel for one. You told me he'd been to see her about your kids' schooling. Or the Rabbi's wife that he's so fond of telling us about. Maybe she was on an emergency chicken-soup and chopped-liver mercy run."

"Hazel wouldn't have been making evening calls. And the Rabbi's wife wouldn't go visiting men on her own, even one as harmless as Dad."

Chloe was wondering how she could bring this conversation to an end.

"Lauren, can you get to the point do you think? Or are you deliberately creating some fictional female admirer for Dad, just to annoy me?"

"Annoy?" Lauren's voice rose an octave which was usually a sign of an imminent explosion, but Chloe felt she didn't really care. If her sister lost it with her then that would at least bring the boring conversation to an end. But it didn't.

"Ok, Chloe, let me intrigue you then. Dad lied to me about it,"

"What *are* you talking about now, sister dear?"

"He lied. L.I.E.D. And yes, he lied in capital letters."

"And you would know he lied, how?" Chloe asked despite feeling she might not like to be a party to this matter.

"Because he said Marsha had popped in. Now, Marsha never pops in. Of all of mother's coven she was the only one who came with great purpose, usually bringing enough food to feed a small emerging nation for a month, not to mention those amazing freshly baked cakes she used to corrupt us all with."

"And?" Chloe asked despite herself.

"I saw Marsha the next day. I thanked her for keeping an eye on Dad."

"And?" Chloe asked again, realising there was no way she could avoid the end of this story.

"And she apologised."

"For what? Coming in to see Dad? Putting him in a compromising situation?"

"No. For not coming. She said she'd been meaning to and felt terrible because she'd been so busy with her own stuff all week."

"So, who did Dad have in for coffee?" Chloe asked after a long pause when the toenails and everything else had been forgotten.

"You know, Chloe," Lauren continued and Chloe knew her sister was really troubled when she spoke to her directly by name and in that tone, "I have not the faintest fucking idea."

Chapter 24

I felt quite ill after I watched Lizzie's car drive away. I went upstairs and drew back the curtains a little, still feeling as if I had something to hide. That was the whole thing about the Lizzie years. There was always something to hide. The excitement, the fear, the adrenalin pounding through my body, the testosterone rushing through my very being, the satisfaction of private cravings, the guilt, the wish for it to be all over, the need for it never to end. If that sounds like a long list of oxymorons, then that is exactly what my whole life was when Lizzie was a part of it. An oxymoron.

There were times when it seemed that without her there could be no life and times when, with her, life was impossible. And after her visit all those feelings came rushing back and I was treading water, just doing enough to save myself from drowning. Yet, with nobody to whom I could wave, I was drowning. And that was what I deserved. I deserved to die, and Helen deserved to live, but we don't always get what we want or what we deserve. The Rolling Stones realised that and the words of that song replayed inside my head. You'd think I was too old to live my life to the accompaniment of pop lyrics, but somehow that's the way it's always been for me. I think classical music is simply the King's New Clothes. I've yawned my way through the odd opera or concert and long to leap to my feet and yell out, "Go on admit it. You're only here because you want to say you've been. You're only here to be seen here. This is just plain boring."

So, there I was looking at the lights of the car disappearing into the distance and thinking "The Night has a Thousand Eyes" and "Because the Night" and "Only the Lonely" and all those great 60's songs that were really just a decade before my time but which still became the soundtrack to my teens because each and every one carried a remembrance of a girl or a night or a lost relationship.

I was doing my best to ensure that neither Lauren nor Chloe noticed anything (Adam was too tied up in his own personal disaster to notice anything and anyway we only FaceTimed) but Lauren had always been sharp when it comes to atmosphere and she and I were living under the same roof.

I'd missed a trick when I'd left those two coffee cups out and I'd told a stupid lie and I wouldn't have put it past her to have followed that one up with Marsha although she'd not faced up to me about it. That made it worse. I'd had all this with Lizzie when Helen was alive. Covering my tracks and wondering if I could remember what story I had told to explain exactly where I had been when I had not really been there at all.

I tried to remember how it had all started. I'd never been unfaithful in all my years of marriage. I'd been tempted, but what man hasn't? I'd had women hit on me at work, at meetings, even in our younger days in our social circle. But I'd just batted them away, sometimes after a bit of mild flirting, the odd coffee or drink about which I told Helen a white lie. Yet, they were always white lies and the lies I told about Lizzie were the blackest of the black.

I couldn't even recall exactly why Lizzie was at the hotel in Manchester when we met. She was a matrimonial lawyer (there's real irony if you like). I think she may have been on a case up there and simply been staying at the same hotel as I was and wandered innocently down to the bar in the evening just to avoid watching TV alone in her room. But then I am not sure anything Lizzie did was totally innocent.

Later she did mention that she'd checked in at the same time as me and that something I had said to the hotel employee had amused her.

It may have been when the girl asked how I would like to pay and I'd said "I'd rather not" which wasn't exactly original or hilarious but she seemed to find funnier than the Eastern European girl behind the reception desk. But then, as we always used to say there is nothing funny about coming from Eastern Europe. Just ask my grandparents.

Anyway, nothing happened between me and Lizzie that night, but we did stay up until the early hours of the morning when the bar had emptied and the staff wanted to close up. And something just clicked and we both knew it. It was mental as well as physical. It was like we had found each other. I mean, really found each other after a long journey through an icy wasteland.

Now, that's not fair on Helen because it makes it sound as if my marriage was awful whilst in fact it was pretty much perfect. We got on well, we were the best of friends as well as life partners, we still made love... yes, we still made love but in the same way we had done throughout our marriage. I lied to Lizzie about that. I told her we didn't, but then I was trying to avoid pain for everybody and if you want to make people feel better then you have to tell lies. Just ask any doctor or lawyer or property developer for that matter. Everybody lies.

Only I thought the lies had all stopped. I thought Helen had never known and so I had saved her the pain. But, looking out the night of Lizzie's re-appearance, into the darkness of an empty street, looking at those stars in the sky, each and every one representing one of my lies, I wondered if, perhaps, she had known all the time and had taken that painful knowledge to the grave. The sins of the past cast a long shadow. As I said, I am not a good person and however many times I visit the synagogue, however many prayers I say, I cannot believe that G-d will ever forgive me.

Chapter 25

Adam Kent walked into his office building, Starbucks in hand, Wall Street Journal tucked under his arm. He could have simply knocked a coffee out of a machine on the twenty-first floor where his office was positioned and grabbed the Journal from the pile by reception. Adam was a man of habit. He liked to rise early, jog in Central Park, shower, shave and dress for work. Smart casual was the mantra at Goldfarb & Hemingway Wealth Management so he could continue to wear trainers and then sit down for a bit near the office, take a few slugs of coffee (saving the rest to take with him), get the gist of what the Journal had to say and then enter the huge atrium of the Bankway Towers building.

He felt more positive than he had done in a while. He'd been out on his third date with Kelly the previous evening and it had gone well, well enough to call it an actual date. The kosher meal had been fun. She had asked all the right questions, made all the right appreciative noises and had wanted to try everything. He now knew that *Gefilte* fish wasn't for her and he'd made her smile by explaining it was made by chopping up a few sundry fishes and turning them into … well, another fish.

He'd taught her that chopped liver was best eaten with egg and onion and pickled cucumber off a matzo cracker and that the matzah balls floating in the chicken soup should properly be called *kneidlach* and anyway needed to be smaller and firmer rather than the fluffy, disintegrating monsters that filled his bowl to over-flowing. He told her that nobody made chicken soup like his mother and he fought back the tears as he realised that neither he, nor she, would ever be able to test that assertion. If she had a recipe it was in her head and her head was in a grave and there would be no more huge cauldrons made for *shabbas* or the Festivals or Passover. No more squabbling over who got the little eggs that sometimes came with the chicken or the special weeks when she had the time to make *kreplech*, little pockets of pasta stuffed with meat. That all belonged to the past and Kelly was no part of that. Time would tell whether she would prove to be part of his future.

They'd parted with a kiss last night. He'd felt that if he had pushed it there might have been more, but he didn't want to face another loss in his life through the wrong move. His mother, his wife and his children were quite enough of a tally to be getting on with. Obviously and inevitably, they'd talked a bit about his case and he was grateful that she hadn't given up on it and still had a few ideas, a few cards to play. But, as she repeated, it was all about timing, all about finding the right judge and maybe even the right venue for any application. She felt that maybe, just maybe, the Gilberts had been too clever in moving the children out of America. Europe generally and France in particular might give them some other options once the family was finally resident there.

Life still had its wrinkles though. He'd had both his sisters Facetiming him together, something that usually only occurred on his birthday and telling him that something was up with his father.

"Of course, something's up with him," he'd said, "he's lost the love of his life, his wife, his partner. Do you really expect him to be behaving normally?"

That had not been good enough for them.

"Do you remember when we were kids, you were maybe sixteen or seventeen, we were horrid teenagers, that there was a time when things weren't great between mum and dad?"

Adam hesitated before he replied. Yes, he did remember. You could have cut the tension in the house with a knife, his father was always disappearing. Either to his office to make whispered calls or to meetings that could only be held in the evening or on business trips to look at a property here a property there, potential foreign investments that never came to fruition. He'd gone to Spain a few times, Florida, even the Caribbean and Mum had always been left behind, ostensibly to look after them even though they'd felt they were quite old enough to be left on their own and had tried to encourage her to go with him. But, the thing was that Dad had never asked. He'd seemed happy, even anxious to get away on his own and although he always returned laden with gifts, not just for them, but for his wife as well, sometimes, just sometimes the presents didn't seem to relate to where he said he'd been.

There had been that one time when they'd surprised him by meeting him at the airport and although he had greeted them warmly, done all the right things by throwing his arms around them for a group family hug, Adam had noticed the way his eyes had wandered to the side as if looking to see if he were being watched. As time passed, Adam began to recognise the signs of the lone traveler and then, casting his mind back to that morning at Heathrow, his father had seemed anything but.

His sisters were not being put off enough by his lukewarm interest.

"Well, Dad's acting just like he did back then. Only it's obviously not Mum he's keeping out of the loop. It's us. He puts the phone down when we come into the room, closes the lid of his laptop, and generally seems to be living in another world."

"Well, maybe Mum is in that other world with him," Adam had said, wanting to talk about his own issues. He'd become inured to his sisters' sense of the melodramatic over the years. Even a bad date was the signal for hours of analysis of what had gone wrong and self-incrimination before blaming everybody but themselves.

"You don't get it, Adam. You're not here spending time with him. You can speak to him, ask him what's going on. He may open up to you."

"Ok. I'll do it when I get a few moments," Adam had replied.

"No, Adam, not good enough," Chloe had said in *that* voice that so reminded him of their mother and then Lauren, sounding far more together than he'd heard her for ages, chimed in:

"Tonight, Adam, you have to do it tonight. Do you promise?"

"There's the time difference." Adam had said hoping to fob them both off. The last thing he needed was a heart to heart with his father which could only end in mutual embarrassment.

"Adam, make it work." Chloe had said and then blown him a kiss and disconnected.

He breezed into his office, smiled at the pretty, black receptionist Lorraine and made his way to where his own PA, Karen sat.

"Morning," he said, pulling the Danish he always bought her from his case. She took it, but without her usual complaint about the calories and seemed distracted.

"Are you ok?" Adam asked. "Is everything set up in Room C for the Kreitzman meeting?"

Leon Kreitzman was Adam's biggest client. He'd made his money out of a chain of West Coast supermarkets and property and had then become a snowbird spending the winters in Miami. He came to New York every other month to go through his portfolio (now valued at three billion dollars) and spend a few days with his much younger mistress at the apartment he rented for her on the Upper Side. After their meetings they'd got into the habit of going out to a little kosher place nearby and having a bowl of matzah ball soup and a corned beef and pastrami sandwich with pickles and French fries on the side. It was a cholesterol nightmare, but Leon, in his early seventies and looking a good ten years younger, felt it was part of the indulgence he could afford himself in Manhattan when his wife of nearly fifty years kept him so disciplined in Florida. His mistress kept him disciplined as well but that was because she knew he liked it.

"The meeting's cancelled," Karen said. "Mr Kreitzman's secretary called."

"Did she reschedule? Is he unwell? Maybe I should call" Adam said, his words blurring into each other. Leon had never missed an appointment during the decade through which Adam had nurtured his money to its current monumental proportions.

"No, she didn't want to reschedule. And I didn't get the impression he was ill. But Mr Goldfarb wants to see you anyway. He said you should go through as soon as you got in."

She glanced at her watch.

"And he did say as soon as you arrived."

Adam did not like the sound of any of this. Donny Goldfarb was the grandson of the founder of the firm and was notoriously difficult to pin down for a meeting. If anybody wanted to see him they generally had to get a date in his diary for some weeks ahead. But here he was wanting to do something with Adam ad hoc and Donny was not an ad hoc kind of guy. None of this augured well and as Adam made his way up to the Executive Floor two levels above and traipsed along, his feet sinking into the thick pile carpet, towards Goldfarb's huge office, he had a terrible feeling of impending doom. His mother had told him never to expect the worst because it didn't usually happen. He just hoped that she was right because, on this occasion, he didn't feel as if she was going to be. And when one's mother was wrong what else was left?

Chapter 26

The fact that we continued to run our property business, David and I, from Hampstead, rather than much cheaper premises nearer to Edgware where I live or Stanmore where David Segal, my friend and partner ended up, was an indulgence.

The rent was ridiculously high for what we had, and parking was a nightmare and all our efforts to buy the freehold had come to nothing. Now, we probably couldn't afford it and the Stamford Hill based Chassidic property company who owned it knew they were on to a good thing. We were excellent tenants, always paid our rent on time and had improved the property no end within the Planning restrictions imposed in Heath Street by Camden Council.

The property had a refurbished glass front with the old door (which we'd had to retain) subtly polished. We'd not even been able to change the brass knocker or the antique bell, but to be honest we'd not really wanted to. Our sign, Kengal Properties Limited, trading as Rosebud Estates, we'd both loved Citizen Kane as a movie, was also a simple brass plaque. The whole atmosphere of the building made a statement. It had been erected as a private dwelling in the late eighteenth century, the floors sloped and creaked, the ceilings were low, but it was a few minutes' walk from both Hampstead Station and the Heath so transportation and meditative walks were on our doorsteps not to mention some really good local restaurants and cafes for lunches and coffees, when we felt there was some advantage to getting out of the office itself.

It had been over four months since Helen died and I realised that I had devoted not nearly enough attention to the business. David had been great and the two lads, Sam Birns and Jason Lerman had really stepped up to the plate, despite their relative inexperience, but David kept urging me to get back on the bike.

"You're doing fine, David, you don't need me moping around the place," I'd said only last week, but he had been insistent that I try to come in every day this following week. It was only Wednesday, but I was already feeling the strain. Not just from the pressures of the deals we had underway or which we were on the brink of landing, but because of the conversation I'd had with Adam last night.

Now Adam and I had never had what you might call the typical Jewish father and son relationship. He'd never shown the slightest interest in following in my footsteps nor did we really share any interests. I'd tried to do all the things that fathers are supposed to do. I'd played football and cricket with him in the garden, despite my sporting limitations, I'd traipsed around things like the Natural History and the Science Museum, Helen and I had tried to get him excited about the theatre from his childhood, but somehow he'd always managed to keep his distance. Well, from me certainly although Helen and he seemed to have secrets to which I was never made privy.

For a while I thought he might have been gay, but Helen assured me he never lacked for girlfriends, although I was rarely told about them until they were toast. Even with Carly, the first time he introduced me to her was when he also told me they were getting engaged. We never really argued, like I did with the girls, but we never really engaged either, to any great depth. So, his call the previous evening had taken me by surprise.

He'd seemed subdued and I'd felt he had something to tell me rather than ask me, but ask he did and when he posed the question it came out quickly as if he'd had to learn it by heart.

"The girls seem worried about you, dad. They've asked me to have a chat with you..."

"Why can't they have a chat themselves Adam? Lauren lives with me and even Chloe seems to be spending more time at the house than usual."

"I think they're finding it difficult to talk to you. They ask you things and you don't answer and it's like you're hiding something from them."

I'd thought I had been less transparent, but clearly I had underestimated my daughters' powers of observation. I'd thought they were both far too tied up with what was going on in their lives to give a second thought to the turbulence that was occurring in mine.

"You know, Adam. It's been hard since Mum died. And there have been some issues with the business that I've just started to take care of..." That was an easy lie but one that he clearly bought.

"Is everything ok? You don't have any money problems do you?" Adam asked, sounding genuinely concerned.

"No, I'm fine for money." I didn't mean to say it but I couldn't help but add, "and I know that even if I was short none of you would be in a position to help."

The silence at Adam's end told me this hadn't gone down well so I tried to sugar the pill.

"Mum had taken out an insurance policy about which I knew nothing and in fact I'm going to be talking to the accountant about how I can give you guys something."

"That's very kind, dad. So there's nothing else going on that you want to tell me?"

No, nothing I'd replied, at least nothing I *wanted* to tell him about.

"But you don't sound great Adam. Forget about me, is there anything I can help with."

No, nothing, he'd replied, but I'd been left with the feeling there was.

So, that conversation was buzzing around my head when David told me that Sam and Jason wanted to talk to the pair of us, together.

We got Amanda, our PA, to make coffees and sent her down to the little deli for some cakes and sat down with the sound of traffic filtering back up from the street. Double-glazing had been another no-no from the Planners.

Jason was a year older, but when the two of them got together it was always Sam who took the lead. Quite frankly, there were times when I found it hard to tell them apart although they looked quite different. Jason was slim and dark, always looking in need of a shave which may have been a deliberate stubble look or it might have been that he looked that little bit older with the faint hint of a beard. He was in perpetual motion, a little jumpy and for a while I'd thought he might have been on drugs, but that was just the way he was. Sam was almost red-headed, freckled, a little chubby and seemed to be constantly eating something. Much calmer and quieter and a follower rather than a leader. I'd settled for 'Stocky Sam' and 'Jumping Jason' to help me ensure I knew which was which although there were still the odd occasions when I'd call them by each other's names.

"Good to have you back, Daniel," Sam began, as if ushering in a new dawn in the business. "we've missed you," and then glancing a look at David he added, "though David has been great. It's just that you two are a team and this whole operation works so much better when you are in harness."

I couldn't help but smile. He was so earnest, so desperate to say the right thing and there was Jason nodding away in agreement and I wanted to reach out and embrace them both, in a way I'd rarely wanted to hold my own son. More guilt. That was a commodity I was beginning to find cheaper and cheaper. Available at every good corner shop.

"OK, boys, is this the time for a group hug?" I asked.

They looked at each other, ignoring my weak joke.

"We just wanted to talk to you both. Don't worry we're not leaving to set up on our own. And we're not looking for more money. It's just this deal has come our way. It's a really good opportunity. Mixed use development out in Docklands, retail, health club, bit of residential on top. It's not over-priced either. Bit bigger than anything we've done before, but we know if something's worth doing that you'll always find the money."

"Sounds interesting," David said, "how did you come across it?"

Sam and Jason shifted awkwardly in their chairs.

"That's the problem. We got a tip off. From somebody on the inside of the current owner. They're looking for a commission on it," Sam said.

"In cash," Jason added.

"So, let me get this right," I said. "Somebody who doesn't work for us or with us and who, in fact is on the other side in the deal, wants a cash payment to make it happen. That's not a commission. It's a bribe."

Sam made to argue, but I cut him off.

"Listen, boys, I know you're both hungry and ambitious and that's good, but this isn't what we do. We never needed to. I just want to put my head on the pillow at night and fall asleep…"

Given the fact that I'd not slept through a night since I'd buried my wife that was a bit rich, but that was certainly the case when I'd had my bedfellow. Helen had always complained that I'd started snoring before she'd closed her eyes. Lizzie, hadn't complained. She'd simply rolled me over and made love to me. But, that wasn't the thought or the picture I wanted at that moment. I just wanted this awkward meeting to be over and it was only when it was and I'd left the office on my own to take my favourite walk across the Heath through the woods, that I realised that David had not said one single word about the proposal. He was there, back in the office, with Sam and Jason and whilst I couldn't really believe they'd do anything behind my back, I understood only too clearly that the only person I had ever met who I could absolutely trust was Helen. Certainly, given my past history and the thoughts now running through my head, I could not trust myself.

Chapter 27

Lauren waited patiently in the school playground for Peta. Callum was in Year 3 and Peta was in the *Gan,* the Hebrew word for the nursery class. They finished at one o'clock and he wouldn't be out for 3.30 pm so she always found herself with a couple of hours to fill in.

Most of the other mothers knew each other well and they'd arrange playdates or have a rota, but she was the outsider. She guessed they all knew her story because a lot of them had grown up in the neighborhood, which was to all intents and purposes a village when it came to gossip. Was it because they knew her background that they didn't bother to reach out to her or was it because they were just a bunch of stuck-up, middle class Jewish Princesses? Probably a bit of each if truth be told and so she usually took Peta off on her own to the park where they fed the ducks or played on the swings and if she was really lucky there was another single child who wanted to connect. Sometimes from the Jewish school, but most often not.

She was well aware she wasn't helping her own cause. She could have struck up conversation, joined in the inanities that swirled around her, found out a few names of Peta's classmates and maybe issued tea invitations. But she hadn't. She couldn't. She felt like damaged goods, like the woman from 'The Scarlet Letter' with something like 'O' for outsider carved into her forehead.

It didn't help that these children had already bonded together for well over a year. Everybody was invited to everybody else's party and when birthdays came in close proximity mothers buddied up to arrange a joint celebration. At this age there was a division of the sexes, which became less blurred in Callum's class. The parties for the little girls followed an almost exact pattern. The kids were bundled into what were obviously expensive designer clothes, escorted to one large house after another, games were played, toys were squabbled over, somebody cried, somebody comforted, the same entertainer did a few tricks, made animals from balloons. If the weather was nice there might be a few paddling pools in the garden or even sometimes an exodus to the park for a picnic.

Callum had already been invited to a bowling party, a swimming party, a laser party and a football party. He told Lauren that he wanted a running party because he was the fastest runner in his class and presumably was confident that he would win every race, but so far she'd not figured out exactly where or how to organise that. However, he had clearly integrated and made friends. He chattered non-stop about them on his way to school and in the car on his way home. Rafi did this, Simeon did that, Brandon was the naughtiest boy in the class, Levi had some learning difficulties but was funny. Peta said nothing.

One of the mothers had felt sorry for her and included her in the class invitation even though Peta could not even remember the name of the classmate whose party it was. Lauren had taken her and watched sadly as she stepped back from everything. She didn't want to play hop-scotch or pass the parcel or musical chairs or even join in a chorus of 'Happy Birthday'. She really didn't want to be there. Lauren had chosen the present, some replica doll from the latest movie that had grabbed the kids' fancies and saw with horror that the child had been given at least four other identical gifts. She had little doubt they would circulate, be re-packaged and move on from child to child until some mother became bored and took them all off to the charity shop, because the film was no longer fashionable.

She glanced down at her watch, suddenly realising she was alone in the playground. One by one the other children had come out, been gathered into the arms of a parent or a nanny and had gone. But no sign of Peta. She felt a sense of panic. Had she been taken ill and had she missed the call on her way to the school?

Parents were discouraged from going inside but she didn't care. She pushed open the doors and walked towards the desk guarded by a slightly threatening woman of uncertain age whose most distinguishing feature was a clearly designated grey moustache above her lip. She dimly remembered her name was Mrs Bloom and she struck terror into the hearts of all the other mothers, who never had a good word to say about her.

"Yes," Mrs Bloom said, "what do you want? You really aren't supposed to be in here unless you're delivering a late child or collecting one early." She might as well have added 'for good reason' but she didn't although the threatening words were left hanging in mid-air.

"I'm Peta's mother. She's in the *gan*. Peta Campbell."

I really should change back to Kent, she thought. I've enough problems here without burdening myself with a name that can't possibly be Jewish.

"I'll just call through to her teacher," Mrs Bloom said, "Just wait there and don't go wandering about please. It wasn't her regular teacher today because she's off sick so Miss Gant took the class."

A few minutes later, the very same Miss Gant appeared. Lauren recognised her as the teaching assistant, but didn't like to point out that she looked about twelve years old herself. She was dressed in the 'uniform' that all the more orthodox teachers wore. Long dark denim skirt down to the ankles, wrist-length blouse and jumper, hair dark, long and shiny but un-styled, make-up minimal. She could have been pretty in a different world, but here, well here, she just looked like one of the pack.

"I'm Peta's mother," Lauren said and saw an expression pass across Miss Gants' face that was pure fear. "I've been waiting for ages and she hasn't come out. Has anything happened?"

Miss Gant was now positively quaking as both Lauren and Mrs Bloom caught her in the headlights of the stares.

"Nothing happened. It was play time. He collected her. She clearly knew him because she threw her arms around him. He told me it was fine, that you were ill."

"He? Who's he?" Lauren almost screamed although she already knew the answer to the question.

"Why, her father of course," Miss Gant replied and at that moment she realised that she had made a career-ending result, whilst Lauren knew that her worst fears had just been realised. She should have known that Luke wouldn't just leave it there, that ignoring his texts would see him off. He wasn't that sort of man and now he had returned to prove it.

Chapter 28

Damien Gold sat in the bar at his tennis club wondering just how he could delay going home for another hour or so. Just how fucked up were his wife's family, he asked himself as he emptied his glass and signaled for another bottle of sparkling water. He could really do with a drink, but he had the car with him and he knew that if he had one glass of wine then he'd have another and then be in no fit condition to drive home.

He'd come straight from work although he knew he should have gone home to help put the kids to bed. But the incident with the porridge was still rankling with him and although he accepted that, perhaps, just perhaps, he should do a bit more at home, that outburst from Chloe had just reminded him of an angry, irrational fish-wife. He'd never quite figured out just why fish-wives had traditionally been selected as a symbol of a harridan and decided to spend a few minutes googling that.

He didn't notice that somebody had now perched on the bar stool beside him. She'd been part of the mixed doubles team that had just roundly beaten him and his regular partner, Holly Lewis. He knew her name was Pippa, but before today he'd never seen her at the club.

"You've got a great first service," he said to her with genuine admiration. "Where did you learn to play?"

"Back home, in Florida," she replied and he noted for the first time the American accent. She'd said little on court and had let her serve, volley and net play do the talking. She'd played alongside Richard Sheringham, the club captain and he should have known that he would have picked somebody who would cover the deficiencies in his own game and guarantee a victory. Richard usually talked a better game than he played.

"Pippa, Pippa Cummings," she extended her hand and then grasped his very firmly when he returned the gesture.

"Damien. Damien Gold," he replied and couldn't help noticing that she was glancing at his hand to see if he was wearing a wedding ring. Which he wasn't. He didn't know many Jewish guys who did. It wasn't to fool anybody. You put the ring on your bride under the *chuppah*, the wedding canopy. You didn't exchange rings and she didn't make any vows either. That was kind of representative of a woman's role in traditional Judaism, although he wouldn't have liked to be the one to persuade a feminist like Chloe of the accuracy of that.

"You're not a bad player yourself," Pippa said.

"Damning with faint praise," Damien said. He inspected her a little more closely. The club was largely Jewish, but she didn't look it although that didn't mean anything nowadays. Look at his nephew and niece, Callum and Peta. Neither of them looked the least Semitic despite their mother who could have been taken for nothing but.

"All I meant was I could see you play. But I could also see you only play for fun and don't really work at it."

"And you don't?" he asked curiously.

"No, I don't play for fun and I do work at it."

Her fair hair was close cropped giving her an athletic, boyish appearance. She had piercing grey eyes now fully revealed as she pushed her Ray-Bans up on to her forehead. He noticed that she was wearing a Rolex watch and the necklace around her neck sparkled with what could only be real diamonds. She had a Lacoste t-shirt on top of designer jeans. He couldn't peer at the label, but he knew it would be from somewhere Chloe would have killed to be able to afford.

Pippa smiled and revealed perfect teeth. She was carefully made-up and had taken the time to do that after her post match shower, so he guessed she must be meeting somebody and then going out. He also looked for an engagement or a wedding ring, but the only one there was on a little finger with a single amethyst matching the bracelet around her right wrist. Behind that there was a small tattoo of a single small flower. Definitely not Jewish he decided. Nice Jewish girls didn't go in for tattoos.

"I went to tennis camp back home. It was all a bit ruthless. My mother was a tiger. Thought I could make it on the circuit. I got ranked in the top two hundred of the Under 16's," she made the statement without seeming to boast, "but just couldn't kick on. Then I hurt my knee and my parents got divorced and my mom ended up marrying a Brit and here we are."

"And you're planning to relaunch your career?" Damien asked, perhaps with a hint of sarcasm he didn't intend.

"I think this may be as good as it gets. A suburban tennis club with a decent gym and bar. Do they make decent cocktails here? I've not had a proper one since we arrived."

"They don't," Damien replied, "but there's a bar in the village that does. Barman's from Canada and seems to know what he's doing."

She glanced at her watch. It was gone six. He should make his excuses and leave now. Tell her he was going home to read his children a bedtime story, have supper with his wife, kiss and make-up and that would be the end of it until the next doubles they played.

But he didn't. All he said was,

"I could take you there if you want."

"Are you sure you've got the time?" she asked as if it was an obligation not to be a burden.

"All the time in the world," he replied, and thought all the time in which I can try to forget my father-in-law and whatever he's up to, my troubled son and my annoying daughter and my wife who seems to care more about her family than me.

Chapter 29

Adam felt in free fall. He'd done what his sisters had asked and had tried to have a man to man conversation with his father. If he'd succeeded then it would have been a first, but he hadn't succeeded. Yes, they'd spoken, but he'd got nowhere and he knew the exact reason for that. On this occasion it had nothing to do with his dad. It was all about him.

His father had realised that something was off kilter and had given him the opportunity to tell him, but he hadn't grasped it. He'd tried to discover the reason for that. Was he still being kind and noble and not wanting to burden his already over-laden father with more problems? Or was it that he was simply ashamed of the fact that his life, which was already a rail-crash, had now burst into flames leaving him only with ashes. He wanted to get closer to his father now he was the only parent he possessed, but somehow he could not figure out the way to make it happen.

He'd not anticipated a good meeting with Donny Goldfarb, but then he'd not anticipated the disaster it proved to be either. Donny's office had views of both the Hudson and the East River. Huge glass windows, reminiscent of the ill-fated Twin Towers, gave him the view that could not but bring with it the feeling that, from his eyrie, he could rule the world. He and Adam's father-in-law both. Was there room for both of them? Yet, despite his vast family wealth, despite the fact that he wasn't much older than Adam himself, he had felt that Donny was essentially a decent person, which Benjamin Gilbert most certainly was not.

When his mother had died Donny had heard and called him immediately, arranged cover for him, told him to take as long as he needed and had even booked a first class return flight to London for him on the next available plane. When his marriage had fallen apart then Donny, the busiest and most inaccessible man in the world, had found the time to take him out for lunch and listen while he talked, telling him that he'd already bought his way out of two unhappy marriages and that there was always another taxi on the rank. Adam hadn't liked to point out that he was in no position to buy Carly off as he didn't want his boss thinking that he was using his kindness to get some more money. But kindness it had been, that was for sure.

Adam had earned that consideration. He'd been a rising star in the company and had made them a lot of money. Yes, Leon Kreitzman was his biggest client, but he wasn't the only one. Adam worked all hours of the day and night. He'd be having a morning meeting on the West Coast and an evening dinner in New York and consistently be able to turn on the charm and convince whoever he was meeting that Goldfarb and Hemingway were the right people to handle their money and that he, Adam Kent, was the right person to care for it once it was there. Usually he succeeded. Their department meetings often reminded him of a collection of double-glazing or life insurance salesmen reporting on their door to door sale successes, but he was still the one with the best strike rate. In typically brash American fashion the company had all sorts of employee of the month awards, though with more sophisticated names than that, such as "The NIAA" which meant the New Investor Award Achievement and they came with a framed certificate and a few thousand dollars of gift vouchers for places like Tiffany's and Nieman Marcus or best seats for the hot shows on Broadway. He'd seen Springsteen's one-man production and 'Hamilton', but had struggled to find suitable female company and had eventually taken a friend from the gym, Ricky, who was very appreciative, but somewhat annoying company. He'd sung along with The Boss and whooped and cheered on his feet at the end of every song in 'Hamilton' and Adam had just wanted to tell him that wasn't how it was done in England. But he wasn't in England and that was how it was done in Manhattan so nobody else objected. Adam was, once again, the odd man out, not Ricky.

Today, though there were to be no certificates, no awards, no bonuses or accolades. Today, Donny merely nodded him into a chair, went through the motions of offering him a coffee, seeming relieved when he refused and headed straight into his agenda.

"I gather old man Kreitzman cancelled," Donny said.

"News travels fast," Adam replied, his tone lighter than he felt.

"It does," Donny said, grimly. "And it spreads. Like bushfire. I don't like bushfires in my company. Hard to put out and bad for business. You always have to rebuild after a fire and we're not in the construction business."

That was a long speech for Donny Goldfarb. The metaphors were unusual as was the lack of four letter epithets. Donny may have been brought up in money, but he'd not been brought up in class.

"Do you know why Kreitzman cancelled?" Donny asked.

"No," Adam replied, although he fully realised from the way the question had been framed that Donny did.

"He cancelled because your ex father-in-law is a powerful man in this city. He warned him off you. And he warned the Seymours and the Edelsons and the Mansfield Foundation," Donny added listing the next biggest names on Adam's client list.

"And they all reached out to you?" Adam said quietly.

"Yes, they all reached out to me."

"And you supported me of course," Adam said, his cheeks flushing, his fists clenched, almost half out of his seat.

"Listen Adam, this isn't personal. This business was started by my grandfather and if he'd had to face a situation like this he'd have told them all to fuck off and take their business elsewhere. But times change. We're a listed company now, I've a Board of Directors, thousands of shareholders to which I'm responsible as Chairman and if I were just to stand by and watch them leave it would be my head on the block. I can't just make decisions like that."

"So what did you tell them?"

"That I'd take a personal interest in their affairs. Andy Myers would be their contact …."

"And they accepted that?"

"No, Adam they didn't accept it. They said they would stay, but only on one condition."

"Which was?"

"That you don't. I'm sorry, Adam but we have to let you go. Don't worry. We'll give you a generous settlement and a reference…."

But Adam was no longer listening. He had left the room and was already in the lift. On his way down.

Chapter 30

Lauren could not stop crying. She just felt helpless. She and her father could rant and rave all they wanted at the school, threaten everybody from the Chair of the Governors through the Headmistress right down to the hapless Miss Gant, but none of that brought Peta home.

She was safe. Well sort of. Luke had been at great pains to tell her that she was well and happy and back with him in the West Country and clearly glad to be back with her old friends at her nursery there. She'd threatened Luke too and after one particular rant he'd told her he'd been recording the call and had every intention of using it in court to prove what an unsuitable mother she was.

She had thought that she would never need to speak to him again, but that was just wishful thinking. The reality was that they were still married, they had children and she'd taken them away without his consent and with the connivance of her father. She had called the police the moment she'd got back from the school on the day he'd taken her. A woman constable had called at the house, listened patiently to her story and then asked if she had formal custody of the children. When she was told that there was no kind of court order she rose to go.

"I'm sorry, Mrs Campbell, but you've given me no evidence to suggest that your daughter is in danger. From what you are telling me your husband has as much right to her as do you. You brought her to London and now he's taken her back to where he lives."

"But he's a vile man," Lauren had sobbed.

"Perhaps he is, perhaps he isn't. He's got no criminal record and no history of violence. I will speak to a local colleague and get her to look in on your husband and daughter, but my advice is to get yourself a good solicitor, go to court and prove that she's better off here with you, her brother and her grandfather, than down there with her father."

Lauren had sat with her head in her hands whilst her father looked on helplessly. She'd spoken to Chloe at hourly intervals and Chloe had been around to visit, but also seemed to have something going on at home that was distracting her. Adam had done what Adam did and had offered his help, but it was a vague gesture and what could he do anyway other than coming back, going to see Luke and beating the living daylights out of him? So, that left her with her father as her only salvation.

"Daddy, can't you do something? You always do something."

She recalled how persistent her father had been in the past whenever one of the children faced a problem. A bully at school, he was there like a shot, a minor car accident and once he was called to the scene he would persuade everybody involved that his daughter was not to blame, a crisis at university and he was there to bring her home. Her mother was much softer, had never liked confrontation, never seemed to need it to achieve her end, but her father seemed to be invigorated by it. That, however, was her father of old and she was hardly recognising the man who was trying to comfort her now.

"Listen, Lauren. You and I know what Luke is like, but he can also come across as very plausible and charming. The school was totally in the wrong to allow Peta to go with him. I've spoken to Hazel who is shattered by the incident and it certainly will never happen again. But that doesn't help you right now."

"I don't want to know what doesn't help me, dad, I want to know what will. Can't you find me a good solicitor? We know that Luke can't afford anybody decent. We discussed that when I first arrived. You deal with lawyers all the time."

"Property guys and commercial ones, yes. But none of those would know anything about matrimonial and children."

"But they'll have partners who will. When I came you told me to ask for whatever I needed. You said you had money. You paid out for that new Mac without blinking. Now, please, just make some calls. You must know somebody."

Daniel hesitated for a moment. Of course he knew somebody. Lizzie had been a rising star in her field when he'd first met her and he'd established, when she'd called to see him, that she was now a partner in a firm that specialised in dealing with exactly the sort of crisis that his daughter was now facing. But, did he want to go there? Could he go there? How would he explain how he even knew this woman who moved in such different circles to his own? Yet, he knew he needed to put his daughter's needs and those of his granddaughter first.

"Ok. I think I know somebody. Let me make the call."

"Do it now, dad, right now, while I'm sitting here. Look at what he's just sent me."

She produced her phone with a series of pictures of Peta. Playing happily at her original nursery, at a birthday party with a mouth smeared with cake, by the side of a rock pool on the beach looking with some interest at a stranded crab. She was impeccably dressed in every one, her hair neatly combed and more importantly with a broad smile on her face at every location. Daniel compared the photos with the miserable little girl who'd seemed so glad to get away from the *Gan* everyday and for a moment, but just for a moment, wondered if perhaps she might indeed be better off with her father. Then, he gathered his thoughts. He was seeing what the devious and cunning Luke wanted him to see. A fiction. These photos were posed, rehearsed. This was not how it really was or how it had been. Lauren had still never told him the whole story of their awful lives with him, but he'd gathered enough to know it had been like living in prison, with hard labour and some physical punishment thrown in for good measure. Now, though, it would be Lauren's word against Luke's. He was the man in possession and children's memories were short. If Peta was happy now she would have forgotten already how unhappy he had made her. In that moment the decision was made.

"Ok. I'm going up to my office to get a number and I'll make the call. But you stay downstairs and play with Callum. He needs you right now and you need to try to help him make sense of what's happened."

That was a rubbish excuse, but there was no way he could make the call to Lizzie and let Lauren hear it from the start. For all that, he owed it to his daughter to help and to help in the best possible way. If that meant reaching out to his ex-mistress, to the woman who had come so close to destroying everything he and Helen had created, then it had to be done.

Chapter 31

Chloe could not believe or accept everything that was going wrong in her life. It was as if the death of her mother had been a signal for chaos. Her brother's marriage was already on the rocks, but now it seemed that he had lost his job as well. Her sister, who'd always been a rebel, was lost and broken since her ex had stolen back her daughter. Her father, well, her father continued to puzzle them all, but worst of all, at least as far as she was concerned, was what was going wrong was her own marriage.

She'd always felt secure in a smug kind of way that although Damien had his faults, could be obsessive and a bit boring at the same time if that were possible, it had still been a good and comfortable union. They were of an age when quite a few of their contemporaries were moving on to pastures new, but Chloe had always served as a shoulder to cry on for her female friends facing matrimonial issues, whilst Damien was known as a good guy to talk to over a drink or a coffee by his male mates in similar situations.

Afterwards, they'd compare notes and although Chloe was not the creative writer in the family, she'd always felt there was a decent sitcom tucked into the situation, looking at a marriage from both sides through two different pairs of eyes. She'd even mentioned it to Lauren who'd made a note in that annoying little pad she always produced when she'd thought somebody had said something worth mentioning. Although there was never any evidence that any of the notes had ever seen the light of day or served a useful purpose. She'd have been better off making a shopping list because whenever Chloe went to visit her and her father, they were always out of something. Milk, bread, cereals, even toilet paper on one embarrassing occasion and she had to leave the house and go on a mercy run to a local store.

Chloe had nobody to talk to her about her current issues and she did not even know if Damien recognised that there were issues of a level that needed discussion. They were hardly talking between themselves. He'd arrived back very drunk the other night, his car abandoned somewhere between the tennis club and home. It had taken him a while to remember and he hadn't collected it until the next evening as he'd felt he might still be over the limit. He'd offered no explanation other than to say he needed a break. That he couldn't take any more of her moaning on about the kids or the latest problem in her family and that he just needed some space.

He'd gone out the next night and the one after that as well and again, offered no apology or explanation. The kids and Tommy in particular were reacting badly to the atmosphere at home. Tommy could not be made to do anything and kept asking for his father. Scarlett had pushed the boundaries of her cuteness far beyond the acceptable and Chloe was not sure how much more she, herself, could take. If only her mother were alive. She would know what to do. But, she wasn't alive and that was that, so she would just have to figure it out for herself. Perhaps, after all these years she'd never fully grown up and was now discovering that she had to, just to survive.

She knew something was up with Damien beyond what he was telling her. She'd tried playing private detective, talking to a few of his friends at the club, calling on the pretext that she wanted to talk to him, but couldn't raise him on his phone. The very phone he'd left in the kitchen one day, but had seized out of her hand just as she realised he had changed the pin password that they both shared. The friends had given her no useful information and his messages and emails were inaccessible to her, so she even thought of following him or maybe hiring somebody to do that. However, that would have been too surreal. The Kent family weren't like that. She wasn't like that. She was just a middle class, Jewish mother / housewife who wanted a normal life.

Normal? What exactly was that? Life had been normal. Friday nights with her parents, shared holidays with the family, school open days, dinner parties with friends when the same old stories, the same old jokes circulated. She remembered feeling a bit bored with it all back in the day, waiting for her big adventure, indulging in creating a bucket list of all the things she wanted to do before she was forty. Damien had done the same and although they'd hardly interfaced, they'd agreed to do their best to satisfy the other. That's what partners did, after all, they compromised, met in the middle and they'd been partners in the true sense of the word.

She had done something she never did during the day. Had opened a bottle of wine and poured herself a glass. Neither of them were big drinkers which made Damien's behavior even more inexplicable, but if he was going to have a tipple (well, far more than a tipple it seemed) then why shouldn't she? Was this how it ended? A sad lonely woman with the baggage of children emptying a bottle of wine a day and hiding it from the neighbours and the refuse collectors? She was being over-dramatic she knew. It was one glass. She'd put the rest of the bottle in the fridge and make something nice for supper, something Damien really liked but rarely got. Maybe some egg and chips. She hated the smell of frying in her kitchen and her chips were never the best, but at least he would see that she'd got the message.

She would text him and apologise even though she didn't feel that, apart from the porridge on the shoe incident, she'd done anything terribly wrong. Tell him to get home early. Have the kids bathed and put to bed. Find something to watch on tv, a serial they'd been waiting to binge with. Avoid talking about anybody in her family. Maybe, even try to plan a holiday.

Then the phone rang.

"Hello, is that the Kent home?"

"Yes," she replied preparing to cut off the caller if they were trying to sell her something.

"This is the Inspiration Wine Bar, in the village."

She knew the place, as she sometimes parked illegally in their car park but had never been inside. Damien and she didn't do wine bars. He always said they were too old for them.

"Is Mr Kent there?"

"No, he's not home from work yet," she replied.

"Is that his wife?"

"Yes, I'm his wife," Chloe replied, totally bemused.

"Oh good. We've had a bit of trouble tracking you down. It's just than when you both were in here the other night he paid by credit card, but our internet wasn't working so we wrote the numbers down by hand and we think we might have got one of them wrong. Maybe when he gets home or when he's passing he could give us the right number. It was a bit of a bill, that's all."

"What do you mean, a bit of a bill?" Chloe asked.

"Well, you had those cocktails and then that champagne, if you remember. We all thought you were having such a good time. You're a lovely couple. You should come in more often. So, will you tell him?"

"Yes, yes of course I will. I'm sorry."

"Well, we'll see you both again soon," the cheerful woman on the other end of the line said and as Chloe thoughtfully replaced the phone all she could think was that the woman would be ill-advised to hold her breath until that actually happened.

Chapter 32

When I called Lizzie and told her about Lauren's problem her first question was,

"Is this wise?"

"It's what you do, isn't it?"

"Yes, but we've got other lawyers here who do the same thing as well."

"Are they as good as you?"

"You know I'm the best at everything I set out to do," she replied and although I couldn't see her face I could imagine that slightly wicked glint in her eyes.

"You always underestimated yourself," I said, continuing the vein of levity that I certainly did not feel.

"Seriously, Daniel, I've been doing this sort of thing for years and I am good at it, but this is an awful responsibility you want to put on me. I mean, your own daughter, your own granddaughter. And how are you going to explain me away to her?"

I'd thought of that already. I'd invented a fictional client who'd undergone a similar trauma and remembered the name of the lawyer he'd used because he'd never stopped singing her praises. Years of my affair had taught me duplicity until, for a while, it had become second nature.

I finally arranged an appointment at her office which was in the trendy part of Shoreditch, not far from Liverpool Street. That hadn't been where she'd practiced when we'd been together so, at least, I didn't have to pretend not to have been there before.

The appointment wasn't until the following afternoon, which did not please Lauren who couldn't understand why we couldn't just drop everything and go immediately. I had to explain that going to see a solicitor wasn't like doing a supermarket shop where you simply turned up and chose what you wanted off the shelves.

"They'll want to see your passport when we go in," I added, "and a utility bill, but obviously you don't have one to hand. So maybe a bank statement or something will do."

She gave me an old-fashioned look as if I might have been asking her to produce the Dead Sea Scrolls.

"In case you've forgotten, we left the house in a bit of a hurry. My passport's still in a drawer in the bedroom (unless Luke has decided to shred it which I wouldn't put beyond him). I'm not usually one for carrying utility bills around with me and I don't actually have a bank account just in my name. Luke made sure everything went into an account where he would know what was going on…"

I mentally kicked myself for my own insensitivity. I was only just becoming aware of how far off the edge of an ordinary existence she had got.

"Listen, don't worry," I said in my most reassuring voice, "we'll get round it. This lady we're seeing is supposed to be really nice. I'll take everything for myself and I'm the one who'll be paying anyway, so why should they worry?"

"I've got my driving licence in my purse," Lauren said as if that deserved a pat on the head.

"Well, that will just have to do," I replied and felt that all the years had been stripped away from my daughter. She was once again a frail, little girl looking to her daddy for all the answers.

I couldn't say that Lizzie knew me well enough to bend the rules, because when we did meet up we were both going to have to give an Oscar winning performance to prove we were two strangers meeting for the first time. I was hopeful I could pull it off. As I said, deception had become second nature to me over the years. It might actually prove harder for Lizzie. There had been nobody she had needed to deceive and to me she had always been a most transparent person, wearing her heart on her sleeve. But then, that was a luxury afforded to a single woman having an affair with a married man.

I actually called Chloe and asked her to come over later that day to keep Lauren company. I wasn't passing the buck, but just thought it would be good for them both. Chloe had also been seeming less effervescent that usual, less concerned with the trivia that seemed to play such a big part in her social circle. She didn't argue and I got the distinct impression she was glad to have an excuse to get out of the house. I was sort of coping, but in an out-of-body experience sort of way, as if none of this was really happening. This was the stuff of TV dramas or the lives of others. Helen would have dealt with all this far better, but having to do it on my own actually made me want to rise to the occasion, so as not to let her down. I didn't want to let anybody down. I'd done that all too often in the past.

I had an odd sort of feeling that this might be some kind of divine retribution. You think you've survived your sin, you think you've been forgiven, have passed through the fire and come out merely slightly scalded at the other end. You've attended synagogue on successive Days of Atonement after the fateful events and abased yourself, scourged your body with sackcloth and ashes (well, metaphorically at least) until eventually you've managed to convince yourself that there's nothing left for which to atone. It's like having some kind of gastric flu. You retch and retch until your stomach is empty and there's nothing more to bring up. Yet, the taste of bile exists and it doesn't actually work like that, because there is always some huge foot, clad in an iron boot, waiting for you up above, waiting to stamp you into oblivion. The wearer has more time than you. He can afford to wait because he has all the time in the world. He created the world and he created time.

What was it they said in 'Jaws'? Just when you thought it was safe to go back in the water?....Well, after all those years post-Lizzie, when I had only given her the odd passing thought whenever something had jogged my memory, like a film we'd seen surreptitiously together was shown on television or Helen and I ended up somewhere that I'd been with her, I'd thought I was well and truly back on dry land. And now, here I was, once more paddling for my life against the tide, for my life and the lives of my family. I was a desperate man and desperate men will do anything.

Chloe duly arrived. Scarlett was off school with a mild cold (the other mothers would ring a plague bell if they saw another pupil so much as sneeze and threaten their precious darlings) and I feared that the proximity of a little girl, someone else's little girl, might set Lauren off again into floods of tears. My children, though, never cease to surprise me. In fact, Lauren made a great fuss of her niece and insisted on playing with her almost to the exclusion of the child's own mother.

I left them all happily drawing and telling fairy stories to fit the illustrations. Lauren was a decent artist. I'd had some hopes that she might turn out to be the illustrator of her own books for children, but like most of my hopes as far as my daughter was concerned they'd flown high for a while before bursting and dying.

I needed to gather my thoughts. For all sorts of reasons tomorrow was going to be a tough day. Not for the first time since Helen had died I missed having somebody to talk to, somebody in whom I could confide, share the burden. However, on reflection the person did not exist with whom I could share the thought that I, the supposed grieving widower, was going to see my ex-mistress in the hope that she could wave a magic wand and restore my granddaughter to her mother.

Scarlett's laughter drifted up the stairs. She obviously still believed in magic despite her veneer of sophistication and world-weariness. I just wished that I could also be a believer.

Chapter 33

Adam had never been unemployed before. There had been times when he had not been working, but that had always been of his own volition. Even during his university vacations he'd found meaningful employment to fund his own holidays, although his parents would probably have happily paid for them.

He enjoyed being independent and even whilst married to the wealthy Carly he'd always insisted on paying his own way. There was no way he wanted to be regarded as a kept man, whether by his peers or her family or his own family for that matter. He wasn't enjoying having to find things to do to fill his day. He'd lived his life in the fast lane, breaking all speed limits, but now he found himself travelling in reverse. That was marginally better than being stationary although either way he wasn't going anywhere any time soon.

At least he had Kelly. That was a consolation and in the general scheme of things, a big one as well. She'd been a real rock to him, more than a rock. Rocks are silent and solid, but she had been feeding him support and good advice. They'd stopped going out to eat. He didn't want to fritter his money away and certainly didn't want her to pay. For the most part she would cook for him in her small New Jersey apartment with its view of the twinkling lights of Manhattan making him realise what he was missing.

She was actually a good cook and she'd been careful to avoid serving him anything that was blatantly non-kosher, even though she knew by now that he was no longer particularly concerned what he ate. That care and concern on her part might have brought a small smile to his late mother's disapproving face if she was able to look down on the burgeoning relationship.

"You need to tough it out, Adam. That fat, vindictive bastard Gilbert doesn't rule the world even though he seems to have a disproportionate level of influence in New York. I've spoken to one of our labour lawyers and they think you may well have a claim for wrongful dismissal against Goldfarbs."

Adam had sighed and shaken his head.

"It's thoughtful of you, Kelly, but that's not the way the industry works. If I were to file suit then they'd tie me down in the courts for years and as somebody once said in some film or other, I'd never work in this town again. Anyway, I can't really blame Donny. It would have taken a far braver man than him to put loyalty to me before a loss of such valuable clients. And they've been fairly generous in the settlement. I can't see them paying the balance of what I'm due once I hit them with an action."

Kelly nodded. As a lawyer she could see the sense in what he was saying, but as a woman who was becoming increasingly attracted to her former client she could feel the anger and the frustration at the injustice he was suffering.

"As I said, Adam, there are other cities in the States. You're good at what you do I'm sure. Outstandingly good from what you've told me despite your Brit modesty."

"It just feels as if they've won and I've lost." he muttered, half to himself.

"This isn't a competition, Adam," Kelly said in the bright tone he'd come to recognise as one she assumed to assure clients, "there's no Olympic Gold for you or them. If they are so mean and small minded as to not want to leave the relationship as a divorce, but to push on to an annihilation then so be it. They simply can't wipe you off the face of the earth. Well, not unless you aid and assist them."

There was an awkward pause.

"Which you're not going to do, are you Adam?"

Another few heartbeats.

"Are you Adam?"

He lifted his head and forced a weak smile.

"That's your cross-examination voice, isn't it, Kelly?"

"It sure is. And I'm not letting you leave the witness box until you give me an answer."

"No, I'm not going to do that. But what I've been thinking is that I might pop back home for a week.."

He saw the worried look on her face and hurriedly added,

"Don't worry. I thought I could get to Monaco to see my children. Can I possibly ask if you can facilitate that through Carly's lawyer. Surely even Benjamin Gilbert hasn't got the power to stop me taking advantage of a court order. I am coming back and this has nothing to do with you. In fact, if you've got any kind of vacation due you could come with me."

"That would be a great idea, but I've got this big trial coming up in a couple of weeks and I've got a room full of papers to go through and half a dozen depositions to handle. And I'm not sure you making a visit to your kids and tagging your lawyer along is going to go down real well with anybody. But, you know what, I think it's a good idea that you do go see your family. From what you've told me they could do with some moral support right now. I will come with you next time though. You've got me kind of curious about what sounds like their special kind of crazy."

Special kind of crazy. Adam rolled those words around in his mind. That summed up the Kent family to a 't'. Except there was no 't' in the four words and that made him smile a little too.

"What's funny, Adam?" Kelly asked.

"Nothing," he replied

"I'm pleased I can make you smile over nothing," Kelly said, covering his hand with hers.

"I think you could make me smile over anything," he replied and then fired up his laptop to see when he could get a flight home. And what was the cheapest ticket he could find.

Chapter 34

I took Lauren for a coffee first in Spitalfields Market. I hadn't been there for years and was amazed at how it had become so gentrified. Stalls and units selling designer jewellery, specialist foods, expensive clothes and shoes; stalls selling just up-market home-made sweets and smoothies, others offering all different kinds of home-baked bread and cakes and even the coffee place selected had enough varieties to confuse anybody, but the most committed bean connoisseur.

I told her it was to calm her down as I ordered us each a vegan cupcake, but it was more to settle my own nerves. I'd hardly slept all night, rehearsing my lines, honing my script. This was not going to be a dress rehearsal in anticipation of a long run. This was a performance for one night (or in this case, morning) only. I realised I hadn't felt guilty enough about Lizzie when we are an item and Helen was alive and here I was now, drenched in guilt just for seeing her in a professional capacity.

"So what's she like, this Elizabeth Gordon woman, we're going to see?" Lauren asked.

"I don't know," I lied, "I've never met her. As I said she was a strong recommendation from somebody who'd found themselves in a similar situation. I checked her out from the firm's website. She looks nice and sounds efficient. Some great client testimonials."

'Nice'. Was that the best I could come up with? Lizzie would have killed me if she'd heard me describe her as nice. In fact, 'nice' had been one of our jokey words that we'd pull out of the hat when we'd had a less than wonderful experience. Like when I'd had too much to drink and tried to be adventurous in my lovemaking and she'd said, "well, that was er... nice," and then burst into a fit of giggles.

We'd had a whole secret language as well as a secret relationship. When we went to a play or the cinema which she wasn't enjoying and wanted to leave she'd run her nails across the back of my hand, giving me the choice of crying out and attracting attention or rising and making my way clumsily to the end of the row, feigning a coughing fit to justify our early departure.

I'd lingered a long time on her website page. She looked mature but beautiful, thoughtful and professional. A lawyer you could trust which I also noted was the mantra of the firm itself. 'Cullens, The Lawyers You Can Trust.' Some marketing firm must have earned itself a small fortune thinking that one up.

Her CV was impressive. She'd done really well for herself since we'd parted. There was no mention of her being married or having children and I realised that when she'd come to visit me I'd not even thought to ask about her personal status. I'd sort of assumed from the very fact that she'd called on me that she was still single and independent, without anybody to whom she had to answer or offer an explanation as to where she was. Yet, there was no real reason why that should have been the case. She could have driven home to a waiting partner, male or female, a husband even, looked in at her child or children, kissed them gently as they slept and then retired to bed and made love. It hadn't felt like that to me, but then over the past few months I'd given up on relying on my judgement.

The office was impressive too. A million miles from the sort of suburban specialist property firms we used in our own business, where all they needed to do was to be able to buy real estate in a way that enabled us to develop it without any problems.

They occupied the whole of the first floor (and according to the signs in the lobby and the lift, the second floor as well) in what looked like a converted warehouse. The reception area opened up on to an atrium with sculptures and huge overflowing planters. The artwork was modern and although I've never been an expert looked as if it was expensive. No carpets, but a highly polished wooden floor that appeared to be have been the original before being expertly regenerated. It looked like the entrance to an office where great care had been taken to assure the clients that those who worked there not only would care for them, but took great pride in their own working environment.

"We've come to see Elizabeth Gordon," I said to the very attractive, well-groomed blonde girl behind the desk who gave me a radiant smile as if my words had just made her day and then answered in what I thought to be an Australian accent,

"Ah, yes. Mr Kent and Mrs Campbell. Lizzie is expecting you."

She pressed a button on the phone, told somebody else we were here and within a minute another pretty girl, black this time, dressed as if for a fashion show rather than a day at the office, appeared and ushered us through to a meeting room.

She gestured to a table in the corner.

"There's coffee, tea, water, biscuits all there. Help yourselves. Lizzie won't be long."

She was longer than I expected, and I wondered if she'd also secreted herself in a washroom somewhere to apply her make up and get into the role she was about to play. Efficient family lawyer dealing with a new client with whom she had no personal relationship whatsoever.

When she did arrive she greeted Lauren first.

"Hi, by elimination I am guessing you are Mrs Campbell. Do you mind if I call you Lauren? I'm Lizzie, by the way."

Lauren smiled and I could sense her relax as if she had found her savior. That was Lizzie's way. She could win you over in a sentence.

"And you must be, Mr Kent." She made to look at the pad she'd brought with her into the room. "Do you prefer to be called Daniel or Dan?" she asked.

"Daniel," I replied, "Always Daniel," Then and now, I thought and we were off and running and once the charade had begun there was no turning back.

"You haven't had any drinks yet. What can I get you?"

"Just some water for me," Lauren said and Lizzie put a bottle of still water in front of her as she took a seat.

"We've just had a coffee," I replied, "but you know what I wouldn't say no to another."

Lizzie poured me a cup and also handed it to me before taking her seat at the head of the table.

I hadn't even noticed that she'd brought a young man with her in her wake,

"This is Paul. He's my trainee. Do you mind if he sits on this? He'll take notes and I'll be able to concentrate better."

Both Lauren and I nodded our assent and as we began and as I took a sip of my drink I just hoped that my daughter had not noticed that Lizzie hadn't seen any need to ask me how I took my coffee.

Chapter 35

"So, Damien, do you want to tell me again about this woman you took out drinking when I was at home putting your children to bed and ironing your shirts?"

Damien ran his hands through his hair. It was a gesture Chloe had found attractive in the past. It had made him look like a troubled schoolboy she'd said, but right now she wasn't affected by it in any positive way and she didn't seem too bothered if he were troubled or not.

"I didn't take any woman out drinking," he said in an attempt to play down the situation, "we'd been playing tennis. In a doubles match. The four of us who were playing decided to go for a drink. I knew you were upset with me, upset over your dad. I just needed some time to get my head together, to work out the best way I could be of help."

Chloe looked him straight in the eyes. It occurred to her that throughout their marriage there had never been a single moment when she had needed to convince herself that her husband had been telling her the truth. Until now. He'd been annoying with his thoughtlessness which sometimes bordered on selfishness, but, he'd never been dishonest. There had been times when she had wished he had. It would have been kinder if he'd said that he had to go to a business meeting rather than choosing to go out with a couple of mates to watch his team play, but then she'd always been prepared to cut him some slack.

He was a good husband on the whole, better than the assortment of men married to most of her friends, certainly better than the ones who'd been jettisoned for their infidelities and other failings. He was a good father, the kids adored him, cherished the daddy time he doled out, perhaps a little too sparingly. He'd been an excellent provider. He worked hard, had built his business up to the point where the family lacked for nothing. A comfortable home, furnished to her taste, the children always well-clothed, over-indulged with toys and outings, at least three holidays a year and his own family taking a back-seat to the Kents because, as he said himself, he'd wished he'd been brought up by Daniel and Helen.

He'd seemed to share her grief at the loss of her mother, well as much as could have been reasonably expected given they weren't blood, but he had done everything possible to cushion the blow of Helen's premature demise. So, now she was into new territory when she continued to look into his eyes searching for the truth.

What colour were they? She'd always thought they were brown. That's how he'd described them whenever he'd needed to put down his facial characteristics on a form. Now, though, they looked more green, a warlock green and she wondered if he had suddenly developed some mystical power to allow him to behave like this. Had somebody put a spell on him or was this the same random demon who had seemed to be dogging the footsteps of her whole family these past few months?

"Please don't lie to me Damien. You've got one chance here to be honest. So for all our sakes can I suggest you take it. Please."

"I'm not lying," Damien replied. "I was really pissed off. That porridge trick was so annoying. You even got the stuff on my trousers as the first people I met with that day took delight in pointing out. The girl who made up the foursome...."

"The girl. Does she have a name this girl?"

Damien hesitated for a split second. So far he'd managed to keep things together. If he told his wife that 'the girl' was called Pippa then that might be a catalyst for all hell to break loose. As long as he could invent an *alter persona* for the American then he could mould the whole story until he could convince himself that his version of events had really happened.

"Amanda. She's not a member. Somebody had invited her along just to play a one off. I can't even remember where she came from or anything about her other than she was a great tennis player. And I didn't take her out for drinks. We all went together. It was just that we were the last two there and the others said to get the bill and they'd sort me out when we met up next at the club."

The narrative was gaining momentum. This was good. This was convincing. This was all going to work out fine. If he believed that this was what had happened, then why shouldn't Chloe? That lengthy good-night in his car was down to his imagination as was her tongue half way down his throat, her fingers unzipping him and her hair falling over his legs as she expertly took him in her mouth. No, none of that happened and if it had then he could erase it. Everything was possible if he wanted it to be. The only question was whether he wanted it enough, because if he did then he would have to find an opportunity to be on his own so he could make the call and cancel the dinner he'd arranged with Pippa that night. That would be the right thing to do, the sensible thing to do. If this stopped with this conversation then it was all over. He could put his behavior down to the drink, convince himself that he would never have done such a thing had he been sober. And that the only reason he'd been drunk was because his wife had pushed him beyond a breaking point.

However, he was sober now and as he held Chloe tight and breathed in her familiar smell, as she kissed him in what was clearly a gesture of forgiveness, all he could think about was what excuse he could find for being out that night.

Chapter 36

It had been a good meeting with Lizzie. She'd pulled no punches as far as the outcome was concerned. She'd been critical, but fair about the way Lauren and I had taken the children from Luke. I'd tried very hard to focus on what she was saying rather than imagine her naked in bed. I forced my eyes to take in every detail of the room, analyse every piece of modern art, anything to avoid the thoughts of the past that simply refused to go away.

I know she told us that we'd not been particularly bright in swooping for the children, but nonetheless she tempered that criticism by saying that she understood why we had done it and how it wasn't necessarily fatal if she could make the court understand the action in the context. The challenge would be for her to be able to show that his unjustified seizure of Peta from school was far worse than what we had done.

"It was," said Lauren, "at least he was there when dad rescued me. When he went to the school he was trespassing and it was bordering on a kidnap."

Lizzie had given my daughter an encouraging smile.

"Have you been reading law books, Lauren? You're actually not far off the mark as to how I might be able to make a convincing argument to the court. But you're going to have to be patient. This isn't going to happen tomorrow. Or next week. Or even next month probably. We can't show that Peta is any danger and it looks like Luke has been getting some half decent advice himself."

"Probably from some mates in the pub or down in the harbour. They're all barrack-room lawyers down there," Lauren said bitterly.

"Listen. The one thing we can't do is underestimate him. Or whoever he has been talking to. Just because you don't practice law in

London or any other big city, doesn't make you a bad lawyer and it doesn't make you wrong. Some people make a lifestyle choice and maybe he's been lucky and found one of those."

"Or we've been unlucky," I couldn't help but say.

"Let's set about making our own luck, Daniel. I've got a really good barrister I use on cases like this. Her name's Maggie Chamberlain. She's a real battler. Judges love her. Other lawyers hate her. She knows how to get right under the skin of somebody like Luke. We just have to find a way of getting him into a witness box and her in front of him. That's my challenge and my problem."

And that was where we left it. Lauren had said remarkably little for her and it was only when we left the office and were standing on the pavement that she said,

"Wow, where did you find her, dad?" she's really impressive. "You must give me the name of your contact who recommended her so I can text and say thank you."

Was I imagining things or was there some agenda in that question? I replayed the meeting over, but apart from the coffee incident, I could recall nothing to suggest we had even met before let alone been lovers. Or was I underestimating a woman's intuition, even that of somebody like my daughter who had never been known for her sensitivity?

Whatever it was I had other things to do, other things on my mind. I needed to get to my own office. The embarrassing meeting with Jason, Sam and David had left a distinct atmosphere between us. David had called me only yesterday to say that we now had the opportunity to proceed with the deal that I had so vehemently vetoed when I had learned of what lay behind it.

"It's ok, Daniel. It's all kosher now. We all took on board what you said…"

I wanted to tell him that I didn't really care what Justin and Sam had or had not taken on board and right then, for all I cared, they could both jump overboard without a lifebelt between them.

"There's nothing passing under the counter and we're paying the market price. The deal isn't quite as chunky as it was, but it still all adds up to a really nice profit." 'Nice' again. The word was haunting me, but David was in full salesman flow and I knew from years of experience it would be hard to stop him. "We can turn it around in about eighteen months, maybe just turn the property itself if the market continues to improve. Helps the cash flow and far less stress. Not that I think this deal is going to be stressful anyway. It'll be in and out before we even blink,"

Long eighteen month blink I thought, but there was a pleading note in his voice. I couldn't tell if it was because David was desperate to do the deal or just wanted to make everything perfectly right between us. I have to admit that when he called I'd been so distracted by the Lauren problem and the anticipatory fear of seeing Lizzie again that I agreed with David. Just like that. I didn't even ask to check all the numbers. I was usually the numbers person. David was the one with the instinct for the deal. So if that was the case why didn't I take the time to check the bloody numbers and kill the project there and then? I was distracted and tired and so it was merely a case of go ahead and be damned. Although, I hoped we wouldn't.

David had always accused me of over-analysing even after he'd decided with that famous instinct of his that the deal was right... Helen said the same thing about me. I'd always liked to take an issue and assess it. Ask questions of others involved and myself. Turn the transaction inside out, pull out the pockets and let the small change and the fluff fall to the floor in my assiduous search for the smallest of details. David said my most annoying trait was blowing hot and cold and I could see why he would think that. We'd missed opportunities in the past when I had taken too long to make a decision and left my initial positive feeling behind and thrown a bucket of cold water over his almost puppyish enthusiasm. Sometimes that's been good and sometimes bad. I've always thought of it as swings and roundabouts, some you win some you lose. As long as the winners outweigh the losers it really didn't matter. Maybe on this one, taking a flyer was a good call even though at the back of mind there was still some discomfort over the way it was first put to me.

I comforted myself with the thought that they'd not try to fool me. They'd been upfront and I had no reason to think they were lying to me now. I've never really wanted to take any wild risks. That's not a great trait in a property developer and all the multi-millionaires who'd been my contemporaries had never shown such caution or restraint. And they'd survived and prospered.

Every deal is a risk of one sort or another of course. But, then everything in life is a risk and certainly I'd taken one after another during my time with Lizzie. However, when you invest money in our business, there's no guarantee you're going to make money. I've always just tried to eliminate the chances of making a loss. At my age, however, I certainly wasn't to take the risk of finding myself in court or even in prison.

I've had all sorts of propositions put to me in the past. Put this man on your payroll, buy somebody else a car as a sweetener, give them a house as part of the development, look after somebody in the Planning Department. Without exception I've always said no. Just as I had originally to this opportunity. Yet, now we were doing it and my partner was assuring me it was all clean and above board. I trusted David. I'd always trusted him, not just him as a person but his judgement as well. That's why we've made such an effective partnership. Checks and balances. Him being decisive, me being hesitant. That's how it had always been. I wanted to forget all about his initial reaction, or rather, his lack of reaction, when Jason and Sam had sort of talked about bribing somebody to gain an advantage. Well, not sort of. They'd asked. That was what worried me that they'd even considered it.

I was prepared to cut them some slack for their youth and their inexperience. They were keen and ambitious. That was exactly what you needed to succeed in this business. David and I, though, we were different. We'd already succeeded. We'd made our money. Yes, it was always good to make more and I accepted David needed that more than I did. He still had a free-spending wife. Alive and still spending. Even when Helen had been alive she'd never spent more than she needed to on anything. She'd been brought up to be careful and respect money and even when we could afford to push the boat out she preferred to stay close to shore. She was always saving for that rainy day. Only it never came and now all I can think of is how many times I said to her,

"Helen, let's do it. If not now, then when?"

But the when was also a question that could now never be answered.

I was so caught up in my own thoughts that I did not even see the Uber I'd ordered for Lauren arrive and simply muttered goodbye to her as she clambered in and then disappeared into the distance. I stayed waiting by the kerb, half-tempted to go back into Lizzie's office and get her take on the situation. Not just Lauren's but ours as well, if indeed the latter existed. I shook my head irritably, annoyed with my own indecision. I needed to focus on getting Peta back, on getting Luke put back in his box and if it took Lizzie Gordon to do that then that was just the price I would have to pay.

Chapter 37

Time was hanging heavily on Lauren's hands. She had to grapple with herself not to call Lizzie for an update even though she knew the lawyer would have nothing to tell her. She tried to calm herself down. Everybody said the process of the law moved slowly and her dad kept saying that in her case it was actually moving very fast. True to her word Lizzie had reached out to the barrister she had mentioned, Maggie Chamberlain and they'd already gone to her chambers for a conference.

Lauren hadn't felt overawed or uncomfortable when she and her father had visited Lizzie. There had been something oddly familiar about everything. She realised that the offices had been designed to achieve precisely that sensation, but then there had also been an inexplicable sense of familiarity in the room during the meeting. She hadn't met Lizzie before and her dad had also said he didn't know her personally, but still that feeling of comfort that comes from a long relationship had prevailed. There was nothing she could put her finger on and maybe Lizzie was just one of those people that when you'd met them once you felt as if you've known them forever. Maybe, or maybe there was something eluding her, just out of reach. She needed to stop thinking about it because some little voice in her head was telling her that whatever it was it wasn't something she needed to know. The firm was going to do a good job for her, Lizzie was a driven and committed woman and those two facts were all that mattered.

There was certainly no familiarity when it came to Derwent Chambers, tucked away in one of those narrow little lanes off Middle Temple or, if there was, it was because the building was pure Dickensian. A dark wooden heavy door, opened off the street and led to a narrow, creaking flight of stairs over which thousands of litigants had passed over the last couple of centuries. On the first-floor landing was the tiniest of waiting rooms into which she, Lizzie and her father just about fitted which meant that another solicitor and his client, waiting to see a different barrister, had to stand awkwardly. Neither party wanted to speak about their case in front of the other and Lauren had been relieved when Ms Chamberlain's clerk (yes, he'd actually said Ms.) was ready for them.

'Ready' was, perhaps, not quite the correct word, because Maggie Chamberlain's room was over-flowing with papers to the point that Lauren was worried that she would not actually be able to find what she'd been sent on her case. The barrister was a big woman in every sense of the word. She looked about forty and must have been nearly six feet tall, with broad shoulders and breasts that were simply eye-catching in their generosity. She wasn't fat, but she wore a tight-fitting black business suit that showed every contour, set off by a mass of red hair that sat uncomfortably on her head as if it had been borrowed from a totally different person. There was no doubt that she would make an impression in a court room and when she began to speak it was as if she was addressing a jury.

"Mrs Campbell," no, Lauren or call me Maggie here, this was a woman with a busy schedule who had a job to do and would do it as efficiently as was humanly possible, "I've read what my instructing solicitor has sent me," so, no Lizzie either, Lauren thought, "and I've formed a few ideas. But I need you to tell me some more about your husband. We have to focus on his weaknesses and your strengths."

"When can I get my daughter back?" Lauren asked.

Maggie Chamberlain rose an invisible inch from her chair as if she had been asked the most stupid question in the world by the village idiot.

"That depends on what you tell me. Tell me the right things and we will get her back. I am confident of that. But as for time, as lawyers often say, so please excuse the cliché, how long is a piece of string? Now, can I please ask you to concentrate. I am advised that your husband could be violent. Did you ever have to go to the doctor or take the children to hospital?"

"I did go to the doctor, but only because I was so depressed. She gave me some antidepressants."

"Did you tell her why you were depressed?" the relentless voice boomed back at her.

"I think so, I can't really remember," Lauren replied, feeling hopelessly inadequate.

"That won't do, I fear. I need you to be sure of things. What about the children?"

"Peta was wetting the bed. We went to the doctor about that as well. That was because her father had been making her eat things that she said made her sick, so she'd become frightened of mealtimes." Lauren surprised herself by how confidently she'd answered that one and got a nod of approval, "And I did tell the doctor that Luke was scaring me with his moods and his drinking and I thought he might also be on drugs from time to time."

"Better, much better," the barrister had said encouragingly, "apart from the doctor is there anybody else who might have known what was going on?"

"I told my friend, Natalie Dennis everything. Luke hated her. Wouldn't let her into the house. He finally banned me from seeing her and I had to wait till he left the house before I could call her or sneak out to see her for a coffee."

Lauren gave Maggie a brief bit of background about Natalie and she could see that the other woman was pleased with the information she was getting.

"Married to a heart surgeon, pillar of the community, all good. Ms Gordon can you please arrange for a statement from her and try to get access to your client's medical records if you will. The other child is still with you?" Maggie asked re-addressing Lauren, "Callum is it? And he's what?"

"He's seven," Lauren said, her eyes filling with tears suddenly. This sort of thing didn't happen to people like her. This was the stuff of movies and television drama, but then, she'd brought it on herself with her acts of rebellion, so she was the one who had to make it right.

"And has he shown any desire to see his father?"

"He's not asked for him once. He's missing his sister though, he does keep asking about her, which is strange because when they're together they don't stop fighting."

She wanted to ask the barrister if she had children, she wore a wedding ring so she assumed there was a man in her life. Or maybe a woman, who knew? But she'd also gathered she was not a woman for small talk, so the question remained unraised.

Maggie Chamberlain turned to Lizzie again.

"Let's see if we can also get some reports on the child, shall we? You know the score on those sort of things. Obviously we will need a CAFCASS report"

Lizzie nodded. She did indeed know the score. The involvement of children was the most painful part of what she did for so many reasons.

Maggie Chamberlain seemed suddenly to be bored with the whole process. She glanced at her watch and swept up all the papers before her.

"Very well, I'd like to be making our application within fourteen days so that the court understands we are taking this whole thing very seriously. Meanwhile, Mrs Campbell, you need to sit down and write the story of your life, or at least the history of your relationship with your husband. Will you do that for me, please?"

It wasn't a question. It was a directive. Lauren got the feeling that as and when this woman asked questions in court that witnesses would feel that they had no option but to answer. If they didn't then the questions that would follow would be even more difficult. She had left the chambers feeling more optimistic than she'd done for days and she'd set to her task with enthusiasm. She didn't know how many words it took to write a book, but she felt that her first novel was now well underway. And it was going to be her autobiography.

She couldn't just sit in her father's house filling notebook after notebook, remembering things that she'd much rather have forgotten. Making endless coffees, waiting for the time when she could leave to collect Callum from school, a school that was tiptoeing around her in anticipation of a legal claim that she had no intention of making. It wouldn't bring Peta back any quicker and it would just make things more difficult for everybody. She'd not seen Miss Gant there since the incident and she could only conclude that the poor girl was under suspension, if she'd not been fired already. Soon, very soon, she might ask to see Hazel Brown, the headmistress and plead her case. She was just collateral damage in the storm created by Luke and herself.

She looked around the dining room which she'd adopted as her workplace. If her mother had miraculously risen from the dead and returned then she would have found the room and indeed the whole house, almost exactly as she'd left it. Passover was not that far off. Her mother had been frenetic from about six weeks before. That's what she could do. She could give the house a spring clean, a make-over.

Together with writing her life story for the barrister, it would fill the days, maybe even the weeks if she did it properly. She'd made up her mind and the sooner she started the better, but like almost every decision that she'd reached these last few years, it would prove to be momentously bad.

Chapter 38

The nights were the worst. They never ended. When Helen and I shared a bed if either of us woke up then inevitably the other would too, but we'd roll over and cuddle or spoon and get back to sleep within minutes. With Helen gone, if I woke and rolled and reached out I reached out to nothing. And nobody. I would sink my face into her pillow which still had a hint of her scent and smell about it, but that just made it worse. I'd even thought about sleeping in one of the other bedrooms, but Lauren had her old room, Callum another and as and when Peta was to be restored to us then she would go back in the little room.

Helen used to love it when all the children came home for either the Jewish New Year or Passover, but then as she said, after days of endless cooking and tidying up after them, she also loved it when they left.

"The disturbance and the enjoyment of a full house is justified by the sense of relief when the door slams shut behind the last of them," she said in one form or other at the end of every stay.

So, I struggled on in our bedroom. Going downstairs to make myself a hot drink (the remedy for everything according to my late wife) or listening to the most boring programme I could find on the radio (BBC World Service consistently won that accolade) or even watching something mindless on the box which unbelievably only seemed to stimulate me.

Lauren had started tidying the house which, although I knew needed to be done, I was finding mildly annoying. Things that I'd known where to find forever and a day were constantly on the move, but so was the dust that had descended on so many surfaces. The weekly visit of my cleaning lady had proved totally ineffective and although I'd tried to be out when she came (to avoid having to sit down with her and actually converse over a cup of tea which she seemed to think was therapeutic) my absence had a negative effect on the end product she achieved. I suspected she needed no company to make herself a drink and eat my biscuits and given that the television was rarely on the channel I'd last been watching I had evidence that she put her feet up in front of that as well. She'd been with us a while and Helen had tolerated her,

"She really needs the money, Daniel. She's got her daughter and grandchild living with her." she'd said.

Well, I'd also got a daughter and a grandchild living with me (I'd have liked it to be two, but that was still a work in progress albeit good progress) and I was trying to find a way of telling her (her name is the unlikely Trixie by the way) that enough was enough. It was either that or I installed video cameras to film her stately inactivity through my house (she was a large lady with, I think a drinking problem as she left an empty water bottle one week and I could still smell the gin she'd had in it) and then confront her with it. Yet, as with everything else in my life it seemed I was putting that moment and the confrontation off. At least until after Passover.

Lauren had decided along with Chloe that we should have the *Seders* at our house rather than at Chloe's (the only serious option) or going away to somewhere like Israel.

"Mum would have wanted that," Lauren said, "she liked to have the whole family around the table." She made no mention of the fact that she'd been notable for her absence almost throughout her own marriage, but I'd learned not to try to score points off any of my children.

As it happened, I did agree with Lauren. Helen *would* have wanted it. She'd worked herself to a frazzle in the weeks before because she couldn't just leave the assembly around our table at just the immediate family. The *Seder* on the eve of Pesach, the Passover Festival was, according to the Christians, the night of The Last Supper when Jesus and the other dozen of his disciples made up the unlucky thirteen and Judas betrayed him. Or something like that. I'd never been encouraged by my parents to know anything about any other religion unlike the political correctness which seems to prevail at my grandchildren's schools, even the Jewish one attended by Callum and until the snatch, by Peta.

Helen would invite friends, neighbours, waifs and strays who had nowhere else to go and whom we didn't see from one year to the other. One year we got to two dozen and even she, dauntless though she was, agreed that was too many. But she loved the challenge, loved it when the youngest grandchild there asked the traditional Four Questions that triggered off the whole of the service that was the prologue and epilogue to the meal. One of the *matzos* (the unleavened bread that we'd eat for the duration of the Festival) was hidden early on and our grandchildren and any other kids who were there fought manfully to be the first to find it even though I think I invariably hid it in the same place. Helen had that covered as well as she always found time to buy little prizes for them all, with which they could play before they either fell asleep in assorted chairs or struggled through as the evening wore to its conclusion with cups of wine and appalling singing.

I'd tried to delay a decision on what we would do this year as well and had the girls not taken the matter in hand then it would have drifted on and I might have simply relied on the kindness of strangers and accepted an invitation to somebody else's house. However, my daughters had, on this occasion at least, risen to the challenge. They actually had a timetable to follow and knew when the china and cutlery would be changed over (Helen had insisted on keeping up the tradition of using nothing we used during the year and which might have been in contact with any bread which was forbidden) when the food shop would take place (I'd agreed that they needn't cook and we'd buy everything in) and which nights they'd be staying as that would involve some room shifting and sharing. It was both a burden and a relief to be so thoroughly organised, because, to be honest (for once in my life) I had grown exhausted from organising everybody else.

When Helen was alive and basically a housewife I'd been somewhat sarcastic when she'd complained of having too much to do.

"Yes, all those coffee mornings and lunches must be absolutely exhausting," I'd said. Something else I wish I could take back. Now, I realised that it hadn't been the social life which had so tired her out (with hindsight that had hardly been a major part of her life). Just keeping everything together, family, home and me, of course, had been the real challenge. It had been a full-time job and I'd simply not given her the credit she deserved. I'd tossed money her way by way of housekeeping, she'd never had to ask before she bought anything for herself on our credit cards and I'd always ensured we holidayed well. Yet, by the time we actually boarded a plane to get away she needed the break so badly that virtually all she was up to was sleeping. On the plane, by the side of the pool, often even over dinner. Had that been a clue to what would finally kill her? I would never know now. All I knew was that, yet again, I had let her down.

And now Adam would also be home for the holiday. He'd called to tell me that he'd be flying over to Europe to see the children and then coming to stay for the whole of Passover and was that ok. I'm not sure quite why he asked. I could hardly say I didn't agree and tell him he needed to check into a hotel. There might well be some comfort in everybody gathering under one roof, however inconvenient that might prove to be. We had a date for the tombstone consecration for Helen now, although that was months away. Perhaps this time together would form some kind of interim closure, if closure was ever going to be possible.

All these thoughts ran through my mind at two in the morning. I'd covered the digital alarm clock to stop its light and taken to wearing eye shades at night. Helen had always mocked me for taking them off the planes along with all the other freebies. I was like that in hotels as well, removing shampoos and skin lotions and even soap if it looked expensive enough. I'd put them in a drawer. 'For guests' I'd said, but they'd lingered in drawers there too, until they solidified and had to be thrown away. Nobody who'd stayed with us had ever used them. Lizzie was a kindred soul when it came to little things like that and would rape and pillage anywhere we stayed.

I pulled up the eyeshade. It was off a Virgin Upper-Class flight and I even remembered which flight. London to JFK when my travelling companion had not been my wife. I held it in my hands as if it contained the secret to the universe, but all it contained was a memory, a memory that had no place in the bed from which Helen was a permanent, nagging absence.

I've no idea what made me do it. Sleep deprivation, insanity, a longing for company, but I took out my phone, went to the camera feature and took a picture with the eyeshade on the pillow. Helen's pillow as it transpired. And then I sent it to Lizzie with a two-word text only,

"Remember this," because I knew she would. As soon as I'd done it, I wanted to recall the message. But that feature did not exist on my iPhone as it did on my computer. Some things you simply cannot take back.

Chapter 39

It had still been cold when Adam left New York and changing planes on his way to Nice to catch the train to Monte Carlo wasn't much warmer. It was typical of Benjamin Gilbert to put his daughter and his grandchildren somewhere that was beneficial to him tax-wise and inaccessible and expensive if you needed to travel there. Adam had little doubt that Gilbert was using Carly's current location to its full advantage and having her indirectly control assets and trusts that were well out of the reach of the IRS in such a tax haven.

Even when Adam and Carly had been an item Gilbert had boasted of having the best tax and trust lawyers in the world to manage his affairs. But, then he always boasted of having the best of everything. He was the sort of man who would have welcomed the election of Donald Trump. Only Benjamin Gilbert did not take to social media. That was not his scene. It would have demeaned him, even if the President of the United States felt differently. As far as Gilbert was concerned if you said something you could deny it. Once you took to the written word there was no way out. He must have been a nightmare to pin down to a legal agreement and indeed, Adam remembered the fifty page pre-nuptial agreement he'd had yet another of his 'best' lawyers prepare for Adam to sign before the wedding.

"Daddy doesn't mean anything by it. It's just his way," Carly had purred in that little girl way that had become so annoying once he had got past its initial appeal (which didn't take too long) "You'll sign it and he'll stick it in a drawer somewhere and it will never see the light of day."

He'd actually had no problem in signing it because he had no intention whatsoever of ever making a claim against Carly's money. Or her father's for that matter. But as for it seeing the light of day almost the first thing that Carly's lawyer, Mark Rockman had said to Kelly was, "you know there's a pre-nup, don't you?"

The financial arrangements, or lack thereof, weren't on Adam's mind as he made the endless journey to the South of France. Given his financial situation he'd booked an Economy flight so instead of turning left on the plane as he'd done so many times when travelling for Goldfarb, he found himself turning right and manouevering himself into the cramped middle seat between a Chassidic Jew and an overweight middle aged man in a creased suit who smelt of sweat, hamburgers and onions. When Adam had left his meal, embarrassed to be sitting next to somebody Orthodox when he'd not bothered to order kosher or vegetarian, the fat man leaned in to him and asked,

"If you're not eating that, can I have it?"

Adam had pushed it across silently. Who on earth actually ate two airline economy meals?

He'd closed his eyes, but sleep wouldn't come and when the Jewish guy woke up at dawn and pushed past him to say his prayers he'd been awake all night. He had a two-hour stopover before getting the plane to Nice and was then faced with a train journey to Monte Carlo and a taxi ride to get to where Carly had designated for the meeting.

Kelly had been surprised that Rockman had not tried to put more obstacles in their way, but Adam had been cynical.

"There's a reason for her co-operation. Neither Carly nor her father do anything without there being an angle for them. That much I have found out."

He missed the opportunity to go into the Business Lounge with his Gold Card for a refreshing shower on arrival and just hoped he'd be able to get an early check-in for the room he'd booked in Monte Carlo. There weren't many cheap options there, but he'd done the best he could for himself. Meanwhile Carly had arranged for him to see the children under supervision at Loews, five star and rising. Quite what he was supposed to do with them there he wasn't sure, but she'd flatly refused permission for him to take them out anywhere on his own.

"Just roll with it, Adam," Kelly had said, "as I've told you, your time will come."

When a nanny he didn't recognise brought the children into Loew's very upmarket coffee shop it didn't feel as if it was his time. He'd been able to get into his room for about half an hour before he'd had to leave for the access meeting. The shower had incomprehensible taps and knobs and all he'd been able to produce was a lukewarm trickle of a slightly dubiously coloured water. He had at least been able to wash off the dust of his travels, change his clothes and then made it to the assigned destination with about two minutes to spare. He sensed that the nanny had been told not to wait if he was five seconds late because she looked at him as if he were something scraped off the sole of her employer's expensive Dolce and Gabbana shoes, then looked at her watch and said with an accent he had trouble placing,

"You have one hour. Madam says not to waste it,"

"No, that's wrong," Adam replied. "I have three hours. Three till six. It was what was agreed."

"One hour," the woman replied, "Now it is three. They leave at four. They have places to go. Things to be done."

"Let me speak to my ex ," Adam said as the children looked on with disturbed expressions on their faces, "I've been travelling for the best part of a day. You can't just give me an hour."

The woman shrugged.

"Not me, Madam. She gives me order. She also tells me not to give you her number. I sit over here," she moved a few feet back, "you be with your children. Enjoy."

"Hi Ben, hi Casey," Adam said wondering whether he should try and hug them although they themselves were huddling together as if meeting a total stranger for the first time. They'd shot up since he'd seen them last. Ben, at seven, was older by a year and for Adam it was looking at an old photograph of himself. Same dark curly hair, same eyes, only Adam had never shown that lost expression now worn by his son to any camera. Adam had only experienced love and affection and he felt so distant from his sons that he had not the slightest notion of what they might have experienced themselves. Carly was not one for touchy feely and their maternal grandfather showed as much emotion as a stone statue.

"I bought you both some presents," Adam said, producing some books and games he'd hurriedly bought at a variety of airports and stations.

The nanny sprang into action.

"Madam says you show me anything you bring before the boys get it."

Adam was nearing breaking point.

"What gives you the right to decide what I can or can't give my children?" he said angrily and something in his tone made her back off a fraction.

"I only follow instructions. Madam and Mr Max they both say this to me. I need this job so I do what they say."

"Mr Max? And who is Mr Max?" Adam asked, trying not to raise his voice as he didn't want to upset his sons who looked quite distressed enough already. He couldn't begin to think what Carly had said to them before this meeting. And now this Mr Max entered the equation.

"Mummy says we mustn't upset, Uncle Max," Casey the younger one piped up.

"Does she?" Adam asked.

"Yes," added Ben, now warming to what was promising to be an interesting conversation, that he thought might be turned to his advantage if he played it right.

"Uncle Max can get very cross if we don't do what he says."

The boys exchanged looks like co-conspirators and the nanny looked even more alarmed.

"You, Mr Kent, you play with the children. Now. I take this things and if Madam and Mr Max say ok to give them then I give them."

Short of snatching them back from her Adam could not see any other option but to do what she said so he changed the subject

"Ok, boys shall we get something to drink. And maybe an ice-cream. It says here," he flashed the menu in front of them, "that they do the best ice-creams in Monte Carlo."

"Ben, he have an allergy. No dairy stuff, Madam say," the nanny intervened.

"Duly noted. But they do sorbets too. So Casey can have an ice cream and Ben can have a sorbet. Would you like one too?"

He was beginning to feel a little sorry for the woman who clearly lived in fear for her life in case she didn't follow her instructions to the letter. And he could do with an ally too if she was the one who was going to bring the children to further meetings.

The woman looked surprised and he guessed she wasn't used to any show of kindness.

"Thank you. Yes, ice cream good."

Adam gave her the menu and she picked something fairly exotic. Casey chose his and Ben and his father spent a while over their selection before deciding on a medley of strawberry, coconut and mango sorbets.

Adam just kept to safe topics. How was school? What sports were they playing? What were they reading? Had they seen any movies? What might they want him to bring next time? By the time the hour had passed the children seemed reluctant to leave and the nanny hesitant about breaking up the conversation.

"I am sorry, Mr Kent. Is right for the boys to see their father. I tell Madam all went well."

"Thank you," Adam said and he meant it.

"I tell Mr Max too," the nanny said, "he will ask."

"Does Mr Max have another name?" Adam asked innocently.

"Rodriguez" she said, "he comes from my country, Mexico."

She seemed to want to say more, but Adam didn't want to push her. Kelly's words were ringing in his ears. Bide your time. He would and he would be back, but when he returned he would be much better informed about Max Rodriguez, the mysterious Mexican who seemed to be so much a part of his children's lives.

Chapter 40

I had half-hoped Lizzie wouldn't have replied to my stupid midnight message, but she did. She just sent me a 'x' and an emoji of a smiley face which quite frankly could have meant anything. Most people, male and female seem to respond with a kiss nowadays and although I'm not an emoji person, I took Callum to see the film which was probably the worst ninety minutes of my movie-going life, and was delighted to see it got the Award for the Worst Film of the Year.

I couldn't decide if I should follow that up but my decision was made for me when Lauren said,

"Dad, can you do me a massive favour. I'm not sure I can trust myself to ask for another meeting with that nice lawyer lady, but you and she seemed to get on fine and you're the one paying the bill so would it be asking too much if you could grab half an hour of her time."

I had to take a subtle intake of breath to try to see if there was any kind of ulterior motive, if this was some test that Lauren had cooked up, doubtless with the help of her more devious sister. However, there was no tell whatsoever. It was genuine and I could hardly say no.

I suppose I could have just gone to see her in the office, I didn't need to suggest lunch, but I did. Whether or not I needed to explain the background to the request or whether she would have come anyway, I have no idea. The fact was that she seemed fine about it, positively relaxed and there was no mention of the picture I had sent her, but then all the arrangements were done by email and I guess she didn't want her PA or the young trainee, Tim or whatever his name was, to start wondering why the father of a client was sending her pictures of Virgin Atlantic eye-shades in the middle of the night.

In fact, it was her PA who sent me the email with the lunch arrangements. Shoreditch House, the private members club near her office. Not my natural habitat. All media, music, film people whenever I'd been to their old flagship venue in Soho. We'd been trying to put some development deal together and one of the investors had his own record label and clearly wanted to show off that he was a member. David had liked it and asked how he could become a member and the young guy had delighted in telling him that he probably couldn't.

"They don't really like property people here. Tends to bring in suits and as you can see the members here don't do suits."

They didn't do age either and I'd felt as if I'd intruded on a children's party as I must have been at least twenty years older (and probably more) than anybody else there.

I have to confess that I was impressed that Lizzie had got to be a member. She was (and still is) much younger than me and I think I had tended to drag her up out of her age bracket rather than be sucked down towards it. As she'd said to me when we were together,

"I love being with you Daniel, because you make me do grown-up things,"

That I did for sure although looking back the whole relationship on my part was totally immature. Mid-life crisis at its worst. Not really a fair description and an easy cop out to describe what had occurred with hindsight. Certainly, not fair to Lizzie. I am not saying I didn't take it seriously and I'm not denying the pain I felt when I brought it all to an end, but her words when she'd come calling that night kept coming back to haunt me,

"You broke my heart, Daniel," she'd said. Did I know that at the time or was I too busy feeling relieved that I wouldn't have to lie any more?

We grabbed a table and just ordered from the bar menu.

"Do you want anything to drink?" I asked.

"This isn't a first date, Daniel." she replied.

"Or any kind of date," I added although my voice rose in that annoying teenage mannerism of making a statement a question.

"You asked to see me," Lizzie said, "and by the way, yes, I will have a dry white wine. They make a good Cosmo here," she added remembering my penchant for that cocktail. That had been another thing for us, me giving marks out of ten for the Cosmos in the various hotels, restaurants and bars we'd visited.

"Though probably not as good as The Regency in New York," she continued.

"That was good. As was our stay there. Do you remember us being so excited that they'd upgraded us to a room with a balcony and then we woke up to thick snow and didn't open so much as a window, let alone the door to it."

A shadow passed across her face.

"Is this intended to be a trip down memory lane, Daniel? I cut you some slack on that stupid photo you sent me. I mean who keeps a blindfold from a plane for what? Over fifteen years?" She paused, "Only you I guess. You can be such a lovelorn teenager at times. But we did have a good time in New York and as I recall we used those eye-things to good advantage in bed as well."

She acknowledged that her wine had been delivered and took a reflective sip.

"I shouldn't drink during the working day. I'm rubbish after a glass or two and I've got a busy afternoon."

My Cosmo came and I tasted it.

"Well?" she asked.

"It's not bad. An eight, maybe going on an eight and a half," I said.

"That's a relief then," she smiled and in fact actually laughed for the first time, making the years fall away.

She looked at her watch.

"Seriously, Daniel I really do have to be back in the office for two. You asked to see me for an update, though we could have done it in a phone call or even by email. Is this your idea of a date?"

I blushed and tried to explain how it was Lauren's idea and not mine, but against the background of my photo episode it didn't really sound convincing. I wouldn't have bought into it, that was for sure.

"Well, we're here now and I do have to report back to Lauren, so where are we?"

"We're getting to a good place I think, Daniel. I've read through all the volumes Lauren sent me. You told me once she wanted to be a writer and I have to tell you that she's good at it. I'm not suggesting she's sent me a load of fiction, but what she's written does make a compelling tale. And a sad one as well. I'm just having my trainee have a first go at turning it into a full-blown witness statement. He's cheaper than me," she added. Was she trying to remind me that this was a solicitor-client meeting or was she just being kind? I used to torture myself with those sorts of interpretations of things said and done all those years ago to a point of obsession and was determined to try and stop myself travelling that particular road again.

"I've reached out to the doctor who was helpful and just needed an authority from Lauren," she fumbled in her bag and produced an envelope, "I've brought it with me if you could get her to sign and then scan it back to me."

"Of course," I said, feeling satisfied that I had something tangible to show from the meeting.

"I've also spoken to that friend of hers. Lovely lady. Very bright..."

"So is Lauren, when she tries. She just had a stupid taste in partners."

Lizzie turned her slow-burning smile on me which could have meant anything.

"Runs in the family then, doesn't it?" she said, with a slightly hollow laugh.

"Anyway, the friend, Natalie, is a veritable mine of information. Seems that your son-in-law has a bit of a reputation locally. He doesn't hold down jobs, he's spent a few nights in the cells for getting into fights, she thinks he might be peddling drugs to keep body and soul together and he's been leaving Peta with his latest girlfriend who also seems to be a bit of a 'good time gal' if that's not too old-fashioned a phrase."

"I'm not sure anybody would have a good time with Luke," I added darkly.

"Well, we have to show that Peta's not having a good time and I'm having somebody dig around locally. We'll need to pay them I'm afraid, but it will be worth it. Already sounding like this new woman would never get past a basic CRB check. And I'm moving heaven and earth to get CAFCASS to move more quickly than they usually would. I've developed a good relationship with them over the years and their report will be critical. So you can report back positively to Lauren. Between you and me we might get this show on the road even quicker than I anticipated."

I wanted to lean across and kiss her but thought that might be taken for something more than gratitude. Just then my phone rang, and I got some black looks from the members at other tables.

"No mobiles here, Daniel," Lizzie said. "It's one of the upsides of the Club."

"It's Lauren," I said, getting to my feet and saying quickly to the caller, "Listen, I'll call you back," but I was given no chance as all she said in a tone I simply didn't recognise was,

"No, dad. Don't bother. I need you back home. Now."

I apologised to Lizzie and we made some vague promise to meet up again, although I'm not sure either of us knew what would be the purpose or thought it would be a great idea. I waited impatiently for the lift and pushed past a couple of girls to get into it, barely waiting for them to follow me before I pushed the button.

"Rude," one of them said to the other, but with her heavily made up eyes on me.

I offered no explanation. I had a bad feeling about the call and as I summoned an Uber outside the club it seemed to me that it was going to be a very long ride home and that my driver, Mustafa from Afghanistan, was not going to be the beneficiary of very much conversation from this particular passenger.

Chapter 41

Chloe felt as if somebody had sprinkled every room in their house with eggshells and the pair of them were tiptoeing around in carpet slippers to avoid cracking a single one. The children, on the other hand were on the rampage, eggshells or not.

"Kids are so much more intelligent than grown-ups," Chloe had said to Lauren on the phone, "my Damien thinks everything is hunky dory. That I've bought into the story he's told me, but the little ones are sensitive to atmosphere and know this is their moment to get anything they want by playing us off against each other."

"So, little sister," Lauren had said, "do I assume that you don't think everything is hunky dory."

"I don't know what to think" Chloe had replied and that was just so true. She'd had a life of certainty of knowing where everything and everybody was and once her mother had died it seemed that all the elements had shifted. It was like shaking a kaleidoscope. She'd had one as a child. It had belonged to her grandmother and it was so well made that it endured everything that all the children threw at it. She could sit and watch it for hours at a time. While Lauren and Adam were glued in front of the children's programmes on the television, Chloe was making her own vibrantly coloured pictures, wishing she could capture each and every one for all time.

She'd had an artistic phase as a child and her parents had indulged her, buying expensive brushes, paints and proper canvases. All they got out of it were her attempts to reproduce what she saw every time she shook her kaleidoscope and they soon realised she might just need a day job. That had been part of her problem growing up in that family where her siblings raised the bar academically to heights she could never hope to reach. They'd sailed through 'A' levels and University whilst she'd gone off to Sixth Form College, had a good time, scraped a few GCSE's and the ability to type quickly and had ended up at a PR Company in Soho often making tea. She made a good cup of tea, but she'd wanted more than that and to be fair, to Eliza White who ran the company, she did get to do more and really enjoyed it. Then Damien came along and the kids and that was sort of that. She could have gone back to work, she should have gone back to work, but somehow with all the chasing around with girlfriends and keeping fit and generally looking after herself, there was never the time.

Damien never kept her short of money so she wasn't hungry for work and until recently she'd felt like the lucky one of the three of them. Lauren and Adam had both made appalling marital choices. Adam was always stressed out with his work as well and Lauren had ended up without a job and on medication. So, now the bar was much lower and yet she still found herself unable to clamber over it.

Perhaps, when things settled down, she would try to get back to a job. Before her life had fallen apart she'd been chatty, presentable and confident enough to sell snow to Eskimos. Now, she wasn't so sure she could even sell food to a starving man.

Normally, she would have confided in the girls who formed her regular social circle. None of them were slow in coming forward about their husbands' short comings. A couple of them were already on to second marriages and had regaled the group with tales of misdemeanors, adultery and in some cases a 'back at you' meaningless shag that had been more amusing than titillating. Chloe had never offered anything on the subject. She realised now what a boring, straight-laced life she and Damien had left. They'd once walked out of a dinner party and never spoken to the couple again when, after some cocktails and too much wine, guests began to swop partners and move off to bedrooms and dark corners. Maybe, that's what had been wrong.

Maybe it was the lack of excitement that had caused Damien to look elsewhere. Though he still maintained that he'd neither looked, nor been elsewhere and it had got to the point of her not only doubting herself for doubting him, but throwing in a bit of guilt for good measure.

She couldn't bring herself to share what had occurred with anybody but Lauren. If the recent series of events had served any good purpose whatsoever they'd at least brought she and her sister back closer together and the children now knew that they actually had cousins. Lauren had been pragmatic.

"Work on the basis that all men lie," she'd said "and if you do that you won't go far wrong."

"Dad didn't lie."

"Well, he was Dad and I just can't see anybody doing anything with him to make him lie about it. Dad is… well, er just Dad."

"Is he still worrying you with the way he's behaving?" she'd asked pleased to have the chance to move the spotlight away from herself.

"A bit. But he seems to have calmed down since he's had my issues to focus on. I think we may have both over-reacted a bit. When you lose somebody you love like that so suddenly and have had no time to prepare yourself then it's not really surprising it hits you so hard after the event. It's kind of PTSD. Like he'd been to war and survived whilst his friends and colleagues didn't. So, I'm cutting him slack and giving him space and we'll see where it goes. And as for your Damien though, I'd give him no slack and no space. Get him back in line, girl. I know you can do it."

Chloe had thought long and hard about the sisterly advice. It was good advice, at least the bit about every man lying. On thinking further about that it was true. In every relationship she'd ever had the guy had told her porkies at some stage or another, so why should her husband be any different? But were the porkies white lies or something far darker? And when Lauren said she could get him back in line what was the best way to do that?

She made herself another coffee. She was drinking far too much of the stuff and the decaffeinated simply didn't do the trick. She'd cancelled a coffee morning with a few of her girlfriends as she just couldn't face the inane chatter. She'd done a double session at the gym instead and was still in her running shirt and sweats. She fired up her laptop. She had an idea that she just needed to know how to put into action. That was the great thing about the World Wide Web. You could find anything you wanted. Find out about anybody at all. It was just a question of what you did with that knowledge when you got it and whether you would use it to good purpose. Or whether it would use you.

Then her phone rang. It was her sister which was odd because she'd spoken to her before she went to the gym.

"Chloe. It's me. What are you doing?"

"Just trying to follow your advice, that's all." Chloe replied.

"Ok. Well this is my up to the minute advice. Get yourself over here now..."

"I need to shower first." Chloe protested.

"No time. I need you here before Dad gets back."

"Gets back from where?"

"From where I sent him and from where I summoned him. Now are you coming or not? We need a few minutes before he gets here."

Chloe almost ran into the bathroom. Washed her face and sprayed herself with a bit of deodorant. She looked at her face in the mirror and without her make-up saw what Damien saw every morning. Her plan would have to wait. Just like her father a few minutes earlier she hadn't liked the urgent and almost desperate tone in Lauren's voice, hadn't liked it at all.

Chapter 42

I'm not sure what I was expecting, but whatever it was, it wasn't the reception committee of my two daughters that faced me at home with cards and notes and an odd collection of mementos spread over the dining-room table.

Of course, I recognised them at once and kicked myself for forgetting I'd kept them. Why on earth had I kept them? It had been dangerous enough receiving them in the first place, but actually saving them had been sheer lunacy particularly when the relationship was dead and buried. Like my wife, I thought, like the mother of these two angry, accusatorial women, facing me in a united front. I wanted to say that whatever they thought I might have done at least it had succeeded in bringing the two girls together, that their mother would have liked to have lived to have seen that, but that was so inappropriate, so far beyond the pale, that all I could say was,

"Where on earth did you find all that?" as if they (or I assumed Lauren) had discovered a long-buried cache of treasure under the floorboards.

"So you admit it's yours?" Lauren demanded accusingly

I thought quickly. What on earth was in it? Stupid little cards Lizzie had sent me, a couple of notes when she'd felt to commit her troubled thoughts to paper, a few bits and pieces that we'd gathered on our travels and I'd not had the heart to throw away. But did any of it actually have my name on it? She'd always called me 'D'. Just 'D'. Who else did I know whose name began with the same letter and what possible reason could I have for hiding these very personal papers. At that exact moment I couldn't even remember where I'd stashed them away, but then Lauren came to my rescue.

"I'd gone up in the loft to see what mum kept up there for *Pesach*..."

Ah, I thought, I knew no good was going to come from my born-again daughter. Yes, it was true that after the Passover every year I had to climb up the steps and put up there some dishes and china that wouldn't see the light of day for another twelve months. Helen had no head for heights and always said that she wanted to die first because she couldn't see how she could ever clear the loft of all the debris I had assembled over the years. So, when I'd put what I could only now think of as my 'Lizzie Box' up there I thought I'd been absolutely safe. Until now. And then it came to me in a flash. I had to take the chance that there were no names on anything that could disprove what I was about to say and that I could get to the poor bastard I was about to put in the frame before my super-sleuth daughters tracked him down.

"They're not mine. David, David my partner had been having an affair. It was years ago. He couldn't bring himself to throw away some of the memories of it so he asked me to keep it for him. And I put it up in the loft and until today I'd completely forgotten about it."

"So, you're not D then?"

"D? I've no idea what you're talking about. I never read them. He just gave them to me in a box and that was that. It's all long past. He never asked for them. The affair had already ended and he just got on with his life. As far as I'm aware his wife, Judith, never had a clue."

My two daughters exchanged a look and I could tell they wanted to believe me.

"So, you don't know who 'L' is either?" Chloe asked. Obviously, she'd been able to bring herself up to speed on the evidence.

I pretended to think for a minute and actually rubbed my forehead and stroked my chin

"I only met the women a couple of times. It may have been Lynne or something. No, it was Laura. Definitely Laura. I think she was Scottish."

I liked that touch, but the girls weren't impressed.

"I can't believe you'd do that, dad. Be a party to your friend and partner cheating on his wife. That poor woman. All these years and she's still with him living a lie. Maybe we should tell her. Show her this stuff. How can you bear to be in partnership with him? If he could cheat on his wife, how on earth could you know he wouldn't cheat on you?"

"It was a few months of madness. Nothing like it has happened again. You know what, let's just throw this stuff away. There's no point in opening up old wounds."

They hesitated. Then Chloe nodded, but not at what I had said,

"Lauren, you are so right. All men are liars. I know exactly what I'm going to do with my problem."

She reached out to me and pulled me into a giant embrace. She felt hot and whatever she'd sprayed herself with couldn't hide the smell of sweat. She took a step back to pull Lauren into the group hug and I could feel my betrayal about to engulf me, not just my betrayal of Helen which had been so brutally brought home to me, but my betrayal of my daughters who'd grown up to the background of my lies and deceit.

"We're sorry, daddy," Lauren said, "we both know you aren't like that. And you're right, let's get rid of all this stuff. But, I'm telling you here and now, I don't want you ever bringing that David Segal into the house ever again. I don't even want him at mum's stone-setting. Can you promise me that?"

"I promise," I said and then went quickly up to my office, closed the door and called David to tell him exactly what I'd done to him. He'd play ball, I knew that. He'd known about Lizzie and disapproved but he'd said nothing. The only thing was that I now owed him a big favour and I had a horrible feeling that somewhere along the line I might be asked to repay that particular debt.

Chapter 43

Adam returned from the South of France to his old family home in a far more positive frame of mind. The children had actually waved goodbye to him and the nanny (whose name it transpired was Teresa) had said she hoped he would come again soon as she too had waved him off.

He'd called Kelly from the airport and brought her up to date.

"Max Rodriguez," she'd said thoughtfully. "And Mexican you say. Looks like he may be a permanent resident in Monte Carlo. We've got some good people in France and I'll be on it as soon as we end this call. I've also spoken to a law firm here, who has offices down there and from what I've been told, for once, Benjamin Gilbert may have been a little too clever for his own good. American courts would have protected American children (as the unpleasant lawyer Rockman had called them) to the hilt. Well, you've sort of found that out for yourself. But American children living in France with a European father who's squeaky clean and is anxious to have regular access and joint custody, that, as we say over here, is a totally different ball game."

He'd left all of that to her. She'd indicated that it might be helpful if he spoke to an English family lawyer as well, one with some insight as to how the French system worked,

"If anybody actually knows," she'd added and he heard her chuckle at the end of the sentence. Her mood had been contagious, but as soon as he got back to London and started talking to his father and his siblings it began to evaporate. Neither of his sisters would tell him what had been happening and although they'd delegated the task of sorting their father out to him a little while ago, it just felt like something else had happened.

He was pleased to hear that Lauren had got herself a decent lawyer and that they were all on the front foot with his so-called brother-in-law, Luke. Well, he supposed he truly was his brother-in-law only it had never felt that way as it had with Damien. He'd liked Chloe's intended from the first moment he met him, but now there was something going on there as well. Talk about Happy Families. This was becoming more like The Borgias.

He felt somewhat helpless, mainly because nobody seemed able to put into words exactly what was wrong. It came to supper on his last evening there. They'd sent out for a Kosher take-away and everybody was there. Chloe, Lauren, Damien and the three kids which made the missing pieces in the shape of Peta and his mother all the more poignant.

"Come on guys, I know I'm not here that much, but please tell me what's been going on apart from the obvious with Mum and Luke and Peta."

Lauren looked at Chloe who looked away. Damien found something pressing to do on his phone and it was left to Daniel to answer.

"Ok. It's all done and dusted now, but let's put it to bed one last time. Your sisters thought I had been having an affair."

"What?" Adam said in a tone between disbelief and choked laughter, "You. While Mum was alive?"

Daniel wanted to ask why his children found it so incredible that somebody apart from their mother could have found him attractive and point out that he couldn't have had an affair once she'd passed away, but decided against it and let everybody run with what they had now decided was so outrageous as to beggar belief.

"I mean, dad, who would have had you?" Adam said.

Daniel wanted to rise to his own defence, but decided that the sort of insult that was being thrown his way was almost certainly a good thing.

"Who was it with?" Adam persisted. "Marsha? I always thought she had the hots for you."

"I don't know," Daniel replied, "your sisters never got that far in their research. Anyway, I wasn't. David, my partner was and foolishly I had sort of covered for him. Well, not really because nobody asked me whilst it was going on."

"Dad was an accessory after the fact," Lauren said, "but as he said it doesn't matter now."

Damien had been unusually quiet and just muttered an apology that he had a business crisis to deal with and the meal trundled to an end with Adam explaining that he had to get back to New York, but would try to be back for Passover as long as he'd not got a job before then back in the States. He decided not to mention Kelly as of any significance in his life. She was just his lawyer of whom he spoke highly.

"We seem to have a great need of lawyers right now," Chloe said, "And Damien can you please stop tapping away at that fu…"

She stopped in mid swear word when she realised that Tommy was still very much awake. He'd already used the odd 'fuck', amazingly, quite often in context so he obviously had a decent ear for dialogue.

"At that phone," she continued.

"Can I play with the phone, Daddy," asked Tommy who delighted in downloading video games and as he knew their Apple passwords all sorts of items kept popping up on their bills despite his assurances that the games were 'free'.

"I need it right now, Tommy," Damien said, "maybe you can use Mummy's."

Chloe shot him a look, but it didn't make him change his mind and eventually she just swept the children up and made for the car, with Damien, still tapping away in her wake.

Adam had kissed Lauren goodbye, hugged Daniel and with one last,

"You an affair, yeah right. Pigs, windows, flying, more likely."

And then he'd gone. Another Economy flight, more endless queues, both at Heathrow to check in and through security and then that slow, solemn unwinding line at JFK where you just felt that you were being watched and then made to feel you had done something wrong.

Because of the kind of visa he had he normally didn't have to wait as long as the poor unfortunates whose entry into the Promised Land could be delayed for anything up to two hours. However, today there was only one window open and the guy in front of him had obviously posed a problem as he seemed to undergo endless interrogation before being taken away for a secondary interview.

Adam knew from past experience that the US Border officials had very little sense of humour and it didn't pay to engage with them. Normally he pushed his passport and his papers through silently, endured the fingerprint identification and the eye iris shot and was then grunted through. Today, he couldn't help but say,

"That looked tricky. At least I'm going to be easy."

The man behind the glass was over-weight with thick glasses that hid any kind of expression or emotion he might show.

"I don't think so, Sir," he said leadenly, "I wonder if you would mind following my associate over there who will take you through for a secondary."

"Through where?" Adam asked, but the man was already attending to the next in line and his colleague was impatiently gesturing him to follow and when he entered a room that seemed full of Asians, Arabs and Hispanics, not to mention the unfortunate man who'd been in front of him at the window and was signaled to turn off his phone and take a seat. Amidst all of that the only two questions he could ask was why was this happening and how on earth he would find his suitcase when he finally got to the baggage hall?

Chapter 44

I wasn't proud of my lies, but what else could I have done? The truth would have helped nobody as I'd said when my daughters wanted to out my innocent business partner, David. All my fessing up would have done was to mean the end of my relationship with my children and probably my grandchildren as well. What the situation had done though, was to make me see the sheer insanity of conducting anything but a professional relationship with Lizzie. Had I thought that I could turn back the clock? Or even if I couldn't, had I truly believed that she might be the answer to my terrible, nagging loneliness? I am really not sure. Sometimes we do things without actually thinking of the end result, but everything we do has consequences. There is cause and there is effect. If I admitted that my cause was the horror of being alone through the night, every night until I died, then would that have justified the effect on my relationship with my family? I didn't think so. But, in any event, just as I had done all those years ago, I had pulled back from the brink.

I decided that, having set David Segal up, the least I could do was to behave a bit more like a partner. So there I was, the very next day, at my desk, looking in far more detail at the deal to which I had already agreed. David and the lads were right. It was a good deal even given the chunky price we'd agreed to pay for the opportunity. My job was to ensure we could fund it without getting ourselves so bogged down in debt that we couldn't function on anything else we were trying to do.

I'd never liked to put all my eggs in one basket in the company. Ideally, I felt comfortable with having some half a dozen projects on the go. We weren't a big concern. I liked to work with what and whom we had. If you started bringing in new faces on a necessity basis then the dynamics and the balance of the office went awry. This deal wouldn't have been the biggest we'd ever done, but it would be right up there and it would have been the biggest we had going on at that moment. So, my knee jerk reaction to agree had to be justified. We'd already signed Heads of Terms so it would have been hard to pull out and I wasn't not looking for a way out. I was merely checking up on myself, given that in the state of mind I wasn't sure I could totally be trusted.

I'd spoken to David straight after my conversation with my children, just in case any of them got straight on to him, but they hadn't. To be fair to him he'd completely understood, although by the time we got to talking the following morning, face to face, he was vastly amused by it.

"I did warn you at the time that it wouldn't end well, if you remember," he said, but not in a preachy sort of way.

As I recalled it, I hadn't told him about it. He'd just stumbled on the relationship when he'd overheard a phone call I was having with Lizzie and I'd had no way back then of explaining it other than to admitting who she was. I'd actually felt better for that, understanding how confession really is good for the soul. At least I had somebody to talk to and looking back, I understood just how self-obsessed and boring I must have seemed to David as I'd analysed my choices and my relationships with wife and mistress.

Helen had really liked David and he'd liked her and although he had nothing against Lizzie as a person (he hardly knew her truth to tell) he had been the Jiminy Cricket on my shoulder urging my conscience to be my guide. Which it finally had. Yet, I'd contrived a situation where the poor bloke couldn't even attend my wife's stone-setting. Brilliant. Another award for Daniel Kent in the Life-Time Bastard of the Year Hall of Fame.

I tried to focus on the figures in front of me. I've always been good with figures when I put my mind to it. Not to the point of wanting to be a Chartered Accountant like a good few of my contemporaries, but seeing a pattern in them, a beauty of form and shape when they all came together. When books balanced, when cash flow worked, when a projected profit actually was delivered within a tolerable margin. David was better at spotting opportunities than me, better at the numbers on the back of the cigarette packet or the table napkin, but I was far better at making them happen, at nursing them through all the administration and as David often said,

"Leave the stuff at the end and the red-tape to Daniel. He's good at all the everyday snores." He sometimes said that I was the cement between the bricks in the wall that kept our business standing, but then who wanted to watch cement dry?

"Do you want a coffee?" David asked and I held up a thumb to signify that was a good idea. Sam and Jason were beavering away in the background and it actually felt good to be back. It all felt like the real world, not the soap-operatic drama that had been going on back at home.

I tapped some figures in on the programme on screen and pressed a button. I shook my head in appreciation. The computer had said yes to everything. It liked it and I liked the bottom line.

"Was I right or was I right?" David said with a big smile on his face. "Can I call the lads over to see?"

"Sure," I replied. Unlike other businesses of our size we tried not to keep what we were making from our staff. They were going to share in it anyway, so from a feel-good incentive perception, it had always proved to be the right thing to do.

Sam and Jason came over and high-fived with a whoop when they saw where I'd got to.

"Excellent work boys, now let's just make sure we've got the money to do it."

For somebody that has no technical talents whatsoever in the home I was surprisingly comfortable with computers, particularly when it came to spreadsheets. It's the matter of numbers again. I just see them so clearly, far more clearly than I focus on people, I fear. I had another programme that connected all our projects, taking into account their current status, what we had in the bank, the cash flows on them and our bank facility. The technical side of this was way beyond me, but I'd sort of developed the principle myself with our external IT geek, Colin, who thought that it actually had some commercial potential if we could take it to market.

I pressed a few buttons and watched what was now coming up on the screen. The others had become bored and moved on. I wasn't bored. I was at first sure I'd made a mistake. So, I started all over again inputting the information. Same result. I looked around the room but everybody was distracted by other matters, probably already having counted and banked our profit. I called up Colin who was always amazingly available even though I knew he had a really good business and serviced dozens of companies like ours.

"Colin, could you do me a favour and screen-share with me for a moment. There's a problem and I'm hoping you'll find the quick answer to it."

I invited him and he typed in the code. There's always something spooky about screensharing when somebody (even when you know them and know where they are) starts flitting about your screen like some Tinker Bell pursuing Peter Pan. I watched as Colin repeated what I'd just done.

"Do you see what I can see?" I asked him, holding the phone whilst continuing to watch the relentless on-screen movement.

"I think I do. I don't know the ins and outs of your business, Danny, (he's the only person who calls me Danny, but I've given up telling him not to. Colin's mind doesn't work like those of normal people. He exists in a series of voids and vacuums and although I'd never visited his home it would not have surprised me if he actually dwelled in some Black Hole in a parallel universe) but it looks to me that whatever you were looking to do, you can't afford to do it. And you can't afford it by a very long way."

I wanted to say that couldn't be right. That we had to have the money. That I hadn't taken my eye off the ball so much or for so long that it had simply de-materialised. But, computers aren't usually wrong, Colin was never wrong and that meant that something very wrong had been going on in the business, something very wrong indeed.

Chapter 45

Chloe felt as if she were playing a role in a thriller. Or, perhaps a spy movie, because that's what she had been doing. Spying on her husband, something she had never thought she would ever do, something that she had never thought would be necessary in all their happy marriage.

Damien clearly thought all was well. That his explanations had been accepted. She had wanted to accept them, they all sounded rational, but at the end of the day, there was a niggling worm of doubt that had grown steadily longer and stronger until it wriggled within her and made it impossible to sleep. Impossible to do anything with any depth of concentration. Wherever she was, whoever she was speaking to, that inner turmoil kept reminding her that there was a problem she had to solve, had to fix and until she had done so there could be no rest.

She had gone over in her mind all the possible options. Damien could be telling the truth. She had been difficult, not just that day, but almost since the day her mother had died. Her darkest fears could all stem from her loss and the irrational thought that further losses would follow, starting with the loss of her husband. He could have panicked and told her a whitish lie. He had gone out with this woman, had a few drinks, maybe flirted a little and that was that. If so, then she could live with it. Or, it had gone further and he'd actually slept with her? Could she live with it? Maybe, if she didn't know for sure, maybe if it was a one off. But, she had to know for sure and then she would know if she could, indeed, live with it.

Then there was the doomsday scenario. He'd already been having an affair, he was still having an affair, because if that was the case, then it really didn't matter when it started. It just was and that was that.

And that would certainly be that for their marriage and she could join her sister and her brother in the line-up of failures that she was, kind of, pleased that her mother wasn't around to see.

How would she explain things to the children? Tommy would react badly and the permanent absence of his father from the house could have cataclysmic results. Scarlett could go either way. Drama or tragedy. She only dealt in extremes. As for her father. She didn't think she could burden him with anything else. What was that line from 'King Lear' she'd learned at school, 'Woe upon woe' or something like that.

The option to do nothing wasn't available to her. Her mother had always said to anybody who might listen,

"You can't fob off little Chloe. She won't rest until you answer her question."

Well, she wasn't little Chloe anymore. She was big Chloe, married woman, mother of children and nobody was answering her question. At least, not in any way that she found acceptable. She didn't want to voice the thought aloud that Damien was lying to her, but the thought was definitely there and if she was going to be honest with herself (and she might just as well be because nobody else was) she did think he wasn't telling her the whole truth.

So, she'd had to do something about it. She didn't want too many people knowing, but her friend, Hayley had been in a not dissimilar situation. There hadn't been a woman involved. For Hayley's husband, Stuart, it had been a question of gambling. They'd already had to sell their house to pay off his debts and then living in a much smaller rented flat he had sworn 'on his children's lives' that he would never gamble again. Hayley hadn't believed him either and had actually slipped a tracker app on to his phone matching one on hers so that she knew exactly where he was every moment he was out of the house.

He'd said he'd been at work but the office where he said he was employed did not in fact exist. He'd left home every day, sat around drinking coffee until the betting offices opened and then he was In Like Flint and losing like there was no tomorrow. When Hayley tracked him down and was waiting outside Corals there was no tomorrow. At least, not for their marriage.

"It's easy," Hayley had told her. "He probably won't even notice you've done it," and done it she had.

For a few days she'd resisted the temptation to look and then for another few days he was exactly where he had said he would be. Only he wasn't right now. He'd told her that he'd been given a ticket to watch Arsenal in a European match and that as he'd be in a box he'd eat there and wouldn't need anything when he got home. The only thing was that Arsenal played at the Emirates Stadium in North London and the app was telling her that he was actually not a million miles from where they lived in Northwood. Or at least his phone was there, if not Damien himself.

She thought of ringing him just in case his phone had been lost or stolen, but she didn't want the pain of the lies he would probably tell if he actually answered. More likely he wouldn't and would claim it had been too noisy when he got home. Calling him would warn him and she didn't want that either.

She called her sister and asked if she could child mind as she needed to pop out.

"No problem. Could do with a change of scene and dad's here and it will take his mind off things. I'll be over in twenty." And she was.

Chloe got into her car and began to drive. It took her twenty minutes of following the GPS before she found herself parked outside a large house that had been converted into what looked like four very expensive apartments. Damien's car was parked in the drive. She felt a shiver inside and settled down to wait. She never listened to football on the radio unless Damien was in the car, but tonight she wanted to know when the match ended so she could have some idea of when he would have got home had he actually gone. The game seemed endless, the commentary loud and inane although it seemed Arsenal were doing well so that would make him happy. But he's not there, she had to remind herself. He's here, a few feet from me doing goodness knew what with goodness knew who, or was it whom? She couldn't remember and this wasn't the time or place to be thinking about syntax or grammar.

Finally, the radio switched to the studio and she gave it another hour. Then the entrance door opened and there was Damien. A window opened and a woman appeared, naked to the waist, grinning at her own daring, waving and blowing a kiss. At her husband.

Damien got into his car and began to reverse, but by then Chloe was behind him, blocking his path with her own vehicle.

Damien got out and she noticed he hadn't even dressed himself properly. His collar was open, his shirt wasn't tucked in and as her eyes diverted to the zip on the fly of his trousers she could see it was half down.

"What the fuck are you doing, parked there?" Damien shouted not realising in the dark who was blocking him in. It was then she got out of the car and despite the poor light she could have sworn she saw him go white.

"How was the game?" Chloe asked and by her tone she left him in no doubt that she wasn't talking about football.

Chapter 46

All the time my family had been falling apart I had felt that the one thing I did not need to worry about was my business. I'd never had cause to doubt my friend and partner David Segal for a moment and throughout all the trauma of Helen's death he had been a rock.

I knew I had placed him in an invidious position when it came to the children confronting me with the Lizzie stuff, but he'd not wavered for a moment and his supporting lies had even begun to have me believing that it was indeed, him, who'd had the affair, rather than me. Now this was something different, this whole issue of the missing money and I had no idea how to deal with it.

I'd taken to filing my problems away these past few months rather than meeting them head on and I suppose I could have done exactly the same with this one. But there was the question of this new transaction to which we are almost committed and the fact that I could not see how we could possibly afford it as things stood. So, there was no real question of hiding this issue under 'F' for 'future problem'. This came under 'I' for 'Immediate'. This was here and now, and I decided I just couldn't wait.

I say that, but I did sleep on it, or rather didn't sleep on it as sleep wouldn't come. Only the what-ifs came and haunted me through the night. What if we did the deal and then couldn't complete? What if we did the deal and David suddenly magicked the money back in from some mysterious source? What if the whole deal was so intrinsically tainted that it would bring down the whole company and David and myself with it? What if I'd got it totally wrong?

Our offices are largely open plan. Only David and myself have doors that close to give us some privacy and privacy was what I needed for the conversation I was about to have. Usually, we'd just wander in on the other, coffee in hand, leaving the door open. Everybody in the place seemed to know what was going on and unless we were discussing sacking somebody (that had happened only once when we found we were employing an alcoholic kleptomaniac) or giving somebody a rise or a bonus or taking on somebody new, our conversations (however heated) were out there for all to hear.

Today I held no coffee in my hand, only my heart in my mouth. I'd consumed too much caffeine in the early hours of the morning. I just marched in on David purposefully, shut the door behind me and spread out the financial information I had printed out. David looked up innocently, but I saw a shadow of something flicker across his face. Puzzlement? Fear? Doubt? Or just resignation to the inevitable? It was hard to tell, but he knew a storm was coming, that was for sure.

I took my time organising the papers into the order that I need to explain what I had discovered and then took even greater time to go through the facts, as I saw them, one by one. All the while David said nothing and I wondered if he was going to deny everything or else offer me some plausible explanation regarding the missing money. If I was waiting for something like that then I was going to be disappointed. Nothing was forthcoming. At the end of my speech he merely shrugged, gave that lopsided grin that normally earned him instant forgiveness and said,

"Fair cop, Daniel. Have to say with all the distractions in your life I didn't think you'd notice. I've not nicked the money or anything…"

"Did I give you my consent? Did I know you were using it? Because if the answer to both those questions is no, then you have stolen it."

I could feel the blood rushing to my face, heard my voice rising and all my determination to keep calm had been blown away.

David still was remarkably cool,

"Listen, Daniel, that deal was too good to miss. I told you we needed to oil the wheels a bit to get it moving. I could see this sort of opportunity was on the horizon one day so I've been getting ready for it for a while."

"Oiling the wheels a bit," I raged, "you've raped and pillaged the business and telling me that you're playing a long game isn't helping your cause one iota. You've paid somebody a huge bribe. You've committed us to a deal we can't afford and if for any reason it goes even more pear-shaped than it is right now then we'll lose everything we've worked for honestly all these years."

I thought I might have rattle him, but he was still ominously calm.

"I think you're over-reacting Daniel. We'll pull this off and you'll thank me when we bank the profit."

I could see he just wasn't getting it and I had I horrible sinking feeling that I knew why.

"I don't need that kind of money, David and nor do you," I said.

"How do you know what I need or don't need? You never even bother to ask. And when did you get to be so holier than thou, Daniel? We've pulled the odd stroke every now and then and it's been fine. It's in the nature of our profession. We're running a business here, not a charity."

"We've never broken the law before, David. Putting one over on our business rivals is one thing, but this, this is something entirely different. I don't want to be a party to this, I really don't," although I kind of knew that unless I went to the police I already was. And I had to admit to myself that I was lecturing him. I was the headmaster, he the naughty schoolboy called to my study for a good dressing down.

"Where were your high moral standards when you were cheating on your wife, Daniel? You asked me to help you out then and now and I didn't hesitate even though I didn't feel comfortable aiding and abetting you in lying to your wife and just recently to your children. I stood by you. And now you need to stand by me."

So that was the bottom line that I had seen coming. The threat I had perceived and now had sort of received was that either I connived in what had been done or David, my loyal friend and partner, would press the nuclear button and blow me to smithereens with him. That was how it seemed to me, that he wasn't making a statement, but issuing a warning. Or was it my tormented imagination running riot. I was in the sort of mental state that I couldn't distinguish truth from fiction.

I needed some time to think although I knew already exactly what I should be doing. I could not be a part of that. There had to be a way out. All that had been proved was that you think you know somebody, but you never do. We don't even know ourselves let alone anybody else. I left the office, without saying goodbye to anybody, not even Amanda who'd been with us forever. I wondered if Helen might have had the same thought, had she ever known about Lizzie. That she'd thought she'd known me, but hadn't. I said before that the sins of the past cast a long shadow. I'd just not realised quite how long that could ever be.

Chapter 47

It was with a mixture of anger, relief and embarrassment that Adam sat on the plane back to London. It could, he guessed, have been so much worse. He'd been kept in the room at JFK for hours along with various itinerant immigrants most of whom did not appear to have showered for several days. It had not been a pleasant experience and it did not improve when he was called into a side room to be interviewed by the most obnoxious Homeland Security officer he'd ever encountered. And he'd met quite a few in his time.

"So, let me get this right, Mr Kent," he'd appeared to choke on the "Mr" bit. "You were trying to enter the United States of America on a work visa appertaining to a job you no longer have."

Adam had sighed. It had never occurred to him that losing his job could have this particular repercussion or that immigration would even have been aware of his change of circumstance. He didn't need more than one guess as to whom might have brought that to their attention. It was so in keeping with Benjamin Gilbert's vindictive nature that the tip off could only have emanated from him. Perhaps that was why Carly had been so amenable to him leaving the country to visit the kids. She and her father knew he would never get back in.

"Look," Adam replied hastily gathering his thoughts. The name tag on the officer's lanyard read "Alfonso Gonzales" and as one minority to another Adam thought he might as well be polite.

"Mr Gonzales, I was recently laid off, but my company is still in essence continuing to pay me. That's what my package was for. Of course, I could have applied for an ESTA and there would have been no reason why I wouldn't have got it… "

"Shall we say, Mr Kent, that's a little presumptuous. Our Government may just have had the last word on the subject. The fact is that the minute your employment ended at..." he glanced down at the paper in front of him, "Goldfarb and Hemingway, so did your right to remain here."

"Technically," Adam began to say, though he was not quite sure how he would have carried on, but he wasn't given the opportunity.

"There's nothing technical about it," Gonzales said, "basically, Mr Kent, you have to understand and accept that in this current situation I am the one calling the shots. I am actually already cutting you some slack by engaging with you and not arresting you for attempting to enter this country illegally. But, as I am a nice person and you've caught me on a good day," (Adam hated to think what might have happened on a bad day for Alfonso Gonzales) "I am just going to send you back home, Mr Kent, courtesy of your favourite Uncle Sam. And when you do get around to applying for your ESTA or a new work visa then please don't forget to mention you've been refused entry. It's on our system now..."

Adam knew when he was being taunted and also knew that this was not the moment to lose it. Deportation was a result given the power that Mr Gonzales wielded in these circumstances. But, it also meant this was probably it as far as him ever working again in the USA was concerned.

He waited impatiently until they told him the details of his return flight. He could have done with a visit to a lounge and a shower, but that wasn't going to happen so all he was left with was the thought that somehow he needed to tell Kelly what was happening and then find a real good immigration lawyer when he got back home. Meanwhile he had some six hours on a plane to think of what he could do to Carly and her fucking father. What goes around, comes around wasn't going to cut it in this case. He would have to go on out there and haul it in.

Chapter 48

It was strange having all the children back under one roof. Even when we were sitting *shivah* there was no sense of permanence of us all being together. Chloe was going back to Damien and the kids every night. Lauren couldn't wait to get home to the West Country (or, at least, back then, had been ordered back as soon as possible by Luke) and Adam desperately needed, if not wanted, to get back to New York.

All that had now changed. Adam had returned although he'd not yet told me the whole story. From his demeanour and lack of communication I was guessing it was not one with a happy ending. Chloe's arrived on the doorstep with so many bags that when she said, "I should have kicked Damien out, but I couldn't bear to spend another moment with him in my sight. So, I've given him two weeks to find somewhere else to live," that it didn't really convince me she was going to stick to that order and return home in the foreseeable future.

She'd not seen a lawyer yet, either and I was sure the advice she would be given would be diametrically opposite to what she'd done. I'd not had a lot of experience of divorce although, when my craziness with Lizzie was at its height, I did check into a few possibilities should I leave or be asked to leave if discovered. The mantra for the wronged wife was do not leave the house unless and until you are carried out screaming pursuant to a court order. And there was my daughter merrily leaving her cheating husband to frolic alone (or maybe, not so alone) under the matrimonial roof.

She made a few noises about consulting Lizzie as Lauren has pushed her street cred way up high. I said little, not wanting to encourage yet another member of my family getting too close to my ex-mistress when things were so finely balanced and delicate in my life.

"Do you think she might do wholesale rates?" Chloe asked over dinner in her Chloe way. "We could throw Adam in as well to get a bigger discount."

A couple of nights in her old bedroom and she was looking better and sounding much more like her old self. She was constantly on the phone. Her friends were ringing the landline when they couldn't reach her on the mobile and if I had to listen to her relate the story of her confrontation with her husband and this woman of his one more time I had decided to grab the phone from her and insist on telling my précised version to whomsoever may be on the other end of the call.

Lauren had her first court application later that week and there'd been a lot of groundwork going on to ensure that went well. I'd had a running commentary on that as well as if my agreeing to pay all the legal costs had also bought me the broadcasting rights to the whole drama.

"Have you spoken to Lizzie, yet Dad?" Lauren asked at dinner. "She's absolutely brilliant. Chloe you've got to get to see her. She'll sort you out, no problem. I owe a huge debt to dad's mystery friend who found her for us. Dad, you never gave me the name so I can thank them." Fortunately, she didn't wait for an answer but just galloped on to say that even Maggie her barrister was growing on her.

I didn't know whether or not she noticed, but I didn't comment or, indeed, answer any question about Lizzie directly. I'd adopted a particular technique to allow me to cope when Lizzie's name cropped up in conversation. I nodded and I smiled like one of those dogs that used to hang in car windows. But, I didn't engage. I found a way to occupy myself suddenly with urgent emails (which were, in fact, becoming fewer and fewer) or go to the kitchen to make myself a cup of tea.

The kids always used to tease me about what they called, "Dad's Tea-Making Ceremony." I just always preferred a cup of tea I'd made myself. I put just the right amount of milk in first as I knew Helen, if she was making it, would add it at the end.

"That's the normal way to do it, Daniel," she'd say, "but then you're not normal are you," she'd add with a smile. I can sort of hear the words today, but the smile is fading just like that of the Cheshire Cat. Anyway, with the tea-bag turning the milk a pleasant shade of brown I'd pour in the water from a freshly boiled kettle, push a spoon down on the bag and when it got to the right colour to satisfy me, I'd whip out the bag and put it into the rubbish bin, usually staining a few work surfaces and the kitchen floor on the way.

Whilst she was clearing up the mess I had created making one simple cup of tea Helen would say,

"If you took as much interest and invested as much effort into cooking just one meal or finding out how anything works in the house, as you do in making one bloody cup of tea, then my life would be much easier."

It was always a light-hearted complaint, something that she knew I expected. She, for her part, never really expected me actually to cook anything, let alone a full meal. Or really do anything domestic for that matter. I can't even remember changing a lightbulb and there were times when Helen would wait until my office was down to one light just to see if I would make the first move. She was never disappointed in the expectation that I wouldn't, as I never did. At least I didn't disappoint in that regard.

I don't know what Lizzie said or how she reacted when my name was mentioned. A part of me was curious wanting to be a fly on the wall, but knowing where my curiosity had led me in the past I preferred to rely on the sensible part of my brain and keep my distance.

I was still finding it hard to accept that the marriages of all of my three children had failed. My genes, not Helen's I feared. It would have broken my late wife's heart to see what was going on with her children. I am not sure she would, or could, have coped with it or the collateral damage to her grandchildren.

Not that my three grandchildren seemed particularly damaged, or at least the three I had under my roof. Callum had grown in confidence every day, shrugging off the dark cloud that hung over him in the shape of his father. Tommy seemed less troubled now that he had his cousins to play with, in a much happier atmosphere than would appear to have existed at home. And Scarlett, now that she had an enlarged group to fuss over as a Mother Hen, was rising to the challenge. Did it really need a death to make us function as a family unit? If so, that was a huge price to pay for something we should easily have been able to attain as sensible grown-ups.

Basically, I let them get on with it. I still had the licence of the fairly recently bereaved, although I know that could not last forever. I think it was that which had probably saved me when my secret cache of Lizzie memories had been discovered. That and the alibi that I'd provided for myself by blaming David. I'd thought of him as poor David at the time, regretted that he was, through no fault of his own, *persona non grata* in my house, particularly once my gossipy daughters had brought Adam up to speed with his fictionalised misdemeanours.

Yet, now there were real crimes that I could discuss with nobody, certainly none of my family. The last thing I wanted was to have them reaching out to David to beat him up, theoretically and maybe even actually, if they thought he was harming me. And he was harming me. I was sleeping even less than before if that was possible. I felt like the detective in that old movie, 'Insomnia'. I didn't know how much longer

I could continue, mentally or physically. I needed help and even thought of turning to a psychiatrist, but he wouldn't get the business dynamics of the problems facing me. I thought long and hard and then decided on what I perceived as the only option open to me, the only person who might just understand and help me find a way out of the complex maze in which I found myself. I called Lizzie and asked to meet her.

Chapter 49

Before Luke Campbell had met and married Lauren, no Jew had ever crossed his path. Of course, he knew all about them from his Labour Party meetings, knew they were all Zios, that they controlled all the money in the world, knew that Israel was the cause of all the troubles in the Middle East and had a good inkling that Mossad was at the root of every terrorist atrocity that could be blamed on the freedom seeking Palestinians. Of course, he did not share any of these thoughts in depth with Lauren. With her he wanted to play the long game. First capture the Jewess, then tame her and make her your slave just as her people had enslaved the innocent Arabs on the West Bank. Then the final solution (he liked that phrase): Use her as a bargaining chip to make her old man buy her back. The Jews were used to captivity and deals to get out of it and Luke's long game plan was merely another example of how to get them to spread their money around a little more to those who were more deserving.

Her father, that slimy Daniel Kent, with his estate agent attitude had long needed a lesson. Needed to be taught that all property was theft. Everybody would come to know that when some radical left-wing politician led the Labour Party to the Promised Land. He liked that analogy as well. Luke had campaigned actively on behalf of Jeremy Corbyn in the election before last, out on the campuses, finding willing young ears who were tired of the way things were. They knew that they would graduate and struggle to find a job, struggle to repay their student loans and struggle even more to be able to buy the smallest of flats. Ok, that had been close, but the election that followed was a disaster. Boris Johnson and his entitled cronies back in power. And yet, a revolution was coming, he was sure of it and the likes of the

Kent family would be the first to be dragged through the streets in tumbrils on their way to the guillotine.

That visit from Lauren's father had messed things up a little. He'd not been quite ready to proceed with his plan, but in a way, it had helped him to accelerate things himself. It gave him some moral ground when he went to the Jew school to recover his daughter. Yes, his daughter who now needed to be re-educated from the nonsense with which her head had been filled during her brief stay away from him. He never thought that Lauren would have had the courage to take him on in the court room. He'd thought that, as always, with the Jews, it would come down to money and that he could strike a hard bargain with her father. Not that he wanted the children all the time. They were a bargaining chip.

Luke Campbell was not a stupid man, even if some of his beliefs and prejudices were idiotic beyond the pale. His perfect result was to get some money from the Kent family and then reach an agreement whereby the children were shared on his terms. Mainly that was that he got them when it was convenient to him and that they had a secular education when they weren't with him. He had a life to get on with and the children did not really fit into that.

It had been convenient when Lauren was around. She would look after the kids and let him get on with his business. She'd never really known what he did and he hadn't told her. She thought he did some manual labour around the harbour, a bit of boat mending, casual crew and anything else that came his way. She had no idea that he was also peddling drugs to the locals and anybody else who heard that he was a good source.

He didn't think of himself as a dealer. He didn't sell large quantities or anything hard like heroin. He merely serviced a need that arose because that one bloody right-wing Government after another, couldn't see that legalising pot was the right thing to do.

When he'd first met Lauren at Uni she'd not been adverse to a joint herself. Maybe he should bring that up in court, though he knew that if he did she'd be back at him in an instant. That might not hurt. At least the judge would see that she wasn't the Snow White character she had been painted by her lawyer in the documents that had been filed.

He'd got himself a local solicitor, Stephen Yarwood, who he knew didn't mind taking a bit of cash and cash was the currency in which Luke Campbell dealt. Nobody bought from him by credit card or bank transfer. The guy was surprisingly good and Luke wondered why he'd ended up in this dead and alive place. But then, it seemed everybody he met had a back story. It was just that Luke, himself, thought he was clever enough to write his own.

"We have to be ready to reach a compromise on the steps of the court, Luke," Yarwood had said, it's sort of fifty-fifty if they get it before a judge. She won't like the fact that you went into the school and snatched the child."

"Will she like the fact that she and her father forced their way into my house and her father assaulted me before they stole the children away?"

"No," his lawyer had said, "she won't like that either."

"Ok, well I am relying on you to make sure she likes that less than what I did."

As far as Luke was concerned that was it. He had done all he could do. Right now he had things to do before he left for London in a few days. One of them involving him going out to the local where he knew a few of his customers would be. The only problem was Peta. He couldn't take her with him and his regular child minder, Mrs Graveson, had already told him that as it was bingo night she wouldn't be available. His latest girlfriend had gone off on some exotic dancing assignment and she'd be back when she was good and ready, probably stoned out of her mind with all the money she'd earned already spent. There was nothing for it. Peta would be going to bed soon. He'd wait till she was fast asleep and then tip toe out. He'd be an hour at most.

He just needed to rehearse her one more time for the interview with the CFCASS woman who'd been allocated to the case.

"You know, Peta, what happens to naughty girls who don't do what their daddy tells them, don't you?" he said and she did know. She knew from what had happened when they were all together and she knew to say nothing about that and to say that Mummy wasn't telling the truth because Mummy had a few problems when she forgot to take her pills.

It was a lot for a five-year-old to remember, but he was confident that she was too scared to forget it and that on the day she would deliver. Once she delivered, once the judge found for him (assuming there wasn't the satisfactory deal to be done outside as suggested by his solicitor) then it would be the turn of Daniel Kent to stand and deliver.

He waited a few minutes after she'd closed her eyes. Her breathing was steady and she was not the sort of child who awoke once she'd fallen into a deep sleep. Then he shrugged on his jacket, tapped the pockets to make sure he had his stock of drugs with him and left the house without a backwards glance. He didn't hear the click of a camera or the softly shod feet that followed him all the way to the pub and continued to track his evening activities on film.

Chapter 50

I didn't have to lie about meeting Lizzie for a drink, but I did. I could have just said that we were meeting to discuss the case, the costs, the chances, the new issues of Chloe to see if she felt she could also represent her. Yet, sometimes, as I'd discovered in the past, the lie was an easier option. And so, I did. I told them I had things to discuss with David about the business. I knew they wouldn't check that one out, given David's current status in the household.

I got a train into town. Lizzie had chosen the original Soho House this time which had undergone a massive refurbishment since I'd last visited as a guest. I don't know if I was supposed to be impressed or not, but at least it was highly unlikely I'd see anybody I knew. She already had our drinks on the table by the time I arrived and I drank mine so quickly that before I'd even begun my story and got past the awkward pleasantries she was signaling for another.

"Try taking that one a bit more slowly, Daniel. I'm not sure what this is all about, but something tells me you don't want to be going home rolling drunk tonight."

Times had changed. In the past we'd have got drunk together and worked on some excuse for me not to go home at all and I'd end up back at her Islington basement flat whilst we made drunken love. On looking back I can't actually remember us having sex stone-cold sober. I didn't think about it at the time, but now I can see that the drinking was to drive the guilt away and make me forget my poor Helen sleeping alone in our bed. All of a sudden this meeting with Lizzie, bringing all that back, didn't seem such a good idea.

However, the alcohol did serve its purpose as I found myself telling Lizzie the whole story, leaving out nothing, not even the more embarrassing parts. I told her about the stuff she'd sent me which I'd foolishly kept. I noticed her blink as I related that and I wondered if it was in despair at my stupidity, or to prevent a tear or just end of day fatigue. I told her about the deal David had found for us and how I'd said no and he'd gone ahead anyway and about how he'd siphoned off the money to use as a bribe and then how I'd used him to cover for me and how I now felt I was sort of being blackmailed into going along with the whole rotten scheme. It all came out in stream of consciousness, with hardly a pause for breath. But at least it did pause my consumption of alcohol for a bit.

"Just seems to me that if I blow the whistle on David then he does the same to me."

Lizzie took another sip of her drink. She was only halfway through her first whilst my tongue was almost hanging out of my mouth for a second.

"Never give people the power over you, Daniel," she said, "I told you that when we were together and you had the death wish of bringing other people into our secret. Showing off your *shikse,* I think I called it. Proving you weren't the boring, respectable family man that everybody else thought you were. Including your wife…"

She watched the effect of that on me and for a moment I wondered if she was going to turn the arrow she had shot in the wound, but she just moved on.

"Anyway, what is done is done. What do you want me to tell you, Daniel? Do you want my advice as a solicitor, a casual observer, a friend or somebody who is sort of at the heart of the problem?"

"Can you manage a combination of all of those?" I asked.

"You always did want the impossible, Daniel," she replied and then did order another drink for both of us.

"You once said that you had to aim for the improbable to achieve the impossible," I replied. I even remembered when and where she'd said that and that was part of the problem because I remembered almost everything she'd ever said, everywhere we'd ever been, every time we'd made love.

After I told her it was over she'd said,

"When you're in the middle of a love- affair, you never do know the last time you'll fuck." She was never scared to call a spade a spade, never scared of anything, never embarrassed or ashamed of her nakedness, whilst I can't recall ever seeing Helen totally naked. I couldn't help but compare them when they were both in my life and now that Helen was actually and Lizzie technically gone, I continued to do the same thing. I couldn't help myself and even as I thought that I realised I'd actually said it out loud.

"That's always been your trouble, Daniel. You really can't help yourself in either sense. You always do what you want without thinking and then expect to be helped out of the mess you've got yourself into."

I wanted to say that I'd not come here for a lecture. I had, indeed, come for help as I couldn't see a way out of this mess, couldn't help myself as Lizzie so succinctly put it.

"What do I do, Lizzie?" I heard the note of desperation in my voice, the words coming to me in a haze through my partially, drink-fuddled brain.

Surprisingly, she put down her glass and took my hands in hers.

"This is what you do, Daniel," and when she went on to tell me, I realised I had known the answer to the question all the time.

Chapter 51

Adam had always been good at making decisions. Before the days of sat-navs and Waze when the family had been driving on holiday, hopelessly lost in France or Italy or even in the English Lakes, he had been the one who would authoritatively say go left or right or carry straight on. Whether it was Daniel or Helen driving they would instinctively do what he said and invariably he was right. However, an intuitive sense of direction was no good to him right now because he didn't have the faintest idea where he was heading. The limit of his decision-making ability was to choose between a plain blue shirt or a striped pink one and then he would dither between which pair of jeans to pull on with them.

Jeans and casual shirts were as far as he was getting in the dress situation. He certainly had no need for any of his suits or ties as he wondered whether he would ever work again, at least in his chosen industry. Kelly tried to cheer him up when they spoke on the phone, but the fact that Facetime or Skype was the nearest he got to being with her wasn't helping either.

"It's early days, Adam," she'd said, "you've not even been back a week. You'll find something."

"I don't want just something. And I don't want to work here."

"You sound like you're seven years old. I don't want. What's that about? Go get 'em, that should be the mantra."

It might have been early days, but the profession had changed since Adam had last worked in England. He was thirty-five and looking in a young man's market. Yes, he had experience, yes, he had a reference from Goldfarb, but he knew that any recruitment agency would want more than that. They would want to speak to people and it was what those people might say when cornered. That was the problem. There was also the issue of travel. Most of the companies he might approach would have offices in the States and he could hardly say that he'd been deported when he'd last tried to enter. However he might try to coat that bitter pill, it would still taste of poison and have the effect of cyanide.

The house in which he'd grown up felt different. He could see that he'd never really appreciated just how much his mother had done. The fridge was always full, the freezer overflowing, laundry always clean, toiletries in reserve, flowers in a vase, biscuit tins full, chocolate bars in the cupboard, spare bottles of sparkling water (his dad like fruit-flavoured, but the rest of the family preferred plain, except for Lauren who only drank tap water as an environmental statement). No contingency was over-looked but he could see at a glance that his father had simply not been coping. The bursting linen basket and the empty larder were significant clues. He wasn't to know that it had been even worse before the arrival of his sisters.

It wasn't just the physical things. There was an atmosphere of incompleteness and that was never going to go away. His mother had turned the house into a home. An old cliché, but true, nevertheless. How his mother had managed to balance bringing up three children with managing a home and her job as an English teacher he had no idea, but manage she had. And not just manage, but totally succeed.

If his mother had been alive, he could have sat down with her in the kitchen over coffee. Unlike his father, neither he nor his mother ever drank tea. She always chose decaf, a choice he could never understand.

"The whole point of coffee, Mum, is the caffeine. It's for the buzz, the kick. It's our drug of choice."

"I just like the taste," she'd replied, logical as ever and it was her logic of which he was in desperate need at this moment. He reached for a blank sheet of paper and scrabbled through a drawer for a pen that worked, wondering how nobody in his family could bring themselves to throw away a biro when it ran out of ink. He hit pay dirt on the fifth one and began to make a list. His mother had been a great one for lists. Maybe that was the secret of her organisational success.

He started with "Find a US Immigration Lawyer" and then struggled with item number two. He supposed it ought to be "Find a job", but as he ran his fingers through his hair he decided upon "Get a haircut." It had been a long time since he'd had his hair cut in England. He used to go to the same hairdresser as his mother. It was primarily a ladies' salon and he'd sat there, listening to the gossip, the inane pop music coming from a radio permanently tuned to Capital or Kiss FM or something of the sort. He wondered if Rikki, who'd finally got to doing his hair just the way he liked it, was still there and again, he missed his barber in Manhattan. Marco, a chatty Italian, who was excellent on the razor cut and from his conversation probably came from a Mafia family who had other uses for razors. There was something comforting about the all-male clientele, the smell of shampoo and embrocation and the fact that they would actually do a wet shave at seven in the morning. So, the next item on his list wrote itself. "Get back to NYC and Kelly." Or was that two separate items?

He was finding the list comforting, but knew that if he added too much, then it would become daunting. There was too much in his life that was daunting at the moment, so he paused there. He could have moved on to "Find out what the fuck is going on with Dad." or "Help sort out my sister Chloe's marriage," "Or actually listen to Lauren and see what can be done to get my niece back," but when he could barely see his own way through the fog that concealed his future he didn't see what possible good he could be to the rest of his troubled family, so he wrote nothing and just sat there, pen poised in mid-air, like an author with writer's block. That was when his phone rang. Kelly on Facetime. He half thought about ignoring it. He wasn't looking for sympathy or platitudes at the moment, but then she was actually the last person he wanted out of his life.

Her face lit up the screen and he felt a sudden upsurge in optimism. It was ten in the morning and only five a.m. in New York so she either really wanted to speak with him or she had something urgent to tell him and he couldn't believe that bad news would have got her calling at that unearthly hour for her.

"Adam, I've found out something. About this Rodriguez character who's shacked up with your ex. You know what I said about timing being the key to you getting your kids back. Well, I think the timing might just be coming up to right o'clock."

She was clearly excited, her words bumping into each other as they raced out of her mouth, her accent becoming increasingly hard to follow even though he'd now spent so much of his working life in the States. When he'd got her to slow down and repeat what she was saying then he understood perfectly and wondered if he should have put "Get full access to my children" on the list because he realised that he now had a chance of at least ticking that one off.

Chapter 52

I'd called a family meeting. That was the stuff of soap operas and radio dramas. Helen always used to listen to "The Archers" and they were forever having 'family meetings' in the twelve minute episodes, meetings squeezed in between the sounds of tractors and harvesters, the clinking of glasses in 'The Bull' and more recently serious frauds, gay marriages and attempted murders. I used to tease Helen when she blocked everything else out at two minutes past seven every night and even listened religiously to the podcasts when we were away. I never admitted to her that I had become just as hooked and I still listen since she's been gone, wondering what she might have thought of the latest twists and turns. The latest family meetings. She'd always said that she had no intention of dying until she'd heard the last episode of 'The Archers'. Well, as the old Yiddish saying goes, *'Mann macht und Gott Lacht.'* Man (or woman) make plans and G-d just laughs.

I had no huge wooden table in my kitchen to seat people around, so I got them seated in the dining room instead. Me at the head, Adam to my left, Chloe next to him and Lauren to my right. The seat at the other end empty, waiting for Helen to arrive and fill it. Only she wouldn't. She would no more arrive than Godot. We were all doomed to wait for her for all eternity, even though what I had to say was for her ears as much as anybody's. I should have made this decision when she was alive, just as I should have told her that I was really in to 'The Archers' so we could have enjoyed each episode together.

What I couldn't say, what I certainly could never had explained to Helen, my wife of some forty years, was that I had reached my decision with the help of Lizzie, my former mistress. It had all seemed perfectly logical when we'd sat together the other evening. I'd thought at the time that the few cocktails I'd had were what was making it easy to accept, but when I awoke the next morning, then despite the headache I always got after drinking too much, the decision still seemed to me to be perfectly acceptable.

"Listen, everybody," I began, my eyes roaming across my audience of three, "I am going to retire from the business."

Chloe snorted derisively,

"You, retire, you're kidding me. Mum always said you would never retire. That your last property deal would be to strike a great bargain for a burial plot."

I smiled. I could hear Helen saying just that, but I could also hear the sound advice of Lizzie ringing in my ears.

"Forget about David turning you in to your family. You ought to be turning him into the police..." She'd seen the expression on my face and knew that wasn't going to happen so she'd continued, " but as you're never going to do that out of some misplaced sense of loyalty the next best thing you can do is put some clear water between you and what's going on at the company."

"You mean get them to buy me out?" I'd asked, "that's not very practical when I can see the company is going to be over-committed by what David's virtually contracted us to do."

"The operative word is 'virtually'. You say he's signed off on Heads of Terms and won't back track. Ok. You haven't signed anything. You get the hell out of dodge. If they can't pay you out right now get some agreement to be paid in the future, though not out of the proceeds of this deal. Now, there may be no future, but you tell me that you're not short of money, that Helen had insurance so, just walk away. No, run away. I know David seems confident he'll get away with it, but although it's a long time since I did any criminal law, as I recall everybody I did come across when I was in training was absolutely sure they'd never be caught. I remember one very plausible con man telling me that he still thought his only crime was being caught and that was after he'd been sentenced to seven years. I've a bad feeling about this. If you found out what's been going on, then the police would do so as well if the spaghetti hits the fan. I can see the pasta coming out in nice thick strands and I can feel the blast from the fan, so just leave it behind."

And that's what I'd told David when I'd gone into see him the next day. He'd been all over me, full of apologies and remorse, sorry it had come to this, but when he realised that he wasn't going to have to write me out a cheque straight away (all I'd asked for was a charge over a property we'd bought between us and tucked away for a rainy day) he didn't try to dissuade me. That was when I knew I'd reached the right decision. It was for all the wrong reasons. If I'd had the courage to do this when I'd had Helen so that she and I could spend more time together and do all the things we'd wanted then that would have been the only right reason.

"So what will you do all day long, Dad?" Lauren asked

"Apart from getting under everybody's feet," Lauren added, but in a tone to which I could take no offence.

Again, I looked around them, really taking in my children for the first time since they were little,

"Do with myself?" I echoed Lauren, "you know what, apart from trying to rebuild my life, I'm not really sure. But as your Callum says whenever I ask him what he did at school, I'll do things and stuff and for the moment, that's going to have to be enough."

I rose to my feet to signal the meeting was over. There didn't seem to be a lot more to say and I just needed to make a start on my things and stuff. Whatever they might turn out to be. That in itself gave me a thrill that I'd not experienced in quite a while. The day of Helen's death had been my first step into the unknown. This was going to be a whole expedition.

Chapter 53

"Fuck you, Damien," Chloe thought and then bit her lip as Scarlett looked up at her as she realised she'd not just thought it, but actually said it. She didn't know whether to gloss over it or to try to explain to her daughter that Mummy had used a bad word and she must never ever copy it. Scarlett, typically, made her choice for her.

"Daddy says it's not a good thing to use naughty words…"

Bugger, thought Chloe, feeling as if she was turning into the worst mother in the world, she actually knows it's naughty so she's heard it before.

"Well," said Chloe, "Daddy should know."

She did not elaborate on that. She knew exactly what she meant as that picture of the woman in the window and Damien's failure even to attempt an explanation was still vividly engraved on her mind. And now he was bombarding her with messages and calls she simply blanked. Now he was faced with starting life all over without her and the children, of footing the bill for their lifestyle and his own, now that doubtless that woman, whatever her name was, had moved on to a better tennis player at the club, now he was telling her he'd made a huge mistake and he wanted another chance.

So, hence the "fuck you" thought, which had turned into the "fuck you" exclamation and was about to turn into a "fuck you" text followed by three exclamation marks and a single raised finger emoji. But something stopped her sending it. Two things, actually. One was that she was bright enough to realise that if this turned into an all-out legal battle that Damien might well use any abusive texts as evidence to show what sort of person she was and how she wasn't fit to have sole custody of the children. Maybe he was right, after what she'd just said in front of a six-year-old. A six-year-old with a parrot-like ability to copy and repeat everything that was said in front of her as well. As for what sort of person she was, well, perhaps a day or two in court would tell her that as well. Probably cheaper than a commitment to a whole series of therapy hours with some expensive psychologist. Particularly, if she got awarded costs against Damien.

Then there was the second reason for holding back. She just wasn't sure she wanted to end the dialogue just yet. Or at all, if she was being perfectly honest with herself. Part of her was angry, very angry indeed, although the anger wasn't just aimed at Damien or the woman whom she refused to dignify with a name even though she'd squeezed the real name out of her husband before she'd left.

"You couldn't even tell me the truth about that, Damien, could you."

No, part of it was aimed at herself for allowing this to happen. She'd seen enough of her friends go through this sort of thing, listening to their whines and self-justification, to know that the breakdown of a marriage was never the fault of just one party. Both of them got the right to have some credit as executive producers as the titles ran at the end.

She'd thought long and hard as to what she could have done to avoid this tsunami that her life had become. In fact, unlike a tsunami, it wasn't a natural disaster. Those you could not stop occurring. You could only take the necessary precautions not to be there when they did. Who went on holiday to Miami or the Caribbean during the hurricane season for heaven's sake? You had to be in a marriage.

Perhaps, that was part of the problem. Neither of them had actually really been there for all those years and as time passed they were there less and less. Damien with his tennis, and his football and his work. Her with her friends, her coven, her ladies who lunched and gossiped, her gym and most of all, her family. There was nothing wrong with her family, she was convinced of that. Both of her parents had got on well with Damien, far better than she'd ever got on with his parents, but then, he'd never really got on with his parents either.

"They come with a Government Health Warning," he'd said when he'd first brought her home and that was an understatement. It took less than an hour to realise that whoever Damien had brought in as a potential daughter-in-law she would not have been good enough for Marion Gold. As far as his father, Stanley was concerned, he was too full of his own self-importance to care. They contributed to the wedding, they were icily polite to Helen and David, but unlike so many of her friends the two families never mixed socially after that. Stanley claimed to have his own Bank, but was really just a glorified money-lender. Marion played bridge and kalooki and canasta and pretty much anything where she could prove to whoever she was playing with that she was better than them. Chloe's family was different and she had made a virtue of that as they gradually sucked Damien in like some giant man eating creature. Eating not for food, but for comfort, loving what they devoured and allowing it to live within them.

So, that had been one cross against her name in the blame game. That, and unwillingness to be experimental in bed. From the off, Damien had wanted sex more than her and before they'd had the children she'd gone along with it. As time went on it was just too easy to fall asleep when he was downstairs watching football or some cricket match or tennis game from a different time-zone. It must have been frustrating for him crawling into bed besides a woman who, as he claimed, snored gently and who simply had become unaware of his presence beside her. Was that what had pushed him into this affair?

He'd denied it was an affair. It had just been a fling, a one off, or when pressed a two off. It had never happened before and it would never happen again, but why should she believe him? If she gave into his entreaties to give it another go, then how could she ever trust him again? She could show more interest in what he did. She didn't actually hate football like some women she knew and a one-day cricket match was tolerable as long as the sun was shining and there was a bottle of wine or champagne to hand. She'd not been a bad tennis player herself back in the day. Before the children. It was a different kind of BC and the AD had suffered because of it. And then there was the AD of her mother. The mourning that was natural, but perhaps she had taken too far.

"I know you're sad," Damien had said a few weeks after the funeral, "but you've got us. Me and the kids. We're all here for you. Isn't that enough?"

She'd just walked out of the room and that was another cross beside her name. And now she just had the kids. All the bloody time. And she had her father, who at times, no longer seemed or acted like the man she'd loved. And she had her brother and her sister and her nephew with hopefully her niece to follow and none of that was enough. She couldn't stay here, that was for sure. She was suffocating within the old family home, within the family and she was beginning to understand what it must have felt like for Damien, an only child, who'd not really been loved by his parents, just worshipped by his mother. So, the ticks against Damien's name were growing in number. She deleted the "fuck you" text and the exclamation marks one by one, thinking all the time what she should say in reply if anything at all.

"OK. Just stop texting and calling, please, I'll be in touch next week and we'll meet for a coffee."

She was going to add the x with which she'd always ended her messages or notes to him, but held back. Instead all she said was, "And don't forget to water the plants." Her finger lingered over the send button for a full minute and then she pressed it.

Chapter 54

It was surreal sitting in the court room next to one of my daughters, whilst Lizzie, who I had struggled to keep a secret for so many years, sat in front next to the barrister, Maggie Chamberlain. My lovely son-in-law, Luke Campbell, sat a few feet away on the right with his solicitor whose name I had gathered was Stephen Yarwood. There was no barrister as Yarwood was clearly as far as Luke could extend in terms of money. I didn't know if that was a good or a bad thing, but Maggie had explained that the judge might cut him some slack as the poor West Country lawyer working on his own against the deep pockets of the Kent family and their no-expenses spared, legal team.

This was the first hearing of the Dispute Resolution.

"They do everything nowadays to avoid full court hearings," Lizzie had explained as we'd been made to jump through all the hoops. CAFCASS (I've always hated acronyms and kept forgetting it stood for "Children and Family Court Advisory and Support Service"), I'd vaguely heard of them before, but now I know what they do. They put children first. I thought that was what we were doing, but the interviews we underwent so they could put in what they called a Safeguarding Report made us both (Lauren and me) feel as if we'd done something wrong. Well, in theory I suppose we had, but then so had Luke and what we'd done we thought had ticked the boxes of placing the child's needs (well, children really as Callum was in the frame too) wishes and feeling at the front of the emotional queue.

We'd already had a without prejudice conversation outside the court. Although Lizzie and Maggie had assured us that it was nothing unusual it had shocked me to the core. What it boiled down to was a kind of blackmail. If we wanted Luke to back off with his personal allegations against Lauren and his assertion that I'd assaulted him, then there was a price to be paid for that. Indeed, as the conversation proceeded it was clear that there was a price for each child as well. If I wrote the bastard a cheque for a quarter of a million pounds then Lauren could have Peta and Callum and all Luke would want is the occasional access when it suited him.

It made everything he'd said in his affidavit a nonsense. In that, he'd shown great concern for the child's welfare, both physical and spiritual. Lauren had always told me that Luke had no interest in religion whatsoever. It might well be the opium of the masses and he'd take the opium but not the bible and churchy bits that came with it. Now, he was keen on Sunday school, desperate not to upset his own deeply religious parents who were mainstays of their local church up in Renfrewshire (Lauren said that on the few occasions she'd met them they'd seemed more interested in their local bingo halls and pubs) and determined not to have his Christian child brain-washed by me and my controlling family.

"Can't we bring all this up in court?" I asked. I couldn't remember ever having been in front of a judge before. I'd always pled guilty to any motoring offences and written an apologetic letter hoping (but always failing) to mitigate my speeding or driving through a red light. This was something entirely different and very new to me.

"All without prejudice I fear," Maggie said, "although I will cross examine him on it. But I know this judge. Sally Hargreaves. She was actually in my Chambers. She's not the nicest and she'll stop me if I go overboard on the aggression with him. We have to ensure that the evidence just speaks for itself. Except, of course, for your ram-raiding your way into his house and taking his wife and child. That's dangerous territory for us and I am sure that his solicitor will make great play of that. I hate to say this (and I'll deny saying it) because I don't like giving in to blackmail, but if you've got two-hundred and fifty grand to spare it might be worth considering. And don't forget that's his starting point. I'm sure he'd take less."

I couldn't explain either to her or Lauren that money was an issue for me at the moment given what was going on in my business. I knew I had Helen's insurance money, but there was no way she would have wanted it to have ended in in Luke's bank account. Under normal circumstances it would have been impossible to place a price upon my granddaughter, but nothing was normal in my life at the moment. So, I just had to take the high moral ground and hope it would convince both the barrister and my daughter. Lizzie, of course, knew of my problem and I could have hugged her when she said,

"It's quite inappropriate to give into threats. Even if you wanted to pay what he wants he'd find a way to come back for more when that ran out. They always do and I've no idea how we would document it anyway."

Which was why Maggie Chamberlain was on her feet painting my daughter as Mother Theresa and Luke as the devil incarnate. I quickly gathered this was a game of which I was totally ignorant of the rules. Maggie spoke, Yarwood objected regularly, the Judge seemed to be keeping count because she alternated her rulings, sustained, over-ruled, over-ruled, sustained. It was like being on Centre Court at Wimbledon. Maggie dealt with the CAFCASS report on the children and asked if there was any need to call the individual who had prepared it. The Judge thought not, Yarwood thought yes as he wanted to ask some questions. This time he got his way and we sat through a fairly boring thirty minutes during which he tried to shake the Case Officer from CAFCASS and she, an experienced woman in her fifties, did not budge. Eventually the Judge became tired of his repetitive questions and called a halt to it. Then Maggie called Lauren.

For once, I was so proud of my daughter. She painted a picture of virtue, of the wronged wife, the caring mother who had landed up in a warm and vibrant home that would offer all the right values to a small child. Yarwood hammered at her over the incident when she had fled with me and when Lauren tried to explain the Judge had to cut her short and told her this was not a matrimonial hearing, but one in respect of the children. I wanted to leap to my feet and say that in this case they were one and the same thing, but Lizzie just passed me a note telling me to keep calm. I felt anything but calm when Yarwood virtually accused my daughter of being addicted to anti-depressants, suggested that there were days when she simply could not function and just stayed in bed, unwashed and not eating. I tried to catch Lauren's eye to assess the truth of the allegations but she avoided my gaze and I wondered just how much there had been in her marriage that she'd kept to herself and how much was now going to come back to haunt her. The Judge herself asked a few questions and I knew my daughter well enough to see that she had reached breaking point and just wanted it to be over whatever the outcome. And then it was my turn to give evidence.

The first part was easy as I'd been well prepared by the lawyers. All I had to do was to tell the truth.

"That should come naturally to you, Mr Kent," Maggie had said without a hint of irony and I could feel Lizzie glancing at me to test my reaction. Yarwood launched into me until I was convinced that by going to rescue my grandchildren, I had committed some heinous crime.

"I gather you lost your wife recently," he stated rather than asked. He assumed a sympathetic air obviously having come to the decision that the Judge was not going to look on him favourably if he didn't.

"So, apart from your daughter (and I've had to point out her personal frailties) there is no 'mother' figure in your household, is there?"

I tried to argue with him, even though my instructions from Lizzie and Maggie had been just to answer questions and not to engage.

"We managed just fine until your client stole my granddaughter. And then tried to shake me down to buy her back."

Yarwood was on his feet immediately,

"That is an outrageous suggestion, Mr Kent. I insist you withdraw that at once."

The Judge gave me a stern look and added,

"Unless you have any evidence to that effect I would endorse Mr Yarwood's proposal. And please don't look to your daughter's legal advisors for advice," she said as she saw me seeking some help as to what I should do.

"I'm sorry," I mumbled. But Yarwood wasn't done yet,

"I believe you work full time, don't you?"

Again, the question caught me off guard. Was this a trap to make me commit perjury? Had they been speaking to my erstwhile partner? Was it better to say I was working and had the money to meet everybody's needs or was there some advantage in saying I had retired and could spend as much time with my grandchildren as was necessary. I knew I had to prove that the children were not at risk with us, but so far we'd not shown them to be at risk with their father either.

While I was hesitating over my answer I could feel it wasn't going to end well. That I was not coming over as I had been sure I would, as the gentle, caring grandfather who could fulfill every need of his grandkids. Then, there was a hubbub at the back of the court. People were handing in messages, the Judge was looking more and more displeased and impatient. I was finding it impossible to understand what was going on and was so confused by everybody talking across each other that when somebody stood up and asked the Judge if they could approach her as there was some new vital evidence I could not even tell if it was a man or woman who was asking. I had sort of forgotten the questions I had been asked and the answers that had come to my mind. Time stood still, the Judge looked at me and then from lawyer to lawyer, from my daughter to Luke and then gesticulated to the lawyers to come forward.

I could hardly hear what she was saying, but when she rose and Maggie and Yarwood followed her to her room I felt stranded in the witness box, like a non-swimmer on a sinking ship without a lifebelt, just waiting for the waves to swallow him up.

Chapter 55

The Kent household was something new to Kelly McGuire. She'd been to London before, of course, but as a tourist. All the usual things, a Central London hotel, well, Bloomsbury actually as her budget in those days hadn't stretched as far as the West End. Then, in no particular order, The Tower of London, the Monument, the South Bank complex, Oxford Street (tacky), Regent Street (not as good as 5th and 6th Avenues, but more pricey), Hampton Court by boat (freezing, but the Maze was fun), Madame Tussauds (cheesy and too crowded), The British Museum (full of noisy school kids, but free so that balanced out the noise levels), a couple of plays (one of which she'd enjoyed and the other through which she'd slept alongside her jet-lag). And then the Tate Modern which had been incomprehensible, but where her crazy schedule had petered out when she'd met a guy who'd distracted her for the rest of her stay.

He came from Santa Monica and she'd already begun to work and live in New York. Eventually time and the sheer inconvenience of a long-distance relationship, when both of them (he was training to be a doctor) were making their ways in their respective professions, just got in the way. It had been a crazy trip with the whirlwind romance thing. Yes, it had been romantic. London was a romantic city and she'd been ready for something like that which could just as easily have happened in Paris or Rome. After that ended, romance hadn't played a big part in her life. She was always too tired at the end of the day to engage in any meaningful way and if she wasn't working on a weekend then she was sleeping. On her own.

Making this on the spur of the moment trip to London and coming out to the boondocks to see Adam (and presumably his family although she hadn't thought it through sufficiently to make them part of the equation) certainly did not have the romantic aura of that earlier visit. She'd not told Adam she was coming and that was probably a mistake, but she had things that she needed to tell him face to face, things that she felt she could not say openly over the phone. There was an element of paranoia about her caution, but then Adam had warned her about the influence and long reach of his erstwhile father-in-law, Benjamin Gilbert. What she had uncovered had taken the situation far beyond his warning. The amber signal had turned to red, a signal that was flashing on and off ever more urgently and she was continuing her journey at her own risk.

She might just be being fanciful, might have watched too many TV movies and box sets, but she was convinced that she was right to be cautious. She was dealing with people who might do anything to protect themselves and indeed might already have done so. They'd taken steps to end Adam's reputation and it would be only one small step to end his life. Whatever the danger, she needed to share what she'd found with Adam and there was also the fact that she had come to realise that, for the first time in many years, she was actually missing somebody.

That was a hard thing to admit to herself. She had become fiercely independent. She had a lifestyle that she found perfectly acceptable and until she had met Adam there had been no room within it for anybody else. She enjoyed the ability to choose to sleep alone when she wanted, to watch whatever she fancied on television (there was that penchant for implausible thrillers, the plots of which she was coming to believe might indeed be credible). She could dress or not dress around her apartment as the whim took her, eat junk food when she was hungry at whatever time she chose, empty a bottle of wine alone when she was down and leave the cups and the glasses in the sink rather than the dishwasher until their stocks were exhausted.

Welcome to the life of a singleton (with occasional off-the-cuff sex) in the City.

There had not been a man in her life apart from the odd itinerant picked up in a bar or a club and just one or two she saw with regular infrequency which she designate her "just in cases". That was just in case nobody better turned up and nobody had until Adam Kent.

So, Adam's greeting of, "What are you doing here?" which had been his first words when he'd opened the door, was not quite what she had expected.

She tried to brighten up the mood by replying,

"Hey, you, what happened to my hug and big sloppy kiss and Kelly, what a lovely surprise. You're just what I needed to brighten up my day and how great is it to see you. That last bit is without a question mark, by the way."

She wasn't feeling great anyway by the time she'd got to Adam's house. She wasn't great with the geography of London and had booked herself into a hotel near Swiss Cottage in the belief that everything north of central London was pretty much adjacent. However, a quick shower an even quicker application of make-up and a comb through her hair, plus a change of clothing hadn't done a lot for her. Then nearly an hour in a cab battling its way through never ending (and mostly never moving) traffic to this mysterious North London suburb, had done even less. So, what seemed to be a less than enthusiastic greeting was pretty much the icing on a cake that had already collapsed under the weight of its expectations.

Adam ran his fingers through his hair, a gesture that she'd come to recognise as one of stress. He glanced back over his shoulder and for a moment Kelly thought she'd made a monumental mistake and she wasn't visiting him, but intruding on his time with another woman. It was then she heard the screams of children (it was hard to tell if they were playing or fighting) and she realised that she needn't have worried. He was actually child-minding and from the sound of it not doing a great job.

"Look, Kelly, I'm sorry," Adam said, still from the doorstep, my dad and my sister are in court today on the child application and then my other sister told me that if I was looking after one I might just as well be looking after three, so," and now he ushered her into the house and dramatically threw open a door with a simulated roll of drums. As she glanced in it looked like a toy shop owner's nightmare. Lego was everywhere, sometimes built into a tower, a road or a bridge, but for the most part scattered like the aftermath of a nuclear attack. Then there were toy planes from what seemed like every airline in existence, colliding with toy trains as if the targets of a random miniature terrorist attack. Cars were frozen in the midst of some gumball rally, Disney characters embraced by vintage tin soldiers manned the ramparts of a fort and atop it all sat a female pig (whom Kelly later discovered was a favourite named Peppa) with a crown on her head, the Queen of Chaos, ruling all she surveyed.

"I think I now understand your lack of enthusiasm at my arrival, Adam. Shall I go away and come back later?"

"No way. I am taking your arrival as that of a volunteer to help combat this mob who, as you will note, have me outnumbered."

He was only half joking. It had been a tough day. He was concerned for Lauren and his dad seemed to be taking it all very seriously, or, at least taking something very seriously. Whatever his somber moods, they could no longer just be explained away by the sudden death of Helen. Tommy was not an easy child to look after and had sensed that his Uncle Adam was a much easier touch than his mother and his currently absent father. Although Scarlett seemed to be behaving herself and playing up to her uncle, she could be the most annoying child with her somewhat prissy, disapproving attitude towards her excitable brother. Callum was adding to the mix by deliberately destroying whatever his cousins made or refusing to obey the rules that Scarlett set down for any game they finally agreed to play.

"Investment banking is a doddle compared to this," Adam said, sweeping a hand in the general direction of the three children who took that as an invitation to race around both their uncle and the new arrival.

"Who's she?" asked Scarlett bluntly, "she's not family. Does Grandpa know she's here? I don't think he'll be pleased. I mean just look at the mess."

Kelly could not help but smile at the small girl's use of a phrase she'd obviously heard her mother use more than once. But as for Grandpa not being happy for any other reason than the mess, well, thought Adam, out of the mouths of babes. His father would most certainly not be pleased if he discovered there was more to the relationship than mere lawyer and client.

He'd been thinking for a while now as to how he would broach the subject of Kelly with his father and the fact of the matter was that now wasn't a good time. And he wasn't sure, given how he knew his mother would have reacted, that there would ever be a good time. Right now his dad's plate was full with the issues of his sisters' marriages, with Peta, with his business, with the challenge of the coming Passover without the organisational genius of his mother and then the tombstone consecration to follow. If he added Kelly to the menu then the plate would surely be over-flowing at the edges.

Only now, with her unexpected arrival, he surely did not have any choice. It would be somewhat tricky to pass off the arrival of his matrimonial lawyer from New York after she'd travelled several thousand miles, not to mention a time zone. He didn't think his father, despite his current distractions (and certainly not his sisters with their sniffer-dog noses) would believe for one moment that she was here just to give him advice regarding Carly and his own children.

He led her into the kitchen and switched on the kettle.

"Electric, huh?" Kelly noted, knowing how he'd sneered at the American domestic fashion of either boiling a kettle or a saucepan of hot water on the hob or else getting what purported to be hot water from a special tap. Neither worked for him when it came to making a cup of tea and he acknowledged in that department at least, he was his father's son.

"Yes," he replied, "how unbelievable is it that in little old England we actually have electricity connected twenty-four seven. Tea? Coffee? Something herbal?" He threw open wide a cupboard door and pointed to the available selection. "My father and my sister may have allowed the food stocks to dwindle, but when it comes to beverages, we could open our own store. My mother seemed to be stocking up in anticipation of a major caffeine shortage."

"Coffee, black, strong and lots of it," Kelly requested.

"We've taken to using the Nespresso machine, but for you..." he produced a cafetière to the accompaniment of an imaginary fanfare. He went to the tin which gave as a clue to its contents the word 'coffee' and scooped in a couple of spoonfulls.

"Put another one in please," Kelly asked "I really need to be awake for the next bit."

Adam duly obliged and with the kettle boiled poured in the hot water, pressed down the plunger and let it brew,

"Apologies again, Kelly, for that non-welcome I gave you."

"It's ok," she replied, reaching out to take his hand and feeling better for the skin on skin contact. "but if your family's out then we do need to talk. I'm sorry to have made it a cliff-hanger over the phone, but without putting conspiracy theories on the agenda, what I've uncovered so far is big, really big...."

She wasn't given a chance to finish her sentence because they both could hear a key turning in the lock and then the front door opened and Daniel led the way into the room, followed by Lauren. A small human tornado raced past them both and a screaming Peta launched herself into the room in which her cousins were playing as if she'd never been away.

Chapter 56

It was proving to be the oddest of days and although I'd had a few of those since I'd become a widower, this one was right at the top of the list. The application which I thought had been lost had been suddenly won like the denouement of a Dickens novel where good triumphs over evil, where long separated characters are suddenly reunited, where there is a promise of everybody living happily ever after. Although I was on a temporary high, I wasn't too convinced that was going to be the case as far as my family was concerned. Certainly, one member would not be living happily ever after as she was already dead.

I had been convinced, particularly after the inept way I had given my own evidence, that Judge Hargreaves was set firmly against us, might even have been a little sympathetic towards the abandoned Luke, but then she suddenly turned on him and as for Luke himself, well it was a bit like the story of Esther on the Festival of Purim where the anti-Semitic, wicked Haman suddenly gets his come-uppance. All that was missing were the gallows on which to hand him.

Lauren's friend, Natalie Dennis from her home in Devon, had been the unexpected catalyst for the sudden turnaround in Lauren's fortunes. It appeared that since my sudden removal of Lauren back to London and the arrival back of Peta after her seizure by Luke, she'd been watching the man like a hawk. She was concerned about his reputation, deeply concerned for her old friend and even more concerned about the child.

It had been sheer good fortune (Dickensian again) that she'd been on her self-appointed vigilante duty when Luke had decided to take a chance and leave Peta on her own. She'd taken a picture of him on her phone leaving the house and had then boldly gone up to the house and had managed to take a picture of Peta alone in her little bedroom at the rear of the small cottage. She'd been sensible enough to knock into a middle-aged lady, Valerie White, who she knew that Lauren had used for baby-sitting in the past. That was before Luke had taken against her when she'd been replaced by the less observant and more alcoholic Mrs Morton who was happy to do whatever Luke wanted as long as he left out a bottle of gin and brandy. Natalie was no lawyer, but she was intelligent enough to arrange for Mrs White to accompany her to a solicitor the following day to swear an affidavit as to what she, too, had seen.

Then, on her own, she'd followed Luke to his favoured local and had quickly grabbed some more photos of money being exchanged in return for little packages which could only have contained drugs. She'd been tempted to buy one, but she didn't exactly look like his usual punter and that was probably a step too far. It was only later when she was with the solicitor and he asked why she had simply not called the police, that she realised that she'd been so caught up in her own drama that she had failed to make it that simple for herself.

Yet, once she had started she couldn't stop. She needed to follow it through to its final scene and reporting the abandonment of the child and the drug peddling to the local constabulary was unlikely to get the immediate result she needed. It was only afterwards that she understood just how horribly wrong it could have gone.

"The Judge could have refused to admit your evidence. Or she could have chosen to adjourn and in either case Luke would have known you were on to him and goodness knows what might have happened then."

What, in fact, had happened, had shaken us all. Once Luke understood what was being shown to the Judge he took the matter into his own hands and ignoring the protestations and the restraining hand of his own lawyer had risen angrily to his feet yelling,

"You fucking Jews, you all stick together." The Judge had flushed and almost levitated from her seat.

"Could you please repeat what you just said, Mr Campbell," she said and a man less out of control than Luke would have noticed the pointed underlining of the 'Mr'. But he noticed nothing and simply did as she asked, but at greater volume, his spittle flying over anybody within range.

He wasn't done yet,

"It's a Zionist conspiracy, Your Honour. You know what they're like" he continued in a wheedling tone as if she was sure to be on his side, "That Jew there and that woman stole my children and I had to rescue my daughter before goodness know what they might have done to her. She'd already been brain-washed, and I was just getting her sorted."

I really thought he was going to give a lecture on the blood libels (without the libel bit as he was the sort of man who might have believed that we killed children to use their blood at Passover) but Judge Hargreaves cut him short. She'd given him enough rope and even without the physical gallows he had hanged himself.

"That's enough, Mr Campbell. Say one more word in my courtroom and I will have you taken away for contempt of court, I happen to be Jewish myself" (that was a total surprise to all of us) "and I can assure you that there are no conspiracies in my court. From what I've seen Mrs Dennis seems to be a perfectly honest and respectable woman who was simply looking out for her friend and unlike you, also for your daughter. Leaving a five-year old on her own to conduct your nefarious business is both irresponsible and unlawful. Mrs Dennis has offered me an explanation as why she did not immediately report both matters to the police and whilst I understand, I do not agree and this court will certainly be bringing them to the attention of the authorities."

She looked at the CAFCASS representative who was looking shell-shocked given the credibility she had afforded Luke in her report and pointedly said,

"I assume you will be preparing a revised report," there was no question mark at the end of the sentence and the woman nodded dumbly.

And that was that. Luke had been foolish enough to bring Peta up to town with him. Perhaps he had thought I would be more likely to agree to pay him off if we could get immediate re-possession. Or was it just to taunt us with her, or even so that he could frighten her by keeping her in sight in case she decided to waver from the script in which he had schooled her. Whatever the case might have been, it worked out perfectly for us as we simply took her home, leaving him ranting and raving at his solicitor who he was accusing of gross negligence and threatening to sue rather than pay.

Then, coming home and finding this total stranger there, in the shape of Adam's American lawyer, was somewhat out of the ordinary as well.

"Kelly," Adam had said, "this is my dad and my sister, Lauren and the blur that just passed us by was my niece, Peta."

Kelly smiled and it was a nice smile.

"Is it a bird? Is it a plane? No, It's Super Peta," and she'd gauged our mood just right and although I was already liking her I still couldn't figure out why she was here in North London and in my house.

"Kelly's the US attorney…"

"His," she added, "not *The* US Attorney," and we all dutifully smiled whilst still feeling part of an audience to a play for which we'd randomly acquired tickets and arrived half-way through the action.

I looked long and hard at Kelly. She was attractive in that hard-edged New York way. Auburn hair, close cropped, a freckled nose that might have had some work done on when she was younger, her chin with a defiant tilt. She was a little taller than Adam, slim and athletic and I could visualise her running circuits around Central Park before work and I wondered if Adam might have accompanied her. There was something in the space they seemed deliberately to keep between them that suggested something that wasn't being said.

"Are you dealing with his divorce, his kids or his immigration issues?" I asked.

She laughed and Adam smiled, and it was then I understood that there was something between them that went far beyond a professional relationship, something that Adam almost certainly hadn't wanted me to know.

"All three, I guess," she replied not noticing the change in my tone.

"Well, I'm still not quite sure what brought you here, but as you are do you want to stay for dinner? And if Adam has no objections then maybe you can bring us up to speed. We try not to have secrets in this family," and the hypocrisy of that statement almost made me choke as soon as the words were out of my mouth.

Chapter 57

Before the fallout from her routine these past few weeks, Chloe had prided herself on her fitness. Yet, now, she still felt like an ungainly blob, beside the Venuses and Adonises who frequented the tennis club. She didn't bother with tanning salons and her pale skin and fair hair made her feel even more of an intruder at this sports centre, which had been at the core of her marital problems.

Damien had no idea she was going to come, but even after their meeting she was not quite ready to give any consideration to what her husband did or didn't want or did or didn't know. They'd met at a coffee shop although he'd wanted to have a lunch. She'd just felt that was too much of a commitment. Them looking at the menu together, the ordering, the possibility of a glass of wine to break down the barriers and the inability just to get up and walk out if things were not going well.

No, a coffee, she had decided would be just fine. It had been awkward at first, like meeting somebody on a blind date and wondering just who they really were and what to say to hold their interest. He'd even asked her what she wanted, although he knew that she always just wanted a black decaf Americano.

"Anything to eat?" he'd asked and she'd shaken her head which didn't stop him buying a packet of two shortbread biscuits and offering her one. She was about to snap at him, to ask him which bit of her not wanting anything to eat he hadn't understood, but something made her take it. She dipped it into her coffee welcoming the mild sugar rush, the slight distraction which made her look at the coffee cup and the crumbs she was spilling on the table as if they were the most interesting things in the world.

"So," she said, "Lauren got Peta back. That no good husband of hers was shown up in court as the disgusting little anti-Semitic shit we all took him for. Except, Lauren, of course, but she knows now."

"Sound like she had a good lawyer," Damien said.

"She did. Dad produced her as if by magic. He said a friend had used her, but we all think there's more to it than that. We wondered if maybe Mum and Dad were having some problems they didn't let on about to us and he actually consulted her."

"What makes you say that?" Damien asked.

"Oh, maybe I'm just letting my imagination run riot, but there was just something in the way that this Lizzie Gordon behaved around him that got Lauren thinking that they weren't total strangers. I'm meeting her myself tomorrow anyway..."

She saw the look of fear in Damien's face and realised what she had said and to what conclusion he had suddenly jumped.

"It's alright, Damien, I'm not seeing her about us. Yet. It's just that Lauren feels so grateful that she's insisted we all take her and the barrister out for dinner." She paused in mid flow and then continued as if half to herself, "and that's another thing, Dad made every excuse in the world to get out of coming. And none of the excuses were convincing. Whether, he just doesn't feel up to socialising or whether Lauren's right in her reading of the relationship I don't know. But, anyway, we are all going, including Adam and his ..."

Damien blew on his coffee although by then it was far from hot,

"Adam and his what?" he asked

"Not what, but who," Chloe said. "That was also really weird. This American woman turned up on our doorstep. Adam says she's his lawyer and was here on business anyway so she's been talking to him about all his issues, like that bitch Carly and her father from hell and the kids and his job and his visas etc, but you know what, we're not sure he's being entirely open with us either. There's something going on between them, Lauren's sure."

"So, suddenly your sister has become Mystic Meg, has she?" Damien said and got a smile out of his wife for the first time.

"Well maybe she's just been able to tune in her radar better after the disaster of her own marriage. Perhaps, I need to follow her lead…"

A flicker of pain crossed Damien's face and she suddenly felt a little sorry for him although he hardly deserved any of her pity.

"Is our marriage a disaster?" he asked.

"What do you think, Damien? You lie to me, you betray my trust, you shag the first American bird who is prepared to spread her legs and show you her tits. Is that a formula for disaster or what?"

"Well, the way you put it, it's not good," he said in a very soft, crestfallen voice.

"It's not the way I put it, it's the way it is," she said trying to control the volume of her voice even though she felt like leaping to her feet, emptying what was left of her coffee over her husband and yelling out, "See that man there, he's my husband and he cheated on me!"

Damien didn't react as he would normally have done, but then the man in front of her was not the same man she'd lived with all these years. He wasn't the man who did exactly as he pleased, went to cricket for days on end with his mates, even took off abroad with them when she was left at home to mind the kids. The man who came home too late for dinner because he'd been playing tennis and then locked himself in his office, because he had some crisis over somebody's website.

"It'll pay for our next holiday," he'd always said, only the holidays were so much shorter than the amount of time he spent working for them and even when they were there, somehow or other she was the one who ended up playing with the kids by the pool, whilst he homed in on the hotel gym or tennis or squash courts. Or even worse sat on his laptop working for hours.

It was then that she realised she didn't want him to be the same man and that if there was to be any chance of a reconciliation he needed to change and he was the only one who could do that. That was one thing she couldn't do for him. However, this visit to the club was her one contribution to the effort. She marched in waving aside the request for her membership card and saw the person she had come to see just getting ready to play a match.

She was also blonde (Damien always had preferred blondes) but her hair was cut short whereas Chloe had hers tied in a somewhat old-fashioned bunch at the back. She was taller than Chloe by a head and looked far more muscular, but none of that mattered as she walked over to her and called her name to ensure she had not made a mistake. But, although she'd seen more of her breasts leaning out of the window than her face there was nothing about her she was going to forget so when she called out, "Pippa" and the other woman turned around she knew there was no mistake. And as she pulled back her arm and smacked the woman so hard in the face that she dropped her racquet, there was no mistake there either.

"What the fuck?" Pippa cried out as a couple of members moved towards the scene.

"What the fuck?" Chloe echoed, "the fuck is that you fucked my husband and if you so much as look at him again I will tear your cute American ass from off your legs and shove it down between your big American tits. Do I make myself clear?"

She put her hands in the air as a couple of men in white tennis gear came closer to her,

"It's ok, it's ok. I've done what I came to say, done what I came to do and by the way please treat this incident as Damien Gold's resignation note. You can send any rebate of his fees to his home address," and as she said that she realised she had decided that although she was going to make his life hell for the foreseeable future she would not be kicking him out and after collecting her clothes and the children from her father's house she, too would be going home.

Chapter 58

In the end it was just Lauren, Maggie Chamberlain, myself and Lizzie for dinner. Chloe had cried off claiming that her own marriage needed more attention than any dinner to celebrate the effective end of that of her sister. As for Adam he said that he and his own lawyer had some urgent business that needed to be attended to whilst the States was awake and anyway, that Kelly claimed that she didn't want to intrude into what was obviously family business.

Lauren had persuaded Adam to make his calls from home so he could stay with the children and he'd not protested despite the stress under which he'd clearly been put during our day's jolly out at court. I didn't like to ask, but I got the distinct impression that he quite welcomed the idea of being alone with Kelly, particularly as Chloe's pair were no longer a destructive influence and Lauren had put Callum and Peta to bed before we left. Callum and Peta. Together again. Chloe and Damien, sort of coming together. It had a nice ring to it. My family was gradually all coming together again, well, not quite all because there was one crack in its surface, one gigantic fissure that would be there for all eternity.

"You choose the restaurant, Dad," Lauren had said, "I've been away for so long that I only know Pizza Express and I don't think that quite cuts it."

"I don't really know either, Lauren. When your mum was alive, we tended to go to one of the kosher places in Edgware or Golders or Hendon and I don't think any of those cut it either. Why don't you ask our guests where they want to go."

She did and so I could hardly be surprised when the two lawyers chose to go to The Ivy, particularly as the last time I'd been there had been so many years ago with Lizzie herself. I just hoped the management had changed and we wouldn't be greeted as a couple as we had been back in the day. I couldn't decide if this was Lizzie trying to make a point, to jog some feelings awake or whether Maggie had been the one who'd made the decision. I didn't have long to find out because as we arrived, all in a sort of heap as it happened even though we'd travelled separately, the maitre'd greeted Maggie as if she were royalty.

"Miss Chamberlain, so good to see you and you have new friends to share your evening with…"

I'd never seen the man before in my life and I realised that my concerns had been ill-founded. It must have been at least fifteen years since I'd been there and 'our' maître 'd had been in his sixties even then. He'd gathered we weren't married with the unerring sixth sense that people in his position always had and fussed over us if every night was our last night together. And, of course, eventually one of them was as it was after one memorable dinner that the wine had not been enough of an anesthetic to block out the guilt and I'd called an end to the relationship.

I just hoped that it wasn't one of those restaurants that kept a computer record of its clientele so they could know exactly what cocktails and what wine they would order; and by being one step ahead made them feel as if they were the most special of all the clientele. That too, was fanciful of course. All those years ago nowhere had been that sophisticated. Times were different and we were also different people. I tried to gauge how Lizzie was feeling at this revisit to the past, but if she felt anything at all she was concealing it remarkably well. She was always a lot better at that than me.

I don't know if Lauren noticed anything amiss. She was positively bubbling and the champagne she insisted on ordering (I assumed at my expense) only lifted her up further. Maggie Chamberlain was surprisingly good company. She let her professional persona slip away and like most barristers clearly had a capacity to match anybody when it came to drinking. We learned she was happily married (to another woman) and they had a child, a ten-year-old daughter. She admitted that she'd had her doubts about our case and did not pull her punches about my contribution to that doubt by seizing the children. It was quite clear that none of my three female dinner companions had a lot of time for men and by the time we got to dessert I was feeling like a persecuted minority. Any sympathy for my plight as a recently bereaved husband was thin on the ground and even Lauren joined in the game of "Kick Daniel When He's Down" by telling me that I'd really not appreciated Helen when she was alive. Now, of course, I knew just what she had done to keep the household and the family together because I was making such a lousy fist of it myself. This time I did see a slight flush rise on Lizzie's cheeks and whether that was the alcohol (she'd been matching the other two women glass for glass) or embarrassment I did not know.

There's nothing worse than being stone cold sober amongst cheerful drunks. Well, Lauren and Maggie were cheerful anyway, although I recalled that Lizzie had actually tended to be somewhat aggressive when she'd had too much to drink. There'd been one night in some expensive hotel (far too expensive for my means at the time, but Lizzie sort of carried me along with her enthusiasm for the finer things in life) when we'd had a row over something trivial, like me being fussy about what I was eating or having the gall to comment on her eating pork and she'd slapped me so hard that I'd had to explain the bruise on my cheek to Helen when I'd got home.

I'd made the mistake of bringing the car, although even if I hadn't, I certainly wouldn't have wanted to get drunk around Lizzie in case I forgot my pre-prepared version of our limited back story. Coming up with reminiscences of our actual history would not have been a good thing in the presence of my daughter, however much she'd had to drink, by way of celebration of the recovery of her daughter and the guaranteed future of both her children.

Maggie also admitted that she'd never encountered scenes such as Luke had produced in court and told us that the Judge had actually called her afterwards so shocked had she been.

"And trust me, in my line of business I've seen most things. Why on earth did you ever marry him?" she asked Lauren bluntly, a question I'd longed to pose many times over the years.

"To spite my parents, well, my Dad, in particular," Lauren replied, adding me as an afterthought, although with a smile, to show that I shouldn't be taking it personally. Her speech was slurred, but the truth was coming out with the wine as the old saying goes.

Lizzie shot me a look as if to warn me against rising to the bait, to cut my daughter some slack, that it was the drink talking and not her, but I knew otherwise. She had never said as much but could it be that her anger had been aimed at me, that she had actually known about Lizzie. Well, not Lizzie specifically but a generic Lizzie. Another woman-type Lizzie.

I politely asked if anybody wanted a dessert, although I couldn't wait to get home and was irritated when they all asked for the menu. I sulked by just having a coffee, but the endless meal was not ended yet by my companions because they all wanted one too, with a liqueur as far as Lauren and Maggie were concerned.

I glanced surreptitiously at my watch and saw it was already past eleven and wondered what time they would ask us to leave, but then Maggie rose to her feet and told us she had some papers to read for a case tomorrow (I wondered how she was going to manage that, but guessed this was quite a normal approach for her) and then Lauren also suddenly felt she needed to get back to her kids and that Adam deserved being relieved from duties.

I went to signal for the bill, but Lauren said not to worry about rushing to leave, she would Uber back and that Lizzie hadn't finished her Irish Coffee and that she would be fine. I wasn't reading my daughter too well since she'd been back and I couldn't be certain that she didn't have some ulterior motive about leaving me alone with Lizzie. Was it too far-fetched to think she was matchmaking? Or was she just testing me out so she could report back to her sisters?

Either way, that was how the evening was going to end. Just me and Lizzie, her well on the way to being totally drunk, me ... well, me with my daughter's guilt-inducing words ringing in my ears and really needing a drink I couldn't have. Story of my life really, needing things I couldn't have.

"That went well," Lizzie said in a half-amused tone.

"It went," I replied. There wasn't a lot more to say and that was another problem. I wasn't sure that Lizzie and I had a lot more to say other than exchanging old memories with a few regrets and recriminations thrown in for good measure.

"Shall I order you a cab?" I asked having settled the hefty bill and wondering just how much was an acceptable mark-up for restaurants to charge for wine and champagne. I'd got out of the habit of fine dining that was for sure.

"I thought you might give me a lift," Lizzie said and although I looked for one, I could find no good reason to refuse.

Chapter 59

After Lauren had left, Callum had insisted on getting up as "Mummy always lets me watch one television programme before I go to sleep." Adam and Kelly had allowed him to do that and resisted his entreaties for ten minutes on Mummy's iPad (which allegedly was another pre-bedtime treat) but given in to his request for a glass of milk and a biscuit, which involved re-cleaning of the teeth and one final visit to the toilet.

"The kid's good, you have to admit it," Kelly said when they'd finally got him settled back into bed with a book and another ten minute extension to finish his chapter.

"I was like that myself." Adam admitted, "I'd do anything to avoid going to sleep however tired I was. I think I just wanted to suck every last minute out of every day."

"Time enough for that when you're really old, Adam," Kelly said, philosophically. They did one last check on the children. Callum had fallen asleep sitting up, with the book in his hands and Peta simply hadn't stirred clutching on to Petey Rabbit (her new favourite bedfellow) as if her life depended on it.

"A drink?" Adam offered.

"I think we may both need one," Kelly replied, "does your dad have any decent whisky in the house?"

"Wow, so this really is serious if you flew the whole Atlantic to drink my dad's Glenfiddich."

"Just get me a glass, please, Adam. No, in fact get me the bottle, I'll make it good to your dad before I leave."

Adam went to the drink cabinet and not for the first time wondered about the huge selection of bottles, when his parents so rarely drank. If they had friends over, one or two might have a pre-dinner scotch or a cherry brandy, but there were unopened bottles of Pimms, Baileys, Vodka, obscure kosher liqueurs and something that had been there so long that its label had peeled off and it had solidified.

He found what he was looking for, the almost full bottle of Glenfiddich which his father had proudly brought back from a trip to Scotland and then hardly touched.

"Ice?" he asked.

"Of course. I'm American," Kelly replied with a smile and waited patiently whilst he went to the freezer and tried to get some cubes released from the tray.

"Do you want some frozen peas and beans with the drink?" Adam asked as he tried to remove the vegetables before he dropped the ice into the drink. "My mother was no great respecter of a division in the freezer."

"Call me choosy, but maybe I'll take the ice on its own," Kelly said.

They'd picked at the same food that Lauren had given to the kids and now Adam just tore open a packet of nuts and put them into a bowl.

"Old habits die hard," he said, "my mum always believed in feeding people before she fed them. Nuts, crisps, dips scattered around the room." He glanced over his shoulder as if Helen might miraculously appear with the nibbles he'd just described, but there was to be no miracle, just some slightly stale cashew nuts, a month past their sell-by date in one of her favourite little bowls that she'd brought back from a holiday in Italy. That was the thing about this house. Almost everything in it had a story.

"Don't break Grandma's vase," his mother had cautioned when he was arranging some flowers he'd bought for her on a Friday night, or "Your grandfather loved that cup (a bizarrely patterned mug with the

Hebrew alphabet on it and a tiny map of Israel) so wash it up by hand and be careful with it."

Now his mother was gone to join her parents he still followed the rules and wondered if his own children might do so and their children after them, although first he had to get them back.

"Ok. Listen up Adam. You lucked out when you chose me as your lawyer although I know you've not yet seen a lot of evidence of that. But I think the playing field's about to be levelled…"

"Isn't that an English expression?" Adam asked

"We have playing fields too. And I've heard you use it and I liked it. Anyway, your clever lawyer (and I know you thought I was too young and inexperienced, even if your English reserve and politeness stopped you saying it) does have some pretty useful contacts. My college year was full of bright people. Some of them work on the Hill in DC, some of them are with the IRS and I've even got a guy who always had the hots for me and is now a rising star with the FBI. So I put out some feelers and couldn't believe what I got back. First of all, this guy, Rodriguez who's the current live-in with your wife and your children. That's not the only name he uses and I've discovered that under one of his other names, he'd be very welcome in Mexico where there's a warrant out for his arrest on some narcotic issues, not to mention people trafficking. So we need to get your kids away from him pronto and I am already on that."

"Are the children safe?" Adam asked, his heart and his mind racing.

"Well our French law firm are taking the necessary steps to ensure that they are. I should have some documents for you to swear very shortly."

"Should I get over there?" Adam offered anxiously.

"You should, but you may have another bit of travelling to do first. Your ex father-in-law may be wealthy but he's going to need every dollar for the shit storm that's coming his way. You can leave some baggage behind if you get to be President but until you do it's always going to follow you. Like The Baggage in those Discworld books you turned me on to. Only Mr Benjamin Gilbert's baggage is not going to defend him or help him because it's more like a travelling hand-made coffin."

"I'm sorry," Adam said, "I'm really not following you."

"Have another drink," Kelly said, pouring him one before he could answer and topping up her own in the process.

"Have you ever heard of Grand Juries?"

"Sort of, though I could never really understand what they did."

"Well, they kind of put you on trial before you know you're on trial and an indictment and a real trial follows as night follows day. The IRS don't like Gilbert's oh so clever tax structure and the lawyer and accountant he used got themselves indicted a few months ago. That led the authorities to investigate all their clients, helped by the fact they both merrily plea-bargained to get their sentences reduced. So, the spotlight goes on good old Ben and then there in the shadows is your ex-wife with all those offshore trusts of which she's the beneficiary. Anyway, this Grand Jury would be very keen for you to give evidence to them…"

"I'm not sure how much I knew," Adam said.

"Well it's good that you didn't know too much otherwise you might have found yourself being indicted as a defendant rather than being summoned as a witness. But there is that pre-nup they made you sign and when I looked at it again it's got some quite interesting stuff in there where you agree to waive any interest in certain trusts which I am reliably informed are off-shore and undeclared to the IRS. And I think they might want to hear about the lovely Carly's lifestyle and how that got bankrolled. And while you're at it you might want to mention how your reputation was destroyed and how you got hustled when you tried to get back into the country and leave them to decide whether there's anything else they need to investigate there so they can add bribery of public officials to Mail Fraud and Money-laundering. "

"And when is this?"

"Next week. I've taken the liberty of assuming you'll do this and they've promised they'll roll the red carpet out for you at immigration. And give you full immunity to boot."

Adam emptied his glass and poured another.

"You are one amazing woman," he said with real admiration.

"I know," she replied and then looking at her watch added, "you know Adam I'm sure there's lots you'd like to show me in your old bedroom. And I suspect that your sister and your dad won't be back for a while so you can also settle my bill in kind."

"I don't need any excuse to settle that kind of account," Adam replied and led her by the hand up the stairs. She paused to close the doors to the rooms where Callum and Peta slept.

"We don't want to wake the children do we Adam?" and then they were removing their clothes with the kind of urgency that only comes when there is not only passion, but real love.

Chapter 60

I'd continued to turn down any invitation to Friday night dinners, particularly now I had the children in the house. Lauren wasn't the best of cooks. In fact, let me rephrase that. She was an awful cook which meant that I would drive out on a Friday morning and go to the kosher shops and assemble a meal. Chicken soup, ready-made *kneidlachs* or matzah balls as Adam had Americanised them, (neither as good as Helen used to make but a million times better than anything Lauren could ever produce) a whole spit-roasted chicken, potatoes, rice, even packages of beans or root vegetable and then into the bakery for an apple or plum pie. Add to that some fresh fruit and non-dairy ice-cream plus some salads, chopped liver and egg and onion and cold meat cuts and we were in good shape, not only for Friday night ,but a Saturday lunch as well with some cold chicken and other bits and pieces over to give the kids on Saturday night or even Sunday lunch. I'm not saying Helen would have been proud of me (when she was alive she wouldn't let me bring anything ready cooked into the house as she took it as an insult to her culinary skills) but I was pretty proud of my own organisational skills, if nothing else.

However, Lauren was starting to get a bit of a social circle going starting with some of the other mothers at the school. A few of them she'd known when growing up anyway and they saw her and the children as a cause. That seemed to involve lots of play dates and party invitations, coffees before school, coffees in the park after school and now she actually had a Friday night dinner invitation from a fairly Orthodox couple whose parents Helen and I had also known socially. The wheel was starting to come full circle.

The couple had asked me as well, but with Adam still back in the States I welcomed the idea of a Friday night on my own. However, it just so happened that when I'd gone to the morning service in synagogue (I'd reduced my attendance to just that one day a week since the house had started to fill up) Rabbi Klein had asked me if I was going anywhere for dinner that night. I couldn't bring myself to lie to him. I was pretty much all out of lies after the traumas of the past few months and so, when I told him I was intending to have a quiet night in on my own, he would have none of it.

"You must come to us, Daniel. Rebbetzin Rachel (he did even realise how funny that sounded, like a character from a children's comic) was just asking about you the other day and saying we'd not seen enough of you lately. It's just the two of us as well tonight, which has to be a first. But the children all seem to be farmed out..."

"Well, don't let me intrude into your peaceful evening," I'd argued, but he was insistent and as his wife said when we sat down,

"I am so pleased you could come Daniel. My husband, like every other Rabbi I've ever known, needs an audience and I'm afraid I'm not really good enough to be one on my own."

Rabbi Ezra Klein had laughed and I envied their ease with each other, the gently mocking, that had absolutely no malice to it.

"The fact is, Daniel, the Rebbetzin has heard every single one of my stories and she needs some fresh material which we're relying on you to supply. The jungle drums tell me that a lot's been happening, but we'd both rather have the truth than community rumours and gossip."

The truth, I thought, do you really want the truth. About how I betrayed my wife and was denied the chance to make it right before she died, how one of my daughters had come to hate me so much that she'd married some anti-Semitic *goy* just to get back at me and as a consequence had caused her mother unimaginable grief and how it was too late to make that right as well. How my other daughter's husband had cheated on her and how, somehow, I felt I'd been to blame for that as well as I'd been so useless in looking after myself that she'd spent far too much time with me to be able to care for her own family. Or how my son was even now in the States with his lawyer who, also just happened to be his non-Jewish girlfriend, even though so far, he'd spared me the revelation on that one, not that there was anything to reveal. We all knew and said nothing about that elephant in the room. Or maybe how my working life had ground to a halt and how I'd been too weak to confront my partner and friend even though I knew he was committing a crime.

So, they were all my truths and this lovely couple didn't deserve to be burdened with any of them on this *Shabbat* evening with the candles burning brightly, reflecting the light from the polished silver on the table and the gleaming white cloth and the smell of fresh *challah* bread beneath the ornate blue and white cover and the bottle of expensive Israeli wine I'd brought as a gift waiting to be drunk from the beautiful wine glasses that had somehow survived a hurried exit from pre-war Berlin by Ezra Klein's grandfather.

I looked at their expectant faces and was silent. I so wanted to tell them the truth about my greatest sin, Lizzie, as I really thought that once I'd unburdened myself it would all be over. I felt an absolute fraud as they continued to think of me as a good man to whom bad things had happened. Yet, how could I tell them that story which had begun all those years ago and had ended as I drove her home from the non-kosher restaurant just a few nights before. And ended it had. She'd invited me in, whether from kindness or from a drunken sentimentality or from a genuine desire to re-kindle something that once burned as bright as these Sabbath candles (an unfortunate comparison I know) but, although I hesitated, although I struggled to reject what was on offer, reject it I did.

I could see the look of hurt in her eyes and I understood for the first time since we'd met up again that she was also lonely and it had been that loneliness that her caused her to visit me. I couldn't even say to her 'let's stay friends' because I knew, just as I'd known all those years ago, that only an amputation would work on this wound. So there it was. The impossibility of a second amputation of the same limb and although it hurt it did not hurt as much as it had hurt before. I wanted it to, because I knew I deserved to feel the pain. I had no idea if Helen could see me, there in that car with a woman who'd had far too much to drink and was offering me certain sex. In a way I hoped she could because she would have known that by saying no, a belated no admittedly, I was really trying to make it right. I didn't deserve to be happy. At least not yet.

Rabbi Ezra Klein and Rebbetzin Rachel Klein still had their faces turned to me and I realised that, what had seemed like hours whilst all those thoughts flew across my mind, had really been a matter of nanoseconds.

"The truth is," I began, "the truth is that I'm kind of shepherding my family back together. They're all beginning to smile again and there's nothing that fills a house like the laughter of children is there?"

Rabbi Klein reached out and gripped my shoulder,

"You're a brave man, Daniel. You deserve to be happy. And now I think the dinner is being ruined so maybe we should make *kiddush* wash and eat. That bottle of wine you've brought us looks very tempting."

And so, I did stand whilst he recited the blessing over the sweet ceremonial wine that my own children had loved when they were younger, and I then washed my hands alongside him, without indulging in the race to be first that had also been a tradition amongst my three and I ate the delicious piece of bread that his wife had baked and upon which he'd sprinkled salt as he'd cut the loaf and said that blessing as well. And I counted my own blessings and tried very hard not to think of Lizzie and whatever bar she might be frequenting this Friday night and whoever she might be with or sleep with later on.

The rhythm of the meal and the conversation with this delightful couple was soothing and therapeutic and I found myself joining in the singing of the Grace after Meals and humming the tune as I walked back home to my own house and my own bed, where I still could not get accustomed to sleeping on my own. Lauren and the children were back and as I locked the door she came over and gave me a huge hug

"Good shabbas and thanks for everything, daddy. And I am so sorry."

We held each other tight and I whispered so softly that I might just as well have been talking to myself or to my dead wife

"And so am I, so am I."

Chapter 61

Passover, the Festival of Freedom, celebrating the exodus of the Jewish People from Egypt. For eight days we eat only matzahs, the flat unleavened bread which at its worst can taste a little bit like cardboard and at its best is a snack I eat all the year round. Less fattening than ordinary bread, biscuits or cakes and really nice if you crumble it into your soup or spread chopped liver or egg and onion on it with some pickled cucumber.

Helen always used to tease me about my methodology in that respect.

"You make such a meal out of it, Daniel that you could make it your *piece de resistance,* your calling card recipe in the cookbook that I am sure you'll write one day. It can stand alone alongside those pot noodles you seem to love. You're the only person over ten years old who actually eats them."

They were easy. Just pour in the boiling water. I could do that. They were my standby then, as they were today. But getting ready for *Pesach,* the Passover was far from easy. Helen had always taken it as an opportunity to spring-clean the house from top to bottom. We had extra sets of crockery and cutlery and cooking utensils which only came out just before the Festival and were packed away immediately afterwards, some in a cupboard in the garage where I was the one who had to get them out and some in the loft, where again I had to climb up as Helen had no head for heights. That same loft where I had stashed the items Lauren had found, the items that were now disposed of finally, just as was my relationship with Lizzie.

The object of the exercise was to ensure that no trace of any ordinary food and in particular bread was left in the house which might contaminate all the special foods we bought for the Passover at great expense.

"They stick a label on a jar of jam to say it's been certified by a Rabbi and then double the price," Helen used to say and she was right but still she did it. She'd also say every year that this was the last time she was doing this, that she was tired of her children disappearing when she needed them and being left to do it on her own and that we would go away somewhere like Israel or Miami or even one of the more exotic locations where whole hotels became Passover friendly for any Jew who was happy to pay their exorbitant prices. I kept promising we would do just that, but like so many of my promises it remained unfulfilled.

I'd never appreciated the effort she put in until this year when the burden fell on me. To be fair the girls did help, they certainly helped their father far more than they'd ever helped their mother, that was for sure, yet I was the one who ended each day of the two-week run up to the big event, absolutely exhausted.

In years gone past, Helen had specialised in inviting neighbours who had nowhere else to go and various waifs and strays in and out of our community who, having come once for some obscure reason, were then invited every year without fail for one of the nights. I had decided, rightly or wrongly, that making the *Seder* dinner for two nights running was a step too far. There was going to be a communal *Seder* at the synagogue on the second night and Rabbi Klein and his wife had been very excited when I had told them I would be coming to that with some of my family. Chloe and Damien were going to friends so it would just be me, Lauren, Callum and Peta and Adam. Oh and plus his children Ben and Casey who Kelly had magically got released from the clutches of their mother.

The House with Too Many Rooms

I was becoming more and more impressed by Kelly, both as a person and as a lawyer, but I'd just stopped short of asking Adam if she might be in England for Passover and wanted to join us. We all want the best for our children, we all want them to be happy, but in my mind the evening I was going to make was in a way a memorial tribute to Helen and I just felt it needed to be family.

It had been a close-run thing, but by seven thirty in the evening we had got everything together and I did feel that Helen would have been proud of me. The best white tablecloth (upon which somebody, or often more than one somebody, spilled wine every year) had as its central setting the Passover plate with the three unbroken matzahs we use for the service, the bitter herb, the *maror* to remind us of the bitter times the Children of Israel suffered under the Egyptians, the *karpas* some vegetable that we would dip in salt to engage the children's interest (I was using lettuce just as Helen had all the years of our marriage) the *horoseth* a mixture of wine and nuts to set off the bitterness of the herb and to remind us of the cement the Israelites had to use to firm up the bricks in the store houses and treasure places they were made to build. Not, the pyramids I'd discovered, as where the nomadic Jews were the ground was far too soft to construct them. I was going to take pleasure in debunking that urban myth as I led the service. Finally a shank bone to remind us that the Egyptians had worshipped sheep which was why the Israelites were told to sacrifice a lamb and daub their houses with the blood so they would be exempt from the slaughter of the First Born, being the last Plague wreaked on the slave-masters, before Pharaoh finally let my people go.

Just thinking all that made me realise what a crazy religion I followed, with all those blind beliefs that symbolically brought back animal sacrifices and the revisiting of the story of the parting of the Red Sea before the waves closed in, like a tsunami on the pursuing chariots of the Egyptians. But, believe it literally or not, it made a compelling story and I'd gone to a mock *Seder* at the school which was now attended by all of my grandchildren and watched the wonder and delight and excitement on the faces of the children as they, too, recreated that mad flight from slavery that began the more modern history of the Jews as an independent and perpetually persecuted nation.

I got everybody seated and having poured out the first of the four cups of wine we would drink during the evening (grape juice for all the little ones except Tommy the eldest, who at 8 took the denial to him of grown up wine as an insult). Then I broke the middle of the three matzas in half and hid the larger part so the children could look for it and get a prize when we had finished the meal.

I turned to little Peta who, as the youngest there, was technically required to ask Four Questions, which would trigger off the lengthy answer which was the background to the recitation and the songs that accompanied and followed the meal. She'd arrived at the school completely unable to read Hebrew and then there had been the upheaval of the enforced stay with her father. He'd made the point of saying (Lauren told me when she was back home) that Hebrew was the language of Occupation. But then he'd said a lot of things that all of us were trying our best to forget, just as we really wanted to forget that he still existed.

She had a go at it, '*Mah nishtana*'... "Why is this night different from all other nights?" and when she stumbled, all of her cousins joined in to give her support and I thought how emotional Helen would have felt seeing all of her family gathered together under one roof, me, the children , the grandchildren, three generations celebrating hundreds of generations past, celebrating her as a wife, mother and grandmother and I wiped away a tear.

We pushed on with the service, my kids complaining about the time it was taking, complaining that I was out of tune , the grandchildren beginning to fidget until we got to the Plagues and I produced little frogs and locusts and mock blood and each of them put on a mask that represented one of the plagues and it was just one big game.

Everybody enjoyed the meal and although I'd bought, rather than cooked it, I gave myself a metaphorical pat on the back that I'd managed to cater for eleven people, including myself, something that I would never have contemplated doing whilst Helen was there to do it all for me.

Lauren decided Peta had had enough when she fell asleep on her and put her to bed, but the other children seemed to have got their second wind. They knew from what they had learned at school that there is a point in the evening when a separate cup is filled for the prophet Elijah who, in a Santa Claus sort of way, is said to visit every Jewish home on the first night of Passover. It's filled to over-flowing and then the front door is opened whilst a special prayer is recited loudly, presumably so that he can hear, although I'd always felt he'd have a fair bit of trouble just standing up after drinking wine at every house to which he came.

There was a brief argument amongst my grandchildren as to who should open the door and inevitably the very pushy Scarlett won. She raced into the hallway, stood on tiptoe to turn the handle and then I heard her call out,

"Grandpa, there's a man here, but I don't think he's Elijah because he says he's a policeman and he wants to talk to you."

Chapter 62

"One of us should have gone with him," Lauren said.

"It's not like going to the dentist to have a tooth out. I don't think that was an option," Chloe replied scathingly. She and Damien had decided to stay the night and had put Tommy and Scarlett to bed. The little girl cried all the way up the stairs and even when put down to sleep was still whimpering,

"But I want Grandpa to come and read me a goodnight story. That's what he always does when we stay here."

Tommy had been much quieter, as if he was grown up enough to understand what was going on and had discovered enough self-control not to throw one of his tantrums. Adam's two boys were just totally bemused. They'd only recently got to know their grandfather and thought it was kind of cool that he'd gone off with a couple of policemen in the middle of the night.

"Maybe he's a spy," Casey, the younger of the two said to Ben, his elder brother.

"Probably a super-hero, gone to help them catch a master criminal," Ben replied. Adam had objected when Carly had wanted to name him Ben, but she had just ridden rough shod over that.

"I don't get all that religious nonsense about not naming somebody after a living relative. Benjamin has been a great name for my father, so why shouldn't his grandson carry it on?"

There'd been a moment when Carly had taken the children and Adam had worried that she might revert to her maiden name and start calling the child Benjamin Gilbert II, but that hadn't happened and it certainly wouldn't happen now. Maybe at some time he could get to using Ben's middle name, Stanton (who called their child Stanton for goodness sake?) but Stan would be unusual for this day and age and much better than anything that reminded him of his ex-father-in-law. Right now, he just wanted the night to be over, the children to get to sleep and to join his siblings and brother-in-law to see what could be done to help his father. When Scarlett had asked 'why is this night different from all other nights?' she could not possibly have known that the answer would prove to be because her grandfather had been arrested.

Nobody had made a move to clear the table. The *Haggadahs,* the books which contained the service they'd been reading, lay scattered, two bottles of the wine they'd been drinking remained, each half-full because Lauren had opened the second without realising the first had not been emptied, Elijah's glass of wine was still full and the *Aphikomen,* the hidden half of the first matzah to be broken was still in its hiding place. Even the children hadn't wanted to look for it and hadn't demanded their expected presents for finding it.

"This all has to be a terrible mistake," Adam said, still shell-shocked, "there is no way Dad could have done anything to get himself arrested."

"I'm not sure he was actually arrested," Lauren said with all her recently gained knowledge of the English legal system. "He said he was going voluntarily to help them with some inquiries."

"But why would they come at this time of night to his house? And during the middle of a *Seder* as well." Chloe added.

"I'm not sure they keep a diary of Jewish holidays down at the police station," Damien chimed in and was shot a look by Chloe which told him firmly this was family only and he'd not fully reclaimed his place there.

"Ok. Enough. We have to get him a lawyer," Adam said firmly.

"I'm going to phone Lizzie. She won't be at a Seder that's for sure," Lauren replied.

"But she's not a criminal lawyer, Lauren" Adam intervened, "maybe I'll go FaceTime Kelly. Her firm has somebody they use here for sure, because she got them involved when we got my boys back."

"I'd rather speak to Lizzie," Lauren persisted. "She knows Dad, they get on and there must be somebody at her firm who does crime."

The others gave up the argument and let Lauren do what she'd suggested. She went to get her phone and returned a few minutes later looking puzzled.

"Was that ok?" Adam asked.

"Oh, yes," Lauren replied, "she called one of her partners whilst I was on the line. A guy called Jack Clarkson, she said he's very good, very experienced and she's worked with him for over twenty years. He's on his way to the station now."

"So, what's wrong? You look even less happy than you did before you made the call," Adam asked.

"Probably nothing. But when I spoke to Lizzie, she didn't sound surprised that Dad had been arrested, she didn't sound surprised at all."

Chapter 63

I'd heard of dawn raids before. Get somebody out of bed half-dressed or naked, get them disorientated, get them down to the police station and get them charged. But, I'd never heard of a raid during a religious celebration or at least, not since the cops disguised as Orthodox Jews, tried to arrest some Jewish gangster in synagogue on Yom Kippur in New York in the Prohibition Era and gave the game away by lighting up cigarettes outside and revealing their guns.

My police officers weren't armed and made it clear that they were merely inviting me to come with them, not arresting me. They were polite and even apologetic, but I was realistic enough to realise that if I'd refused there might have been a change of mood.

"Shall I phone Lizzie?" Chloe had asked "she's sure to know somebody."

I didn't know how to say that I didn't think that was a great idea and given that I had a shrewd idea as to why I was being summoned, I didn't think our regular lawyers in the company were a good option either. Most of the solicitors I knew were Jewish and were either away for the Passover or at a family evening of their own and none of them were criminal lawyers anyway. Criminal lawyers, who'd ever have thought that I'd have need of one of them, but who would ever have predicted the labyrinth route that my life had taken since the death of Helen.

"Listen, don't worry, they say we're going to Barnet. I'm sure there must be a duty solicitor I can talk to. Just finish off the evening between you and get the kids to bed. I'll be back before you know it."

I sounded more optimistic than I felt. In the car nobody spoke to me and I guessed that was also part of their game. Leave the guilty man to his own thoughts and he'll entrap himself. I wasn't guilty though. I'd distanced myself from whatever was going on, I'd left the firm,

gained no reward and indeed cost myself a lot of money in the process.

I didn't even have time to ask for a solicitor before Jack Clarkson turned up and I realised my children had totally ignored my instruction not to phone Lizzie.

"You probably don't remember, but we met before. You picked up Lizzie from work one day and she and I were the last two in the building. I was trying to set the alarm and managed to set it off instead. Lizzie sort of introduced us. We all knew what you were though."

"What was I?" I asked, even though this probably wasn't the time or place to take a stroll down Memory Lane.

"You were Lizzie's married man," he replied, and I surmised that he'd been one of the shoulders she'd cried on when it all came to an end.

"It's good of you to come," I said thankfully.

"Lizzie asked me. I wasn't going to refuse her," and in that moment I wondered if Jack Clarkson had offered more than a shoulder in comforting Lizzie back then. Or, even now when she needed a shoulder yet again.

It didn't really matter as I repeated all I'd been thinking to the lawyer.

He looked a bit older than Lizzie, built for rugby with a broad, but solid upper-body, topped by a bull-like neck, a nose that appeared to have been broken more than once, a mop of thick unruly hair as if he'd just been aroused from his bed and I realised I had no idea of what time it actually was.

I told him the whole story from the moment the deal had been put to me, to my rejection, to my being told they'd cleaned it up and gone ahead anyway, to my discovery that it still looked dirty and to my resignation and departure.

"I don't know if somebody told you to do that or if you decided on your own, but it was good advice." He paused and I didn't like the pause and the short silence that followed. "The only caveat is that if you knew a crime was being committed they will say you should have reported it and if you didn't then that makes you an accessory."

"But..." I began and he cut me off before I could continue, choosing to finish the sentence himself, "but you didn't know a crime was being committed. You just didn't like what you suspected was deception by your partner and your employees and given the emotional strain you were under from the death of your wife and the case going on to recover your grandson, you decided it might be a good time to call it a day. You weren't short of money so your financial settlement was going to happen when it worked for your good friend and partner David Segal and that was that.... Wasn't it?"

I nodded dumbly. It was as good an explanation as any and not a million miles from the truth and given my relationship with the truth, likely to be as close as I might get.

"Ok, let me talk to them. All I know so far is that they pulled in your partner David early this morning together with the two kids who worked for you and they've been hammering at them all day. Seems they'd got to a convenient moment in the proceedings when what they were saying reminded them that perhaps they ought to be talking to you as well. Early mornings, late evenings, Jewish holidays, all the same to them, as long as they put you on the back foot. Have you said anything to them at all?"

"Nothing," I replied feeling weary beyond my years, wondering how I was going to explain all this to my children and grandchildren.

"Good. Keep it that way. Now just try and relax and let me do my job."

Again, I was left on my own for what seemed like hours. A woman PC came in to ask if I wanted a drink and then kindly brought me a cup of tea. I didn't even have the strength to reject it although it was probably the worst I'd ever drunk and somebody had added sugar without even asking. Maybe everybody who used this room took sugar. They certainly smoked, because the smell from stale clothing hung heavily in the air and I felt myself struggling to breathe. It was only when the cup was empty that I remembered it was still Passover and even the tea, the milk and the sugar were forbidden to me to drink as not being kosher for the Festival. Another three nails in my coffin and if you added the ordinary cup that made four. I muttered an apologetic prayer and thought those might just actually be the least of my sins for which I was being punished.

At first I just didn't care what might happen to me. I had got to the point of thinking I deserved every storm that raged around my head. It was never going to end, this constant pursuit by justice, by revenge, by all the curses I had brought down on me by my past behaviour. Just by not falling again into temptation with Lizzie, wasn't going to be enough to clean the slate, nor were all the good deeds I'd done or attempted to do for my children. The writing was in blood, not in ink, the writing was on the wall in ten feet high letters and I just felt that whatever I said or did, however good my solicitor might be (and he was a man who exuded confidence) that I was doomed.

It was then that I had the picture implanted in my mind of my family gathered around the table earlier in the evening. It seemed like a lifetime ago, rather than just a few hours. I could hear the children laughing, reciting what they could, emptying their cups dramatically, hopping around pretending to be frogs, making wild beast noises. I couldn't just give all that up lightly. I had no idea what David may have said to save his own skin, he could have tried to put the blame firmly on me, but I wasn't going to give up without a fight, I wasn't going to go gently into any good night. I was going to do what needed to be done to get back to my family, now I had my family back.

Another half an hour passed and then I heard footsteps stopping outside the door. A policeman opened it and there was Jack Clarkson with a poker player's expression on his face. Before he spoke I could hear a church clock chiming. Midnight. The witching hour, was it the end of one day or the beginning of another, the end or beginning of my life as I had known it? I waited as the solicitor began to speak, hardly daring to listen, holding my breath until I felt faint, and offered up a silent prayer and a plea to my betrayed wife for forgiveness.

Chapter 64

Even with the sun shining over-head, with leaves on the trees and the grass looking healthily green, the cemetery was still cold. Whenever I had been there, whichever season, there always seemed to be a wind blowing across and amongst the tombstones. My calendar told me that we had buried Helen on a hot summer's day, but all I remembered about it was the chill that ran down my spine as the earth hit the lid of her coffin. That and my thought of the domino with the mark of the dog's teeth. The double-six. I think my wife deserved better memories than that of the day we put her to rest, but maybe others had them. As for me, there was a whole lot more she deserved and I failed to supply, that was one awful truth I had learned in the eleven months since her death.

It wasn't the only thing I had learned. I now knew with a terrifying certainty that there was a vengeful G-d. And a forgiving one as well. His vengeance had been wreaked on me that night I had been carted away by the police and his forgiveness had been proven when I was told that I would be a witness in the case against David Segal and Sam Birns and Jason Lehman, his two willing helpers.

I took no pleasure in it, nor in seeing them all sentenced alongside another individual who had been their man on the inside in the transaction and who had received the bribe to make it happen. I breathed a sigh of relief when, with his impeccable past record, David's sentence was suspended although the fine was hefty. Only the beneficiary of the money received a custodial sentence, but our business was finished and there would be no pay-out for me. I accepted that as a punishment, not for the fact that I hadn't turned them in when the opportunity was there, but for all the other crimes of moral turpitude I had committed. There was an Old Testament justice about it all and strangely enough I found that satisfying.

There was no longer any fear that David might seek retribution by telling my family about Lizzie. That was because I had told them myself. When I finally got home after my hours with her partner at the police station I felt ready to confess to anything and so, when Lauren demanded to know why Lizzie seemed to have known more than them about the Sword of Damocles that has hung over my head, I just told them the truth. It was easier and I was so tired of lying, to them and to myself.

It wasn't an easy conversation, confessions never are, but I was shocked to hear some home truths about how the kids had heard their mother cry herself to sleep some nights when I was away with Lizzie, how, now they really thought about it, they'd all had some suspicions even back then, that their father, whom they'd all worshiped, had feet of clay. As I say, not easy, but cathartic. There had been a final closure of my years of deception and although there were silences and meaningful looks, not to mention sarcastic comments, from Chloe in particular, eventually we seemed to have reached an acceptance that what had been had been and that none of us had the power to change the past. If there was to be a future then we had to move on and we did. Slowly for the first few weeks, but now, gathered together at my wife's and their mother's tombstone consecration, we were united in our loss.

I thought at first that Chloe was the most blameless and had the most justification for despising me for what I had done. She'd been the daughter who'd conformed, who'd done well at school, married a nice Jewish boy (well it had seemed that way at the time) and had then been dumped on in every way possible from a great height. Her mother's death, her husband's infidelity, her father's adultery. It wasn't fair, so everything she threw at me I accepted and would willingly have taken even more.

However, I then got to thinking about Lauren and how she had deliberately set out to hurt both Helen and I and I realised that with what she had pieced together from her childhood, she had every reason to hate me and that it was just unfortunate that her mother had become collateral damage. It was the same with Adam. How, could I have even been upset with him that he had ended up with somebody non-Jewish when I had done exactly the same myself? Hypocrisy of the highest order and I mentally flagellated myself even more.

In a way what I had done to Lizzie had been even worse. She could have had her pick of suitable men, but she had chosen me with all the baggage I brought, baggage I had refused to remove from my home to move in with her. I know that's what she wanted, but she was too good a person ever to ask me to do it and in not asking she wasted some of the best years of her life. If I had decided to break up my marriage, rather than her heart, then it would have had to have been my decision. And it was a decision that I could not make. Which was both to my credit and my shame. Lauren had kept in touch with her, even knowing what she did about her past relationship with me and she told me that for a while she had been seeing Jack Clarkson and they were now engaged. I don't know whether she told me to inform me or to hurt me, but what I did know was that I could see the irony in that. Perhaps it was her call to him to help me that had cemented their relationship. You know, I would really like to believe that was the case. There wasn't just an irony in it, but a symmetry as well.

That day, at the cemetery, there was no coffin waiting to be wheeled out to be buried. Just a space where one had been and where others would follow until I, myself rested there. I hoped all my children and my grandchildren would be there and would think kindly of me, despite everything. I'd said it before and I would say it again, that I had not been a good person, but I hoped to be a better one. I had discovered the value of truth and the pain of loss and they were both elements of healing and improvement.

Rabbi Klein officiated at the service in the internment Hall. He spoke from the heart and I heard how others outside of the family had respected and loved Helen. There was an amazing number of people there, not just our family and neighbours, but people within the community who I saw at synagogue, people outside of the community to whom she had extended innumerable acts of kindness. I simply could not take in everything that was said to me, but the voices all merged in a chorus of approval of a life well spent even if it was a life tragically cut short.

We walked in procession to the grave side where the Memorial Stone had already been erected. The bare facts carved upon it in black and gold lettering. Her name, in English and in Hebrew, her date of birth and death, in English and in Hebrew, beloved wife of Daniel Kent. I took a deep breath. My name there, for all to see. For some reason when my parents had died, all it said was that they were mourned by their only son and somehow I had remained anonymous. Mourned by her adoring children, Adam, Lauren and

Chloe, her grandchildren, Tommy, Scarlett, Callum, Peta, Ben and Casey. A true *Aishit Chail* a woman of worth.

And that was it. There was no more to say. People stood around, still talking about her, how they could not believe she had gone, about how brave we all were and how we were admired for getting on with our lives. Little did they know. But then, that's always the case. Nobody really knows what goes on in the lives of others. Not unless we invite them in. The Rabbi did announce that everybody was invited back to my house for something to eat and drink and the girls and I had been getting a table ready since the small hours of the morning with the help of Helen's old friend Marsha and a few other neighbours she'd gathered together.. We had enough food to feed the army of a small emerging nation, but that was exactly as Helen would have wanted it. At least that was what I hoped. For once I had done her proud. And by some miracle I'd pulled her family back together into some recognisable shape. I'd made my peace with my children, with her children. All I now needed to do was to make peace with myself and my Maker.

Epilogue

I sold the flat in Brighton first. The children didn't use it and I didn't feel comfortable going back there on my own and awakening memories, not just of Helen and the excitement we had shared when we had bought it and fitted it out, but also of Lizzie.

I got a decent price and simply divided it amongst the children with a chunk of Helen's insurance money that I didn't need. There was enough for a deposit on a small house for Lauren and her children in Bushey, which claimed to be in Hertfordshire, but was really just another North London suburb with a thriving Jewish community. She loved it there, as did her children and she developed a nice circle of friends including one particular man called, Robbie to whom I was actually introduced, which I regarded as a statement of intent.

Chloe was expecting again which was an even greater statement. She and Damien had become closer than before The Fall as I had come to think of the whole series of disastrous events. That was hardly surprising as Lauren told me (and yes, we became very buddy, buddy) that she hardly let him out of her sight. They played table-tennis together at a local club and won the mixed doubles at a tournament there. I gathered he'd given up his season ticket at Arsenal and hadn't been to watch any more Test Matches. He was focusing on his family and his business and they had some massive offer to buy his company out so I didn't have to worry about them financially. Nor emotionally, it seemed.

Adam went back to working in New York at his old firm with a much improved package and a Vice-Presidency (which came with a groveling apology from the Goldfarb man, as I had taken to calling him after he appeared to have behaved so badly). He moved in with Kelly who was actually working on a conversion to Judaism. Adam said it wasn't just to please him (or me) but because she had been so impressed by the legacy that Helen left behind her. That said so much that she could reach out from the grave to be a good influence. You couldn't say that about many people.

I'd put the main house on the market. The proceeds of sale would see me and the family through in a comfortable manner for the foreseeable future. Although, who can really foresee the future anyway? I found a nice flat, sort of equidistant between Lauren and Chloe and I seemed to spend a fair amount of my time collecting sundry grandchildren from school or taking them to swimming, ballet, football, tennis or cubs. Who knew that kids could keep up with so many activities? I found it tiring just watching them, but they seemed to have boundless energy, the energy of children, and although they wouldn't really understand exactly what I mean by it, the optimism of having so much ahead of them.

As for me, I'd lived longer than I was going to live. I joined a gym and lost weight and became fitter than I'd been for years thanks to a ruthless fitness trainer. When I found somebody to buy the house they were a lovely young couple with three small children. They reminded me of how Helen and I were at their age. I knew they'd cherish the house and it would cherish them. They bought some of the furniture, but none of my memories. Those travelled with me to my new place. I had spare bedrooms there for the grandchildren to stay over when necessary, but it was nowhere near the size of where I'd been. Why would it need to be? At the end of the day, after Helen left me alone, after the children moved out taking their kids with them, I realised what I should have realised from the moment Helen died. For me, on my own, it was no longer a family home, but just a house with a roof and four walls and far too many rooms.

Copyright

A House with Too Many Rooms copyright © 2020 by Cara Samuel Books. First edition August 2020. Published in the United Kingdom. Illustrations by the author. All rights reserved. No part of this book may be reproduced in any format, print or electronic, without permission in writing from the copyright holders. For further information, email melstein13@gmail.com.

About the Author

Mel Stein lives in North London with his wife. He has been an author and sports lawyer for nearly forty years having published some 19 books across the range of novels, sports biographies, faction and self-help books.

His fiction career began as long ago as 1980 with "Danger Zone" published as an original paper back by Fontana and then followed with critically well received books such as "Rags to Riches", "The White Corridors" and "Race Against Time".

He has also written a trilogy about ex-professional footballer Mark Rossetti, "Marked Man", "Red Card" and "White Lines" and a horse racing thriller "McGovern's Horses" under the name of Tim Elsen.

He wrote the biographies of Paul Gascoigne (Gazza) and Chris Waddle and the Faction book "Football Babylon".

He has also written two self-help books, "How to Complain" and "How to be a Sports Agent" which have led him to be a regular broadcaster on radio and television on sports and consumer related matters.

The House with Too Many Rooms

Copyright © 2020 Mel Stein
All rights reserved.
ISBN 978-1-8381770-2-7

Printed in Poland
by Amazon Fulfillment
Poland Sp. z o.o., Wrocław